COMFORT

"A historical drama with savagery and grace. *Comfort* is one of those novels that unnerves the reader, the characters are vile, beautifully rendered, and it action unfolds cinematically."
—Scott Whitaker, *The Broadkill Review*

"Compelling from beginning to end, *Comfort's* rich characters, swift-moving narrative, and twists of plot surprise and pull the reader deeply into this novel. Comfort is a must-read."
—Gordon Weaver, author of *The Eight Corners of the World*

COMFORT

A Novel of the
Reverse Underground Railroad

H. A. Maxson
and
Claudia H. Young

Parkhurst Brothers Publishers
MARION, MICHIGAN

www.parkhurstbrothers.com

Parkhurst Brothers books are distributed to the trade through the Chicago Distribution Center, and may be ordered through Ingram Book Company, Baker & Taylor, Follett Library Resources and other book industry wholesalers. To order from Chicago Distribution Center, phone 1-800-621-2736 or send a fax to 800-621-8476. Copies of this and other Parkhurst Brothers Inc., Publishers titles are available to organizations and corporations for purchase in quantity by contacting Special Sales Department at our home office location, listed on our web site. Manuscript submission guidelines for this publishing company are available at our web site.

Printed in the United States of America

First Edition, 2014
2014 2015 2016   2017   2018   16 15 14 13 12 11 10 9 8
7 6 5 4 3 2 1

Library of Congress Cataloging in Publication Data: [Pending]

ISBN: Trade Paperback   9781624910449
ISBN: e-book   9781624910456

Cover model	Morgan Williams
Cover model photography	Maureen Maxson
Cover and interior design by	Linda D. Parkhurst PhD
Acquired for Parkhurst Brothers Inc., Publishers	
And edited by:	Ted Parkhurst

112014

DEDICATIONS

For our grandchildren:

Alison, Lauren, Kristin
H.A.M.

Cody, Clellie, Cruce, Bella and Emma
C.H.Y.

SUMMER 1816

The nightmare thundered into Esther's sleep. It pounded and flashed. Indistinct images ripped across her field of vision. There was light, then no light, only the guttural bursts of sound that arose from pain. Here and there a woman's long hair flashed. Then an arm.

Esther tossed fitfully on her tick. Images swirled, light came lightning-like. Then there was only dark. No colors played across the dream. Just black and white, black and white in a rising tempo that even in sleep began to make her nauseous. And there was the breathing—labored, heavy and quick—that washed the jagged pictures in sound.

The voice, those strangled scraps of sound, she thought, could break your heart. Esther struggled to escape, to wake and leave behind whoever was fighting for life against whatever forces had entered her sleep. To wake is to save her, she vaguely perceived.

She sat bolt upright. Sweat poured from her forehead and her nightgown was soaked. She stared into the dark of the cookhouse. Not even a star threw light into the tiny window. And the cold. She concentrated and tried to banish the nightmare images, the cold, smudged, black and white and loud corruptions of sleep and sanity.

CHAPTER 1

Cuff walked unsteadily down the street; Comfort was embarrassed to be seen with him. Rose was spending more and more time with Esther in the cooking shed.

"You ain't got enough sense left to bow your head when these people speak to you. Just grin and tip your hat to 'em. They got to know."

Cuff stopped suddenly and glared at her.

"Every day you goes on at me. Why'nt you stop it? I'm tired a hearing what I doin' wrong. No wonder men slap they wives aroun'."

"Cuff Mifflin, you ever even raise a hand like you goin' to hit me, I'll be all over you like darkness at midnight. I swear. You ain't the man I married. Such talk, and you become the drunk of the town."

"Won't be takin' it fo' long," he mumbled under his breath.

"What?"

"Nothin', woman."

"Where you takin' me, anyway. I don't know this part of town, and I don' like it."

"We jes goin' for a walk, tha's all. We can do that now. Tha's what people do." Comfort was silent. More and more she was certain she had to get away from Cuff. He'd turned mean with his drinking. He rarely had money to buy food, and Comfort had to take in more sewing and knotting so they wouldn't starve. She kept her freedom money, untouched and well hidden. If Cuff ever found it, it would be gone. She never breathed a word about it, even to Esther, who was becoming a second mother to Rose.

"How far we goin' to walk, Cuff. My legs is tired and I'm gettin' hungry. We got to go get Rose from Esther, and here we are stomping aroun' Wilmington like we had a house full of servants fixin' dinner and what not. This is just another crazy idea you got floatin' aroun' in your head—drink whiskey, bet on cocks and horses, drink more whiskey, go for a walk. What in the world is there for us out here?"

Cuff was stoic. He kept his eyes straight ahead and his gait as steady and forward moving as he was able. His strides were long and Comfort had to hurry to keep up. He seemed to have a purpose beyond just taking a walk with his wife. Besides his state of mind, he seemed genuinely worried about something, but what he had to worry about, except losing his wife and child, she couldn't fathom. His walk was purposeful and mechanical, almost like he was unaware of her presence.

"Cuff," she said, stopping, "we got to go get Rose."

"Not yet."

"Where you got to get to in such a hurry? I almost got to run to keep up."

"Then run."

"Cuff, I'm goin' back for my child."

"Our child, and no you ain't." He spun and faced her. His eyes glistered cold and black. "No you ain't goin' nowhere, and no you ain't doin' nothin' unless I says so. You my wife."

"But I ain't you damn slave. I been that, and I ain't ever gonna be again—not to you, not to no one. I ain't for sale. Now you get that through your head 'cause I'm one step away from leavin' you."

"You won't ever leave me 'less I say so."

It was the most cruel look he had ever given her. His face turned to sheer anger and rage. "You ain't got no say so in any of this, you hear what I'm sayin'?"

"Ain't got no say in what?"

"Nothin'," he said, his face melting from anger to worry.

"I ain't got no say in what, I asked you. Get it out of your head that you owns me."

A large hand clamped down over Comfort's mouth, cutting off her sentence. Another grabbed at her stomach and pulled her into his body. The air went out of her lungs and her eyes grew to silver dollars. When the two sets of hands slackened for a moment, Comfort whirled her head toward Cuff, pure damnation written across her brow. Then they were at her again. Cuff stood by and watched, little emotion showing.

"She's a wildcat, ain't she," Joe Johnson said with a hint of admiration. "She sure as hell ain't gonna lay down and die."

Comfort slipped one hand free and struck at the other man, catching him firmly on the cheek. He reddened, then punched her hard in the stomach.

"Lay off the merchandise," Johnson snarled at him.

"But she ..."

"Wouldn't you? Get her legs tied 'fore she kicks your manhood."

Comfort twisted in their grasp, growling and squealing the best she could against the attackers. Her hair flew and she was vaguely aware of stitches popping in her dress. Don't let them see me naked, swung through her consciousness, then departed. She was fighting again, and harder. The two white men were finding it more and more impossible to control her.

"You must be some man, Cuff," Johnson grunted, out of breath. "She do you like this in bed?" He smiled. But nothing seemed to register on Cuff's face. He watched as if seeing a nightmare come to life. It wasn't real, couldn't be, he told himself. But there she was, fighting two big white men for her dignity, her life, and she was wearing them down. Maybe she'll get free, run away. Cuff thought for a second. What I do then, I got nothin' lef' to pay wit' but my life.

In a moment of swirling hair and dress material and bound arms and legs, Comfort was hoisted above the men's heads and forced into the wagon bed. And she began the rhythmic, outraged kicking against the wagon boards that she would continue for hours, days, until she passed out from fatigue.

Joe Johnson climbed into the driver's seat and took up the whip. The other man climbed up alongside him and nodded. Both were worn out and utterly disheveled. Johnson looked over his shoulder at Cuff. "Debt paid," he said, and drove off. Comfort's kicks and muffled screams were all he was left with.

CHAPTER 2

Pompey stayed close to the edge of the woods. He had no blue flame to sell, Cuff wasn't even with him. He liked to watch the horses run, though with his income cut off he could not place even a small wager. Still, no one seemed to mind his being there. A few men made the long walk from the track to where he was leaning against a tree and asked to buy whiskey, but all he could do was shrug and show them empty hands. They left disappointed.

As the afternoon moved on, Pompey drew closer and closer to the track. Something about the powerful muscles and the raw energy of horse and rider made his heart race. No, it wasn't like it was with Cuff, who worshipped the bet and the thrill of filling his pockets with cash, Pompey liked the race no matter who won. He wondered what it must be like to mount one of those horses and ride it around the track, he imagined after that that walking would forever be too slow. Running would be too slow. He might, he admitted to himself, become addicted to the speed and find the world off a horse's back a lazy, daily disappointment.

His fancies came to a quick end when he spied Joe Johnson stumbling toward the track. Cuff spotted Pompey at the same instant and made a motion as if he were drinking. Pompey quickly wagged his head no and retreated towards the woods again. The last thing he saw was Johnson raging on the far side of the track, kicking up clouds of dust and threatening anyone who tried to calm him. Then he was gone.

Pompey had decided it was time to return to Wilmington, and scanned the crowd across the track but could not find the dirty, lumbering slaver. Attention seemed to have returned to the race, so Pompey cautiously made his way back to the railing. He smiled broadly, as he always did when the horses shot past him into the curve. He allowed a fragment of his imagination to return to wondering what horse riding must be like, but he did not allow himself a return to a full-blown daydream.

Johnson had merely lurched his way back toward the wagons where a few deadbeats had gathered around a jug of third-rate moonshine. Pompey heard him before he saw him. His voice boomed into the woods.

"Remember that nigger used to sell that blue moon," he began, loudly. "Blue flame," someone corrected.

"Well, he ain't so lucky anymore. Sold whiskey. Picked winning horses. Then it all went to hell on a hobbyhorse. It did. I watched him in that clown suit. Rich nigger to poor he went. And tha's when I knew I had him. Could'a stole him and sold him right down to Virginnie quicker'n a blink. But I tole myself, hold on there, he got somethin' more valuable than hisself. He got a young wife he's all the time braggin' on."

Even a few of the deadbeats turned and walked away from the braggart who stopped mid-story to gulp down some more rum. Those who remained listened intently—perhaps out of fear, perhaps out of a strange admiration for the man known throughout the state for his raids of free black communities where he snatched free people and took them south to Virginia or the Carolinas and sold them into slavery. He was reviled by most, revered by a few, recognized by everyone. He was tall and always filthy. A black scar ran across his cheek and disappeared behind his ear and snaked through his black hairline.

He was Patty Cannon's son-in-law and was not supposed to be allowed in the state of Delaware. But that didn't stop him from coming to the races or making late night raids as far north as Wilmington. And it did not stop him or other members of their gang from trafficking heavily in human beings. He had been caught once, convicted, and stood for several hours in front of the Georgetown courthouse with his ears nailed to the pillory. But he escaped jail soon after and went right back to stealing and selling human beings.

Now he would sometimes slip into Smyrna late at night and camp out in the woods before the races. The others who came were not the types to alert the law, and the law turned its back on the races. So Joe Johnson, drunk and feeling particularly proud of himself bragged on.

"He got the bettin' habit first. Then he took to his own hooch. Didn't know when to quit either one. I jest watched him slide both feet into hell." He laughed and a few of the men laughed with him.

"What'd ya do to the nigger, Joe?"

"Oh, I didn't do nothin' to him. I just give 'im the rope to hang hisself."

"And he did?"

"Done it up right, he did. Started borrowin' a little money here, tried to pay me back in 'shine. Sometimes I played along and he thought he had me figger'd out." He took another slug and smiled the smile of a clever and contented man. "Then I called in the debt."

The men standing around looked confused.

"His wife bought her freedom a few weeks ago. She was a free woman, and he turned her over to me. I sold her down Pocomoke way. Farm belongin' to some fella named Osborne. He calls it a plantation. But them Virginnie men think they's all bluebloods." He nodded at each man in turn, nodded to the nobleness of his deed.

Pompey sat motionless behind a tree about ten yards from the cluster of drunks by the wagons. Comfort stolen and sold ran through his mind over and over. Cuff paid a debt with his own wife. At that moment Pompey could have killed with his bare hands.

He sat until the group broke up, then got in his wagon and headed north. His brain was too busy to begin thinking about what he had to do.

CHAPTER 3

Pompey ran the old horse hard from Smyrna to Wilmington, stopping only a few times to give him water and a handful of grass from the side of the road. His mind raced too. Who could he tell? Mistress Mifflin was dead and Cuff was sinking daily. He heard stories from people all over town, and they weren't good, and nobody was laughing.

If the bastard Johnson had taken Comfort, had he taken Rose also? Could Cuff stoop that low? Paying off a debt with his wife was horrible to think about, but a daughter? His own flesh and blood. Pompey thought again that if Cuff were there right now, standing, or crawling, in front of him, he would beat him to death and feel no guilt.

But those thoughts were not going to answer his questions or solve any of his problems. Esther, he thought suddenly. Of course. Who else could he go to? But could he get past Clendaniel? That man was known as pure evil in the free Negro community. Then he remembered something Comfort had said once, merely in passing, about how Esther practically owned the cook shed of her master. No one but servants went there except on very rare occasions. Perhaps he could get to her there without having to get past the Master.

❧

Esther held Rose on her lap and rocked slowly and steadily. She murmured in the crying girl's ear. "I don't know why your Mama ain't come for you, I truly don't. It's been nine days and your Papa ain't come for you, neither. I pray every night to get a message, but I'm afraid of what it might be. It weren't no fun bein' an orphan. I was one, or nearly one. If it hadn't been for Namby, I'da had to raise myself up." She knew Rose would not understand what she was saying, but she also knew just the sound of a familiar voice could take some of the fear away.

In a little while Rose was cried out and went to sleep in Esther's arms. When she was certain Rose was fully asleep, she placed her on the pallet on the floor that she had made for her the night neither Comfort nor Cuff came for their daughter. They were supposed to finish clearing out Mistress Mifflin's house the next day, but that was more than a week ago, and Esther had been sick to death with worry ever since. Dead, the two of them dead, would blunder into her head often during the day, and she would fight to run the idea off.

She would think of the recipes for poultices or decoctions. Some were complex and required a great deal of thinking, thinking that left little room for sadsome ideas about the death of her friend. Rose slept, and Esther busied herself with early-in-the-day preparations for the evening meal. She took her daily sip of the quassia infusion and began to calculate the number of days more she would have to sip and build up her tolerance to the herb. She was surprised that she was very close.

She took a second sip. It was a dangerous thing to do, but there was no other way to find out if she could take a full dose and not be harmed, or at least not incapacitated by it.

She went back to her preparations, but her mind remained on Rose sleeping in the corner, and the missing Comfort. She also monitored how she was feeling. And she felt fine.

CHAPTER 4

Esther was deep into her dinner preparations, and her mind was steeped in worry. Every time Rose stirred in her sleep it reminded her anew that Comfort had simply vanished. Nothing like it had ever happened before. She and Rose had never even spent a night away from one another. Every day brought pain from uncertainty that was so deep that it almost stopped her from moving. But a slave couldn't stop, was not allowed to have concerns or worries or even feelings. That was not her job.

Just before five o'clock Esther heard something she had heard only once or twice before. There was the faintest knock at the cook-shed door. It was open, of course, but before she turned, her heart racing to see if it was Comfort, she mumbled a short prayer. It was not Comfort, and her heart sank. It was that friend of Cuff's.

She stood stock-still. She could no more move than reach

up and touch a star. She was suddenly certain that he brought news of their deaths. Tears began. Pompey mimed writing on the palm of his hand. Esther watched him, confused. They had seen each other only a few times, and Pompey was uncertain that she was even a Negro, let alone a slave. He remembered she was fair, but not this fair. What he did remember clearly was that she had a most remarkable feature—one eye was blue and the other was brown. This was the woman he had seen.

He mimed writing again, and Esther wondered for a moment why he did not speak. Then she remembered, he was dumb. She fumbled for something to write on and with. She found some fragments of paper that Comfort had used to wrap her dress. She gave him some charcoal from the ash bucket. He sat at the preparation table.

He strained, like a very small child, to fashion the letters. Even then they were awkward, almost grotesque shapes. After several minutes he handed the paper to Esther: cumfrt sol. She stared at the letters and their true horror washed over her slowly. Her free hand flew to her mouth and she stared at the little man.

As soon as she could, she whispered the words, "And Cuff?" Pompey took the paper back. Did it, he wrote.

Esther looked at him, not comprehending. "Did what?" she asked almost in anger.

Pompey pointed at the first two words. "Cuff sold Comfort?" She shook her head in disbelief. Pompey nodded sadly. How do you know this and why didn't you tell me before?"

Pompey pointed at his ear. "You heard it. Can it be true?"

Pompey nodded again. "Do you know where?"

Pompey wrote after much thought: vrgina.

Later, with prodding and help, Pompey revealed the best he could the rest of what he'd heard. Esther was patient with him after she got over the initial shock of Cuff's betrayal. But she's alive, she kept thinking, and Cuff will never get this child from me if I have to kill him.

CHAPTER 5

Esther opened the trunk in Rachel's room and found all of her clothes neatly folded and arranged by seasons. Imagine, she thought, having different clothes for different seasons. It struck her as odd and funny all at once. Only rich people would think up those kinds of excesses. The rest of us is too busy just stayin' alive.

She took everything out of the trunk one piece at a time. It was all her things, and none of Thomas's. Rachel had seen to that. She knew no one should be burdened with a lot of knicks and knacks that only meant anything to her and her dead husband. It had taken several days, but when it was done she felt a kind of exhilarated exhaustion. And she had space. Not that she would need it now. But there was freedom in creating space, nudging a little a bit of openness where there had only been clutter. Rachel felt like she could breathe better despite the growing heaviness in her chest.

Now Esther thumbed the same dresses and shawls and snoods that Rachel had worn only weeks before she died. Comfort had written a brief note to Mistress's distant niece and she was coming for her aunt's possessions. As Esther began to return the clothes to the trunk, she noticed some papers at the very bottom. She lifted them out and placed them on the dresser. She could read a little, but only what she'd taught herself sitting in the cooking shed with Namby. The old woman had insisted she learn and purloined a few primers and readers. Esther asked no questions and delighted in the pictures and the lines, dots and squiggles that eventually she recognized as letters and words and sentences.

There were two sets of papers. The older ones were two copies of exactly the same document that had been cut in two along a wavy line. When Esther laid the two pieces end to end, the wavy lines came together perfectly, and she smiled at how ingenious that was. She could read very few of the words, but the age of the document suggested they were important— why else keep papers around for that long. Perhaps they were Rachel's indenture papers, Esther thought. Maybe her niece would like to have them. She put them back in the trunk and looked at the others. These she recognized as Comfort's freedom papers, she had shown them proudly to Esther the day of her release from bondage. Esther had felt a twinge of jealousy when she took the papers in her hands. It was painful that they were not her own, and she had come so close. Twice she had prepared to go from the Clendaniel household into the free community. And twice he had slammed the door and said she was too valuable to go so cheap.

She refused to let him see her cry, to see any more wrinkles in her dignity. She wanted that in whole cloth, smooth, straight and clean. So she had returned to the cook shed, prepared another meal, served, and returned to the shed to weep the entire night. That close, she said over and over to the darkness, only to be snatched back from the threshold on a white man's whim. Paid in good faith, denied on bad faith. And the twinkle in his eyes when he told her, the infinitesimal upturn at the corner of his mouth might as well have been a full-throated roar.

Now Esther held Mistress's copy of Comfort's freedom papers. Would the niece want those too, she wondered? For what, she thought before putting them in the trunk. Instead, she refolded them and put them in the pocket of her apron.

When everything was packed, Esther backed out of the house, perhaps for the last time. The niece would pick up the trunks and parcels and haul them away. The house would be sold.

That's the way lives go, Esther thought. Things just pass on to the next person with the good fortune, good luck, or enough money to possess them. That's the way lives go.

CHAPTER 6

Comfort huddled in the corner of the small, dark cabin she had been shoved into. Some light fell in through chinks in the rough boards. Besides the fear and disbelief of what Cuff had done, she felt an overwhelming sense of warmth. She had no way of knowing where she was, but it had to be south, for there actually was some warmth in the sun.

The cabin had little furniture. As her vision had adjusted to the dark, she began to make out a rough chair and table, a pile of straw in a corner, and perhaps a blanket to lay on top of the straw. There were some pegs in the wall and a cracked bowl and pitcher. That was all.

She had kept to the same corner for what seemed like days. No one had come for her. Her stomach hurt, to say nothing of her heart. Rose was a constant in her thoughts. She wondered if Cuff had taken her from Esther and gone north, or if he had abandoned her. If she could have imagined what would be best, she would have, but what would be best; to live with a father who had sold his own wife, or be left without a mother and father? If Rose was still with Esther, Comfort knew she was all right, but what would happen when Master Clendaniel discovered the little girl? Comfort curled deeper into herself with that thought. The world beyond these walls crawled with monsters.

She had not dared to sleep for a long, long time. She did not know where she was or what she was to do. Her fingers ached for something to do, but she had no string or thread.

Her dress was in shreds. Johnson had made short work of that the first time she tried to run away. He caught up to her in a few strides and grabbed the back of the dress. When he pulled her back, the seams split and the material gave—the back was torn away. She hugged the remaining material to her.

Johnson laughed because now she could not run unless she wanted to go naked in the cold August air. But he had figured her to be more modest than that. Still, he was cautious. Nothing he thought he knew about her had held up. She was not timid and weak. She did not cry, did not beg him to look at her papers, did not try to bargain. She lay crumpled in the wagon bed, but not like one beaten and discarded. There was a kind of rebellious dignity in the rhythmic beating of her feet against the side of the wagon.

It was annoying to the two men who were stealing her south and again into slavery. But not as annoying as the simpering souls they sometimes took who wailed or moaned for days at a time. Utterly broken, they would be worn out and worthless by the time they reached Richmond, much less Roanoke Rapids or Raleigh.

This one had spirit, perhaps driven by a hatred of the one who sold her. But whatever the source, she was defiant and kept up the kicking until she passed out from lack of food and energy.

Only hours after Cuff's betrayal, Comfort had vowed to herself that she would not go quietly or easily. She would find a way back to Rose, and she began to plan what she would do to Cuff. He would be an easy target now that he had begun to drink that damned blue flame alcohol, and she could use that to her advantage. For long stretches she lay in the strips of sunlight and imagined varieties of torture.

Cuff could not swim, so she daydreamed ways to introduce rivers and streams into his death. Simply holding his head under water would not do. He would easily overpower her and drown her instead. No, she would need to be clever and turn his strength against him. But how? She didn't know offhand, but she knew she would have time to imagine every detail and revel in every painful misstep until she had it perfectly planned.

She turned next to fire. She could not think of a slower, more painful fate. Cuff had spoken of the woman on the road from Smyrna who was hung and burned. It was with absolute horror that he told her of the way the woman dropped, prematurely, into the flames, but would not give her persecutors the satisfaction of a scream, and went silently to death, the mouth that refused its voice, a hole in the fire and smoke damning them all forever. Cuff burned alive in a stupor had a certain balance of justice and pure revenge. Cuff burned alive fully conscious had a satisfaction all its own.

At times she would marvel at her own devious thoughts and shudder away from them. But then she would think, except for murder, and perhaps rape, what crime was worse than selling another human being into bondage? Especially a wife? No, revenge was justified.

And she imagined suffocation. Her hands on his throat, watching his eyes bulge. Her bare foot on his throat and the terror of airless moments and the world going blank and black. A stick at his throat and her knee in his back working in opposite directions.

And then she would cry. Cry that he had driven her to these thoughts, to this place where the sun threw down bars on the floor and taunted her. Cry that she would have to face someone, face outside, face the unknown and the future alone. No one would buy a slave only to have her molder away in a half-dark cabin. That she had been there for so long confused her. Was it out of kindness such as Mistress might have shown her? But—why? A new owner owed her nothing. Perhaps it was to show her she was property again. And property does not question.

For a long time she cried, and did not think, but reveled in the gray nothingness that seeps like a fog into the brain and dampens thought and feeling and time.

CHAPTER 7

Esther woke suddenly. She wasn't sure where she was, but it was black in the room, and cold. She lay on the floor, she knew that. When she rolled on her side, it all came clear. Rose lay sleeping in the very faint glow of the last embers dying in the fireplace. It was not the usual warm glow, this light, like this season, was stingy and brittle.

She had made herself a pallet out of blankets and straw. It was too early to rise and stoke the fire and get breakfast started, so she lay thinking. Comfort was in Virginia, sold back into slavery by her own husband. It made her feel physically ill. But she had to do something. But what? Get her! Get her! Get her! Began in her head and soon fell in syncopation with her heart.

It was a crazy idea, a slave woman going south to Virginia to steal back another slave woman. The idea was lunacy of the first order, she realized. But she also realized that so many forces in her life had been gathering for just such a situation. Hadn't Comfort encouraged her, even helped her prepare, to walk away from the Clendaniel household and head for Pennsylvania? Hadn't Comfort made her two dresses fit for a free woman? Hadn't she been born almost white, even having one blue eye and very light hair? Why would God send her all of those things if she was not supposed to put them together and find Comfort? Maybe there was some sense in all of this after all.

Get her! Get her!

But going north and going south were very different ventures. That thought kept intruding. Lying in the dark she could feel the words dissolving into rhythm.

Get her! Get her! Get her!

Words becoming, not a pattern like her heartbeat, her heartbeat.

Steadily, over a half an hour as false dawn came and went, and then the first stray rays of sunlight streaked the sky. It transformed utterly and completely, and she could no more turn from it, or stop it, or forget it than she could blink and stop the sun from rising.

Get her! Get her! Get her! Get her!

So Esther got up with the sun as she always did. Rose's dark shape lifted and fell with her breathing, and Esther willed her heartbeat into the girl as vague, frightening plans began to form in her head. A troubling array of questions appeared and disappeared. Appeared and were solved. Appeared and seemed to have no solutions.

Get her! Get her!

Get a wagon. Learn to be white. Take Rose. Give Master quassia infusion. Take the dresses out of hiding. And on and on. But rather than feeling oppressed by the impossibility of what she was suddenly planning, she felt light, energized and hopeful in a way she had never been before. She was certain that everything that had been massing like storm clouds, were foretelling what she would someday have to do. And like the storm, that day had come.

CHAPTER 8

Comfort drifted in and out of a light, dreamless sleep. She did not need the blanket, it stayed warm through the nights. A very large full moon took up the job of the sun and lay narrow planks of light across the floor, and over Comfort. She would awake with a start, accustom her eyes to the light and dark, and her brain to where she was, or where she thought she was.

Sometimes she thought she saw an animal in the room, other times she imagined others sleeping around her on the floor. But they were all figments. She was utterly alone.

Then, there was someone there. He was a tall, stout woman standing over her, hands on hips, and a face lost in shadow. "I hear tell you're clever with yer han's. That true?" she barked. "I could use a seamstress 'roun' here."

Comfort had awoken with a start and lay still, afraid to move. Most of what the woman said to her rang in her head, but she was unsure how long she had been there and how much more she might have said before Comfort rose to consciousness.

"Ma'am," she muttered.

"I asked you could you use a needle and thread. From the looks of what's left of your dress, you know quite well."

"My Mistress let me earn money sewin' and knottin' when I wasn't busy makin' her collars and such," Comfort said quietly.

"Mistress?"

"Yes'm. Mistress Mifflin of Wilmington, Delaware."

"Yer a runaway got caught?

"No'm."

"Then that Johnson son of a bitch snatched you from this Mistress o' yourn?"

"No'm. Ain't how he took me."

"Get up," the woman told her. "Get up and look at me. You'll be seein' me for a long time. Frankly I don't care where you come from, or who snatched you, or any of the rest of it. That part of yer life is over. You belong to me and I expect to get my money's worth out of yer black hide."

"But my baby," Comfort cried.

"Baby—I ain't seen no baby. Didn't hear tell about no baby. He's gone, and fare thee well," she said coldly and without a hint of feeling. "I'll make those fingers work like they ain't worked before." She turned and stomped out of the door. After the door slammed she yelled, "I'll see you out here ready to work at sun up. Be late and you get the whip. Be late twicet and you go in the stocks. After that, God protect you."

And she was gone.

Comfort slumped to the floor, dazed. Mistress had never spoken to her like that in her life. And now she might as well be an animal.

The casual days of knotting beside Mistress's fire were gone, the conversation, the stories of Ireland, the newspaper articles about exploding mountains seemed years ago, if not delusions of a life never lived.

There were clothes piled in a corner for her, she'd been told. She was reluctant to take off her freedom dress, but it was tattered and would not stay on her unless she hugged it to her body. She searched the room until she found the slave dresses and a second hand pair of slave shoes. She swapped them out, an old life for a new.

CHAPTER 9

Esther pulled the dresses Comfort had made for her out of their hiding place in the wall. She placed the knotted snood on top of the dresses and stood back trying to decide what else she might need for traveling. She didn't have that much, she concluded, but she needed to give the appearance that she was well off if she were stopped and questioned.

There was a Bible in the hallway, she could filch that at the last minute, and perhaps a parasol out of the stand. There were so many there, one would never be missed. Mistress rarely went outside in the daytime, she would merely need to secret it out of the back door.

She took the mother of thyme infusion down from the

shelf and placed the bottle in her pocket. She had increased her intake to a quarter of a cup a day, far more than she would need to put in Master's wine.

Esther carefully measured out two teaspoons of the liquid and poured them into Master's wine cup, then she poured the wine to blend. She sniffed, but there was no odor. She placed the cup on a tray beside the decanter, straightened her dress and headed for the parlor where Master took his wine at four in the afternoon while Mistress continued her sewing, or knotting, or staring off into the infinitely fascinating ceiling.

She poured a small draft into her tasting cup, making sure he saw every movement. He watched how much she poured, and when she had drunk it down, showed him the empty cup. Only after he had nodded, did she pour his wine. He hesitated.

He knows, she thought. He knows. Her hands began to sweat, and she thought she could see the tray shake. He will whip me right here in this room before Mistress, she thought. Then he nodded the almost imperceptible nod she had come to watch closely for. She poured the wine then left the room. She would return, until he stopped her, every fifteen or twenty minutes to pour more wine.

In the cook shed she prepared the rest of the evening meal. Sometimes he bellowed for her to come pour, other times he waited patiently until she returned. Today he waited. As she worked, Esther wondered how it would begin, thirst, diarrhea, sweating. Perhaps vomiting. Whichever came first, the other symptoms would follow quickly. She wished she could be around for the ultimate result, Master would come to hate alcohol in any form.

She returned to the house and waited to be summoned from the doorway where she stood, arms at her side, no expression on her face. Master raised his right hand and motioned twice with his pointer finger for her to come to him. She took the cup from his hand and poured another draft of the wine.

As she handed him the cup, was that a bead of sweat she saw on his brow? Sweat in these cold times?

CHAPTER 10

The fabric she was handed looked so much like the fabric she'd used to make Rose's dress, she began to cry as it passed through her hands.

"'Less you wanna wind up a field slave, I'd suggest you quit the tears and start sewin'."

Comfort wondered if there was a soft place anywhere in this woman—in her heart, her mind, her memories. She had daughters, surely that must mean something between women who had shared the pain, the risk of death. Women forever share a bond because of birth, Mistress Mifflin told her once. She believed it. Women were cursed. But the tears still came. The images of Rose just kept rising in her brain like the child was right there and she could see her in the warm sunshine playing with her dolls.

"I'm warning you," Mistress barked.

"But my daughter," Comfort said throwing her hands into her lap in frustration. "I got a daughter."

"I don't see no daughter. Ain't no daughter come here with you. Joe Johnson said nothin' about no daughter. If this child exists, then get her demon outta yer head, she'll ruin you here. From now on you had no life before you come here. All this sniffin' and blowin' is on my time, and I don't like it."

"But she's real."

Mistress rose heavily from her chair and stood in front of Comfort. "I said you had no life before you come here. You born again," she laughed. "You got no daughter, you ain't drawn a breath 'fore you got here. No daughter, no man, no life 'fore. I'll even give you a new name. I call you Virginnie," and she laughed.

"Tha's what you are, a virgin in Virginia." She seemed proud of herself to make a complicated connection. But just as suddenly her smile fled.

"Hear me and hear me good, nigger Virginnie, next time you'll be out in the field." With that she slapped Comfort hard on the left cheek. It stung, but she would not cry, crying was only for Rose now.

CHAPTER 11

Cuff had not seen her for weeks. He might never be able to face his baby. What would he say? Nothing he could say now would make much sense to her, but later, when she asked about the mother she only faintly remembered, what would he say then?

Let her go now, he said to himself. It's easier now, 'cause I got to make some money. I'm runnin' low and I sure can't do my business with a little girl hangin' on my back all the time.

What he truly feared was facing the wrath of Esther. What would he tell her? The truth? He didn't trust her with the truth, her knowin' Roots and all whatever kinda voodoo some women know'd about. Comfort had told him stories. He knew what she could do.

Tell her a lie? Those women were half witches at least and could see straight through to the other side of a lie. That would be worse. She was just plain nobody to mess with. But he knew Rose was safe with her, if she could just keep the child away from Master Clendaniel. That man had one of the worst reputations among slaves and free blacks. He was evil itself.

Cuff gave up drinking from a cup, he just raised the jug to his mouth and gulped. That way he could justify not going to see his daughter, it wouldn't be right to see her when he was drunk. And it was a way to keep him away from himself as well. This was not the real Cuff Mifflin. He'd gone off somewhere, this one was just here to visit awhile, then he'd go.

That thought sloshed around in his softened brain until he was convinced it was true. Gone off. Gone fishin'. Gone to hell.

He had not been back in the house since that night. He couldn't face what he and Comfort had begun to make together. Too, anyone looking for him would come there, and by now someone may have caught wind of what he'd done. He knew Joe Johnson would no more keep his word than give up slaving and find religion. Sooner or later he'd start to brag, and there was nothing lower in the community than someone in league with Joe Johnson and Patty Cannon, traffickers in human souls.

Cuff kept to the woods mostly. Visited the cockfights from time to time. But his luck had turned completely and he refused to get in debt again. If he continued to lose, he was afraid he might have nothing left to sell but his own black soul.

CHAPTER 12

It was not, Esther decided, a symptom. It was too early. But perhaps he was beginning to question his treatment of her, a slave who held his life in her mouth every time she sampled the food she'd prepared and brought that food to table. Perhaps that was the source of the sweat on his upper lip.

The first real symptom struck William Clendaniel about an hour after he had finished supper. He was standing on the porch facing the street contemplating a trip north that he was about to make. He had made arrangements for the livery to deliver his horse and buggy in the morning. Suddenly he realized that he was very thirsty. He went to the cook shed looking for a cup of water. He dipped a cup and drank it straight down. He dipped a second and then a third, but nothing seemed to slake the thirst. Very odd, he said to himself.

On his way through the house, the sweating began. This is most peculiar, he thought, and continued back to the porch. As Master passed her, Esther could make out the glistening on his face. She had watched him go to the cook shed and stood paralyzed with fear. She did not know what he'd gone there for, because it was a place he never went. Esther could recall once, maybe twice, Master standing outside the cook shed talking with Namby. But he had never come, that she was aware of, as long as she had been doing the cooking.

But Master returned quickly. It was not as if he had been snooping. He did not seem at all as if he had even seen the dried herbs and tinctures and decoctions and infusions set in neat rows along the shelves. He had gone for water merely, and she sighed.

Esther stood deep inside the house and watched Master who was framed in the doorway, the last light making him look like a shadow of himself. One moment he stood erect, dark and severe. The next he seemed to teeter, just a little, but a crack nonetheless in the severity of his posture. Ester broke into a brief smile. She wanted to hold on to the moment, not let the full effect come on too quickly so he might come and find her and beat her and beat her and beat her until his strength ebbed with the vomiting and awful, painful diarrhea. No, let it work slowly. He had the thirst, now let the hunger come.

Master returned to the house. "Esther," he bellowed, not knowing she was only a few yards away. She entered the room slowly. "Was there any food left from dinner."

"Yessir."

"Fetch it for me," he said gruffly.

"Yessir, must mean Master liked what Esther cooked."

"I'm hungry. Simply hungry. All it means is you didn't feed me enough. Now go."

"Yessir." And she was gone to the cook shed, smiling as she stepped from the porch.

She had, in the darkest corner of the building, a bundle made up of the fine dresses Comfort had made for her for her eventual freedom, or for her escape. It was wrapped in the same paper Pompey had written on to tell her about Comfort being sold. She had secured the bundle with some string. She hoped no one would question a fair woman walking down the street with such a package. She hoped.

Esther gathered the remainder of the food and brought it on a tray into the dining room. Master attacked it, not even bothering with a knife. He grabbed the cold chicken with his hands and devoured wing, thigh and leg. The stewed tomatoes he drank from the bowl. Bread he tore into large chunks and chewed voraciously. The pie he lifted from the pan and held in front of his face. He seemed to not chew so much as swallow whole every bite he took.

Esther watched in wonder. She had never seen a soul eat so much and so quickly and without the least bit of self-consciousness. Even though she stood in the doorway awaiting orders, he did not notice her. His eyes, his absolute focus was on the food, as if the world had been reduced to what lay on the table, and the supply was dwindling by the minute.

She racked her brain to recall if there was anything else that might even pass for food in the cook shed. More bread perhaps, water, the tainted wine. Then, for a moment, the spell seemed to break. He paused, a chicken leg about to go into his mouth.

"Drink," he said, and the chicken leg disappeared. And so did Esther. She nearly ran to the shed and grabbed the water and the stoop of wine.

She set bucket, stoop and cup on the table. Master dipped a cup and poured it down his throat. Then wine. Bread. A wing. The last of the pie.

Then, as quickly as this maelstrom of eating began, it stopped. Master rose from the table and returned to the porch. There he stood, wavering, teetering on shaky legs.

And then he vomited, violently and continually.

Esther watched from the dark recesses of the house. Now she could smile broadly. The sun had set its cold, thin remaining light, but there was still enough for Esther to see the outline of Master bent at the waist. And she could hear, as well, the awful retching and heaving of the monster who had raped her since she was a young girl.

He moaned as the diarrhea began, and he could not make it to the outhouse. He held his stomach and fell to the porch. He could not move. Could not stop or even slow the sustenance escaping him above and below.

Esther exited the house, returned to the cook shed and sought out the bundle that contained everything of earthly value she owned. She put on her freedom dress and the snood Comfort had knotted for her.

She left the cook shed and did not look back.

CHAPTER 13

Pompey and Rose sat on the stoop of his little cabin. Rose's face was resting in her hands, elbows on knees. She had asked for her Mama so many times, Pompey was about worn out. He kept a jar inconspicuously next to him. Since there was no more blue flame, Mingo had scavenged enough parts to build his own still, and Pompey was the official tester of every batch.

When Rose turned her head to look up the street, Pompey would test the content of his jar. It was no blue flame, but it beat plain water. Mingo was even servicing Cuff's old customers. Cuff dared not go out among them now. Any number of people had sworn to kill him if it meant their own freedom, or even their life.

Esther had made up a little bundle of Rose's clothes, her slave clothes, and it sat on the floor next to her. Pompey had loaded what little he owned, mostly stopped jugs and bottles full of Mingo's concoction, into a sack. It hung from a nail next to him. A woman turned the corner into view, and Rose leapt to her feet and began calling Mama, Mama. The woman smiled at her as she passed by.

Rose sat back down and began to softly cry. Pompey stroked her hair gently, he hugged her a moment, unsure what to do. He'd had little to do with children in his life. In the dark he grimaced hoping Esther would appear soon. They would only be able to travel under darkness. And that carried even odds that it would get them killed, or at the very least, sold south.

CHAPTER 14

Just as Rose cried at Pompey's, Comfort sat on the steps of her mean-looking cabin and sobbed. Isaac sat next to her and let her cry. He knew why. He was old. In his life he'd seen about as much meanness as one human could heap on another. There would be no freedom price for him, no, for him the only freedom price was death.

Isaac marveled at how long this girl could cry. But he

knew that burden. One son sold at age five, a daughter as soon as she could sew, and another son bludgeoned for trying to escape. Imagine, he'd often thought, rather kill a man for trying to escape and lose his back and sweat and muscle. The whole thing made so little sense he'd given up trying to understand it.

Isaac was tired. With the sun down, he wanted sleep. They worked into dusk, and would have worked him well into darkness if they had light for the field. But he wanted time to himself, and Fillis, his common-law wife. They were separated daily when he went to the fields, and she, after forty-three years, to work in the kitchen house.

But this girl needed him more tonight. He was afraid she might just lie down and die, and to do that meant no hope. At least with light in your eyes, he knew, there was always hope.

In the patch of woods across from the steps they were sitting on, a large black dog appeared. His tail wagged and he woofed softly. Isaac spied him and smiled. He reached down to the ground and felt around for a chicken bone or some discarded gristle.

Comfort's bout of crying seemed to be coming to an end, and Isaac said, "Look."

Comfort wiped her eyes with the back of her hand, then pulled a rag of a handkerchief out of her sleeve. "His tail's a waggin'," she said.

"He's a good old hound. Been aroun' here fo' years. Name's Clancy."

"Strange name for a big ole dog."

"Best anyone kin remember is he showed up about the

time a big pack of Irish moved through here. Field hands called all the Irish Clancy. And some of them boys was pretty dark. So when the dog done showed up, they called him Clancy as a joke, and it stuck. Likes to have his head rubbed."

He let it go to silence. Let her watch the dog. Let her put out a tentative hand toward him. The dog had snatched the bone from Isaac's hand, and the man laughed. "Done that since he was a pup, like he was afraid you might change your mind and take it back. Don't mean nothin' by it. Tha's how it is when you don't know where your next meal's comin' from. Gets like that here from time to time. Food goes up to the house first, scraps come back. But it's good to have connections in the kitchen." He winked at Comfort.

While he spoke, the dog brought his head up under her hand and closed his eyes as she stroked him. "It feels so good to touch something tha's alive again, Isaac."

Isaac nodded his white head. "Ever'thin' needs to touch and be touched, I guess."

Clancy lay down with an "oomph" next to Comfort like he had no plans of going anywhere, like he knew she needed to be needed.

CHAPTER 15

Esther sat tall with her back very straight on the seat of the wagon. She wore one of the freedom dresses Comfort had made her and the snood covered her hair. She looked very proper. And white. Rose sat or lay on a thin blanket behind her. Even in her sleep, at times, she murmured "Mama, Mama," and Esther could feel her heart break just a little more. She had not yet allowed herself to question the wisdom of a trip into slave country to steal a slave. It was simply what she had to do.

Pompey drove.

The roads, such as they were, were little more than wheel ruts in the sand and clay. He had allowed himself to think about the foolhardiness of this trek south. But bolstered by Mingo's rum, he kept his fears to himself. He would occasionally feel his pocket for his papers, but they could do him more harm than good now. He was a slave being taken to Esther's brother's plantation in Virginia. Rose was his daughter.

If anyone asked, she would tell him or her that story. Why were they traveling at night? Her skin was fair and burned easily in the sun. But this was the year without a summer! Yes, but in a letter from her brother she was told it was not like that in the South.

Esther had pieced together every interrogation she could imagine, worried hours, even days, over answers until even she believed the story. She didn't sleep much in the days before she walked out of Master Clendaniel's house, picked up her bundle, some herbs, and marched down the street toward Pompey and Rose under the benevolence of darkness. The few people out and about did not seem to question her being in that part of the city, didn't notice her at all. But she refused to grow confident, she had seen whites turn in a second and pounce on her emotionally, verbally, and physically.

Among whites, she wore caution like a cape.

The wagon moved slowly, but there were no other travelers. When the moon moved out from behind a fast moving cloud, Esther had a sharp intake of breath. Pompey put his hand on her to calm her. She slapped it off of her. "Remember who we are. Touch a white woman like that in front of a white man, he'll cut your hand off." Pompey withdrew and hung his head. He had forgotten.

Esther instantly wanted to take back the gesture and apologize, but she dared not. Perhaps the brief event had woken him to the danger they had put themselves in. He could not make that mistake in front of anyone, it might mean eternal hell for Comfort, and death for the three of them. No, Pompey would have to remain embarrassed and hangdog.

Esther hardened. But she kept her fear from Pompey and, of course, Rose. She turned and looked at the little girl sleeping in the moonlight. This had to work, she thought. She turned forward to watch the road, her back straightening a little more.

She tried to summon every movement, every rhythm of speech, every nuance of hand and mouth and eye she had ever seen in a white woman. She was, for all of their sakes, becoming white—outside, if not in.

CHAPTER 16

Cuff, drunk, rapped the jug on the rear tavern door. Hard and impatient, he knocked and knocked and knocked until the angry tavern keeper yanked open the door.

"What the hell is your problem?" he shouted before he even saw who was making all the racket. He stopped before saying anymore.

Cuff held the jug out to him. When the tavern keeper did not respond, Cuff shook the jug in his face. "Fill it," he said unsteadily.

"Who you givin' orders to, boy?"

"I ain't no boy," Cuff said with only a veneer of control on his words.

"You're right about that. You used to be a boy. Now you're just a drunk who sold his free wife into slavery. And I will no longer serve scum like you. Take my word, there are any number of people ready to hang you up—black, white, bond and free. Watch your back, and don't ever come here again."

Cuff raised the jug above his head and smashed it on the

lintel only inches from the tavern keeper's face. Pottery flew, a large shard glazed the man's cheek. Blood began to flow. He wiped it with a finger and stared at it. Cuff turned and walked away.

"Thinks he can talk to me like I was some slave? I'm a businessman just like him." He spoke out loud. "Good as him, good as anybody. Hang me? We'll see about that. Find my proper dog tooth and I'll come back and buy that old tavern, then I can serve who I want." Get my Rose someday to work with me, he thought.

Cuff found his way into the woods and sat on a fallen tree. His head spun, he was beginning to sober and he didn't like it, not a little bit. But with this clearer head he remembered that he had heard that Mingo had combobulated a still for himself since he had stopped making blue flame.

He smiled and stood up. "Got to go see my man Mingo." Then he headed towards the road.

CHAPTER 17

Mingo rose from filling a jug and nearly dropped it when he saw Cuff standing behind him. Anger rose in him instantly. "You got no business 'round here no mo'. Go on 'fore I beat you."

Cuff stood his ground belligerently. "I'm thirsty, Mingo."

"I s'pose snakes git thirsty too. But I don't want my rum in your belly." He spit near Cuff's shoes and dared him to come after him.

"I ..." he began, but Mingo cut him off.

"I? Let me finish that fo' you. I—sold my wife to Joe Johnson, miserablist man ever lived. I—left my daughter and never went to get her. I—used to have a business, make money, care about my family. Have I got it about right, Cuff Mifflin?"

"You don' ..." Cuff began again.

"Don' tell me I don' understan'. I understan' you gonna burn in hell for all eternity. I sure do understan' that. I understan' that as low as Johnson is, you lookin' up at the soles of his boots. I understan' you the shame of black folks all over this town, bond and free. Answer me this, Cuff. Where did you bury your dignity? 'Cause I want to go piss on its grave."

CHAPTER 18

Mistress watched her on the sly, watched her practiced, artful hands as the shuttles looped and clicked through knots and picots, double knots and rings. Delicate, perfect, beautiful white flower-like designs bloomed from her hands. And she was, Mistress observed, quite aware of her own superior talents. Didn't she almost smirk when she observed Mistress's handwork? Didn't she condescend to inspect her work and pronounce it "so pretty," or "so fine?"

How could a Negress—a mere slave—learn the art of knot-ting, let alone master it, she wondered. The more she watched and saw that Virginnie did it almost unconsciously, the more incensed she became, until she could not control the rage-fu-eled shaking in her hands. Her voice wavered when she spoke, clipped, nearly spat out.

"Stop. Stop it. Put it down."

Comfort looked up at her, perplexed. "Yes'm," she said and let her hands settle in her lap.

"It's wrong. All wrong."

"Yes'm, if you say it, it must be so."

"It. Is. So. By God," she hissed through pursed lips.

Mistress rose slowly as if she were deciding what to do with each movement she made. Comfort watched her carefully. This was nothing like the comfortable room in Mistress Miff-lin's house, with two rocking chairs beside the window, a fire in the grate. This was a working room with no comforts at all. It was dim and all business. Mistress rarely came there except to fetch some work Comfort had done, or berate her for some imagined offense. And Comfort preferred it that way because Mistress took no pains to hide her distain for slaves, for blacks in general. "Stain on this country," she would mutter to one of her children who were quickly learning their mother's hatreds.

"It will not be anymore," she screamed. Comfort was utterly confused. This large, powerful woman now towered over her with rage turning her face and neck into burgundy blotches. Her whole body seemed to quake. Comfort cowered and would not look into her eyes.

Before Comfort could rise from her chair and seek safety

away from her, Mistress snatched the knotting from her lap and slammed it to the floor. She reached for Comfort, but she backed away.

"Virginnie," she howled, "stand still." She grabbed Comforts right hand, and in a single, swift motion pushed her middle finger back until it snapped loud as a green stick and touched her wrist.

Comfort slumped to the floor and passed out.

"Now you'll work the fields," Mistress said, calming, and walked out of the door.

CHAPTER 19

Comfort lay unconscious. Mistress huffed and stormed from the room. A few minutes later Sabra, Mistress's other domestic slave, rushed into the room and immediately knelt next to Comfort. She had been sent to tend to her finger, but she had learned a long time ago to be low keyed in everything, excel in nothing, and these were the wages of that sin. Mistress had done the same to her, twice.

"Comfort," Sabra said in a near whisper. "Comfort." It was as she had hoped, Comfort was fully unconscious. Even when she blew softly on her eyelids, there was no response. "Won't feel nothin' now you're out."

Comfort's middle finger was bent grotesquely backward.

It seemed limp and impossibly angled. Sabra shook her head from side to side. "How can a woman be so mean?" she said softly. "Answer to that is she ain't no woman, she's just some horrible beast."

Sabra sat on the floor and took Comfort's hand in hers. She took hold of the middle finger and quickly pulled it up and forward so that it came back into alignment with the other fingers. She had brought a piece of rag torn into strips. She wrapped a length around Comfort's ring, middle and index fingers so would not be able to use any of them for a while. If she regained the use of the finger, though Sabra never had, Comfort would probably never be able to knot again, or sew.

Sabra sang softly while she waited for Comfort to come to. It was a field song she'd learned as a child. Her mother sang it incessantly and unconsciously as she taught Sabra to cook, and sew, and bake, anything that would make her invaluable inside the house, not in the fields where days were long and hot, or long and cold, the work dirty, the cycle without change—seed, tend, harvest, seed, tend, harvest—until you died.

Inside, at least, there was variation and protection. Though for Sabra, the protection seemed only as good as a fickle Master or Mistress, or worse, both.

Sometimes she hummed, sometimes she sang. But she was patient.

Comfort came to with a start. Her vision was cloudy for a few moments, but when it cleared she started to stand up. Then the pain knocked her down again. "Lie still, Comfort," Sabra said. "I promise you you're gonna hurt. She broke that finger good." She shook her head.

"I shoulda warned ya, I guess. She don't let nobody do nothin' better than her. She probably saw how good your handwork was, and it made her mad."

Comfort stared at her hand, then at Sabra.

"She done broke two of my fingers, so Mistress sent me to tend you. I put your finger back in place like somebody done for me. Keep the piece of rag on there awhile. It'll keep you from usin' that hand."

❧

Isaac cradled Comfort's hand in his own while Fillis tried to coax spoonfuls of carrots into her mouth.

"She done it again, Fillis," Isaac said, as if the very idea was so monstrous that he had never entertained the idea. Sabra had been damaged, but she was so willful that she remained in the house. Her mother had taught her well. Others had been whipped, burned, tied to posts in the mid-day sun stark naked. But much of what Mistress inflicted was swift and unpremeditated. She angered in an instant, and struck in the heat. She did not burn slow and plan her punishment. She lashed without thinking and slashed, slapped, scratched or broke whatever came most readily to hand. And she had no guilt.

"We're jist animals to her, Comfort. Animals. She'll ride us hard and plant us when we die. Tha's all she's obliged to do by her way of thinkin'."

The pain cut from her fingers and radiated up her arms. And as if by some intimate connection between hand and eye, the tears flowed, and dripped from her cheek and pooled in Isaac's palm.

Fillis cajoled some more carrots that had been cooked to mush and flavored with a little molasses. Clancy chewed on a stick nearby, rarely leaving Comfort's side since their first meeting. "Don't know what that dog sees in you, but he sure is stuck on ya," Isaac chuckled.

"He's my baby now, I 'spect. Mistress says I didn't have no life 'fore I come here. Even took my name away, named me Virginnie."

"Comfort," Fillis said putting the spoon in the bowl and sitting next to Comfort on the cabin step. "She can't take anythin' you ain't willin' to let her take. Ain't nobody can take your past, your name or nothin' else you carry around in your heart or head. She could take your clothes or your food, but that ain't nothin'. Comfort be Comfort always."

"Amen," said Isaac. The white haired man was fifty-two years old and looked seventy. He was bent and scarred from years in the fields. And his skills with crops and people made him the defacto overseer. Someone stepped out of line, it was Isaac put him back with only a glance. This Master and Mistress believed if one slave acted up, all were punished, and Isaac had grown accustomed to getting regular rations, his yearly clothes and shoes, and the roof over his head. He didn't fancy sleeping outdoors among the mosquitoes and snakes and the occasional bear because some young hot head decided to act up. He didn't fancy going hungry or watching his wife go hungry because someone didn't put their whole back into a job.

He'd think each time somebody became the recipient of his stare, hate me if you want to. Rarely words. The eyes spoke loud enough and without breaking his own work rhythm.

Soon the loudest things around the three were the crickets and Clancy chewing his stick.

CHAPTER 20

A heavy mist clung to the grasses and lower limbs of trees. There was barely enough light to see the roadway, but the horse seemed to be walking in his sleep anyway, so Pompey put his trust in the animal and just kept his hands lightly on the reins. Esther had been dozing for the past hour and Rose snored lightly in the back among the bundles they had brought with them. The horse walked noiselessly on the soft earth. Pompey might have dozed too, and trusted him to a straight line, but his senses were keened. This was enemy territory. His whole life he had heard stories of atrocities in "the South," the states whose existence depended on owned workers.

He instinctively tapped the pocket where he kept his papers, but they did not console him as they did in the border state of Delaware. Not that he was danger free there, but he felt like less of a target. And Esther was in even more danger, a runaway slave deliberately traveling south. A shiver ran through him.

The sun beginning to show to his left told him his instinct had been right through the night. They were indeed traveling south. The orange rim of the sun shimmered above the mist and looked close enough to ride to, to touch in an hour. There was no heat to that sun, and it would take a while for the mist to burn off and the chill to get run off by the new day. But there must have been something in the new light, for Esther's eyes shot open, her head swiveled around in confusion. Pompey's first thought was to reach out and assure her, but he pulled his hand back before he could touch her. He remembered the lesson, and his hand still stung.

"Where are we?" Esther asked.

Pompey shrugged his shoulders and pointed at Rose. She looked behind and frowned. What if she were taking Rose into as much danger as she feared? What if they all wound up slaves? What good would that do Comfort? She felt fear, like some bad meat, in her stomach. She looked at Pompey and knew he was feeling the same thing.

"I wonder how long it'll take Master to get a runaway notice in the newspapers." Pompey shrugged again, and pointed behind him, to the north.

"What?" she asked

He jerked his thumb over and over to the north. "Oh," said, "he wouldn't think I'd run south?" Pompey nodded in agreement.

The horse followed the bend in the road at his steady, slow pace. Then he startled. On the side of the road stood a white man next to his horse. He rose up out of the mist and shocked them all.

Esther had a quick intake of breath. The man touched his hat to her. This was what she had feared, this was where her story, her nerve, her voice and her skin would keep them moving south, or to some farm where they would never be heard from again.

"Ma'am," he said. "Out awful early, ain't ya?"

"Sir," she tested her voice and it was working with no telltale squeaks or breaks. "We have traveled the night."

"Must be in a hurry. Ain't really safe to be travelin' at night with just a nigger for protection. And a picaninny sleepin' behind you."

Esther blushed. "Believe me, I wouldn't travel if I didn't have to. But my brother..." She broke off and wondered if she dared to tell her story without being asked.

"Brother?"

"Is sick and I'm taking my man and his little daughter down to help out. He's only got one slave and the work ain't gittin' done. His wife is frail, too."

"What's your name, boy?"

Pompey shook his head and stared at Esther.

Esther sat up straighter. "Name's Pompey. He's mute. Dumb."

"That right, boy?"

Pompey nodded.

"But he ain't deef."

"No, he can hear."

"Must be lonely ridin' all night with nobody to talk back to ya, and it too dark to see him flappin' his hands around."

"Yessir." But it came out too much like slave talk, and she could feel the fear firing up again, but he seemed not to have noticed.

"So where's this brother of yours live at?"

"Virgin..." She broke off having almost said Virginnie. "Virginia," she corrected.

"That's a big state, ma'am. You'll have to be a whole lot more specific if you plan to find him anytime soon."

"South of Pocomoke and north of Oak Hall, his letter said. Near the Osgood, or Osborne plantation."

"Don't know it myself, I stay in Maryland mostly. But I'd say you're going in the right direction."

Rose woke up and rubbed her balled fists in her eyes. When she saw the white stranger standing only a few feet away, she started to cry. Esther's first instinct was to grab up the child and hold her, talk her fear away, But she caught herself before she made a move. Moments stretched uncomfortably. Rose began to crawl toward Esther. Pompey watched and knew this was not going to look good. He jumped down, and the stranger sprang back.

"He just wants to get to his daughter, Sir. She's been in and out of fever for the past few days. He doesn't want to lose her like he lost her Mama."

Pompey picked Rose out of the back of the wagon and held her. Esther was making up more of the story than she had originally planned out and he feared she might stumble or forget what she had said. What then?

Pompey took her hand and began to walk away. "He'll walk her just a little bit, legs probably got cramped up. It was a tad cold last night. Had on three shawls most of the time."

The stranger climbed onto his horse. "You be careful. Near'st I can tell you're goin' right."

"Thank you," she said softly.

He turned the horse and started up the road they'd driven all night. He cantered past Pompey and Rose and stared hard down at them as he passed. It was then Esther saw the rifle he carried strapped to the saddle. She went cold as Pompey kept his head down like he was studying Rose as she tried to communicate with him. Then the stranger was around the bend and gone.

Esther closed her eyes and prayed.

CHAPTER 21

Comfort dreamed. She dreamed a dream of death—but not her own. No, she dreamed the death of everyone she'd ever loved and some she'd hated, and their bodies lay humped or stretched in the fields she worked by daylight. In the dream there was no daylight, or moonlight or starlight, only dream light, the light that emanates from everything and is everywhere, even and constant and pure.

Above the fields a mist hung at head height, below it in the depth lay the bodies, most of their faces hidden by posture or arms or clothes. But she knew each and every one of them. Here was her mother, beside her lay the bundle with her freedom clothes she never wore. Comfort paused, then knelt beside her. She straightened the collar on her mother's dress, brushed some hair from her forehead, rose and moved on. There was her father who wandered off and never returned. He looked neither pained nor confused, merely relieved.

Mistress Mifflin lay dead, but not as Comfort had known her, old and gnarled and deeply in pain. Here was the lass with burnished hair and pale skin lightly freckled. Her hands were straight and slender. Thomas, though she'd never seen him, slumped nearby.

Esther lay near Rose, both as dead as hope. And in the dream Comfort cried. And far, far away on the pallet in the corner of the cabin she cried. Beyond these that were so dear to her, lay Master Osborne and Mistress Osborne as though trying to escape, and scattered around them their sons and daughters. Their eyes were frozen wide open. Whatever killed them brought fear first.

Sabra lay face down, Beck slumped against a boulder, eyes shut at last. Isaac lay by Fillis, arms intertwined as if they slept.

Comfort wandered the dream-lit fields until she woke. She felt nothing, the hollow ache of nothing. She opened her eyes and saw only darkness, not even the shafts of moon and starlight that usually seeped through the cracks in the walls lay on the floor. Darkness upon darkness that her eyes did not become accustomed to billowed out in all directions.

She closed her eyes until the images of death returned to her mind, and for the longest time she did not know if she slept and returned to the dream, or just remembered it, detail by detail. Did it matter, she asked herself? The images of death were the same in memory or dream.

For a moment Comfort thought she saw herself hunched

over a hoe strapped to her wrist, but that couldn't be, it was someone else. The scene glowed with light of its own making, but no one and nothing cast shadows. She wandered from body to body, and when she had seen them all, she began again, moving slowly, feeling every loss as if for the first time, feeling relief for Mistress and Master whose lives were worse than this death. Their bodies were finally near enough to one another to touch each other, though they didn't.

Night crept on, and the dream or the memory of dream crept with it without relief, without a glint of hope. The mist covered the fields, did not burn off, or settle. Her head above the mist obscured the crumpled heaps of bodies below. She walked awhile with her head above the mist, but there was nothing to see in the sky. No sun, no moon, no stars, no clouds, no birds. There was nothing. There was no sky. No wagons made their way along the road that split the fields in two. Nothing slithered, slinked or crouched among the bodies.

Comfort ducked beneath the mist and beheld again the landscape lifeless, bereft. Only way across the field did she catch a glimpse of someone moving among the tress. It was Cuff, and he refused to come out.

CHAPTER 22

The cabin door slammed open, and the paltry pre-dawn light seemed to crawl across the floor then climb slowly over Comfort cowering in the corner, more huddled into herself than a beaten dog. Mistress Osborne clumped unsteadily up the rickety steps and loomed in the doorway. She leaned forward and strained to see Comfort across the small room.

"Virginnie," she called, hatred building with each syllable.

"Yes'm," she whispered, and instinctively drew her broken hand under her for protection if the woman struck again.

"Talk so I can find you," she demanded.

"I'm here in da corner on my pallet." Mistress followed the sound across the floor that Comfort had swept and scrubbed until it shone in the sunlight that eventually found its way in. "I got a fever. I couldn't sleep ..."

"Shut up. I found you. I don't give a damn about your fever or your sleep or any other damn thing. I came for one thing only."

At that moment Comfort saw for the first time the bundle in her Mistress's hand. She tried to shift deeper into the shadows, afraid of what she might be holding. Had she come to kill her, since she was useless now for doing what she did best? Mistress swung her left arm and turned on her heel and started for the door. In that split second something hit Comfort full in the face. But there was no pain, only the surprise that sucked her breath out.

Mistress was back in the doorway, facing Comfort. "They's your new clothes. You can throw away them house clothes, you won't be back in my house. You a field slave now. A field slave," she said more slowly. "You had it easy all your life, I understand. Well mop that outta your mind. It never happened. Like I tole you, you had no life before you come here. You was in limbo, just waitin' for someone to bring you here."

Comfort whimpered.

"I catch you wastin' my time in the field cryin', you'll know what pain's all about. My husband 'spects you in the field by first light with the rest of 'em. He don't tolerate much from niggers, and he sure don' tolerate bein' late. He'd kill ya sooner'n look at ya if he hadn't some money tied up in ya."

"I can't hold nothin' with my hand," she started to complain. But Mistress started back across the floor, her hand raised, her eyes wide and face screwed up into a look of absolute disbelief that this insolent slave would protest a direct order.

"Why you," she screamed and lashed out. But in the dim light she could not calculate depths and distances and the blow struck the wall. She wailed like someone impaled in a dull knife, and stumped out of the cabin. "You wait," she threatened when she reached the ground. "You ain't never nightmared a life like you just walked into. You wait."

And she was gone into the gray unpromise of false dawn.

Comfort heard her walk heavily away, her moans were barely audible above the frog sounds, and human sounds of those just waking and entering another moment in the cycle none of them could see the end of, except, perhaps, those awaiting death.

Comfort rose and dressed hurriedly in the chill morning air. There was not yet enough light to see herself in that shard of mirror someone before her had attached to the wall. She knew the clothes she was putting on would be dull and shabby and shapeless and rough, she had been around Cuff long enough to know what real slave clothes looked like, especially after years of wear. The sudden thought of Cuff caught her up short, and she allowed herself a moment to think about him, trying desperately to keep Rose in the way back of her consciousness, not out in the daylight where she jabbed like a pin and hurt her into inactivity—something that now, more than ever before, could get her hurt worse, or killed.

Cuff hung in the dark air in front of her, and she seethed, wishing she could reach out and slap him and smash him senseless. She stood motionless, tensed, and watched him like he was really there, until her shoulders drooped and her arms went limp and she allowed herself a moment of pure hatred at the betrayal, at the heartless act of deception that took her from freedom and love and dropped her off in hell.

Comfort gathered a few pieces of bread that she had saved from yesterday and stuck them in her pocket. She was not sure how she could work in the field, but she would not let the others suffer because she was hurt. Outside she could begin to learn the geography of this place, if there were roads or woods nearby. Did anyone patrol looking for runaways? How closely would she be watched, except by Isaac?

That she would one day run away from this place and find her way back to her freedom, was not a question. Somewhere there were papers that declared her a free woman under the law. And if she grew as old as Mistress Mifflin getting back to them, then she would wait, hoping Cuff would live that long so she could have the satisfaction of his shock at her being alive, and then she'd kill him. She wished him a hell worse than hers.

CHAPTER 23

Cuff squatted deep in the woods, trembling. His movements were jerky as he swatted at dark forms that seemed to come at him from all angles. The innkeeper had refused to sell him whiskey, even Mingo had threatened him and would not consider selling him any. He was afraid to return to his own still, and, besides, it would take too long.

He stood and paced the little bare spot in the midst of the woods outside of Wilmington. He had not been to the races or the cockfights in weeks. He had no money left, and he could not stop the trembling in his hands. The bobbing, flashing, whizzing dark objects would give him no peace. He swung at them, ducked them, closed his eyes so he could not see them, yet still they came, giving him no chance to rest. Not even when exhaustion took him down did they stop.

They might be some combobulation from my brain, he thought, but if they aren't, one of them might knock me cold. So he lashed out, put his hands in front of his face to fend them off. He acted like a man who had disturbed a nest of hornets.

CHAPTER 24

The three rode the wagon deep into the woods after they had passed a small town at a barely-lit hour of the morning. "If we don't stop and ask someone, we'll never find that Osgood place," Esther said to Pompey. "Osborne," she corrected herself.

Pompey drew back and pointed rapidly back and forth to himself and to Esther.

"I mean me. But I'm too scared to go alone." Pompey nodded in agreement and pointed to his stomach which Esther surmised felt like her own, knotted and twisted and always on the cusp of a spasm. She had known fear all her life thanks to her Master, but nothing like this. This was different. The demon in her Master was a familiar monster, known and, if not predictable, at least unsurprising. But riding into an unknown town pretending to be a white woman in the South was fear harnessed to terror. One slip and someone might see through her mask. Her imagination would not let her go any further, but it could come to no good end.

She tried to concentrate on what she had done right in the encounter with the stranger on horseback. She had held herself straight-backed and tried to remain calm. She spoke without breaks in her voice and watched her pronunciations. Being on her own among many whites, as she imagined the encounter proceeding, would place her, a stranger, at the center of all eyes. One stranger was easily fooled in a bad light and or mist of an early morning, but now she might have to address many in good light. And worse, there would probably be women among them. She refused to follow that thought as well.

"Well," she finally said to Pompey and Rose, "Standing here thinking is torture. Sooner I go, the sooner I gets back." Pompey's eyes widened. He made a pointing gesture with one finger.

"Yes, I know," she said to him. "Won't change a thing me standin' here five more minutes of five more hours. I got to do it or we may never find that plantation and Comfort and get on outta here."

Resigned, she climbed into the wagon and took the reins Pompey held out to her. "You take care of that child. I should be back in an hour or two. The town ain't that far back." She tapped the horse tentatively and began moving forward. Then the horse stopped. Esther stared straight ahead, "If I'm not back by nightfall, get Rose out of here. Stick to the woods at night. Find her a home." And she started moving again.

The town was even smaller than it had appeared from the road through the trees. There was a tiny bank, a saloon and one store that sold everything else. Most folks didn't have money to put in a bank, and the saloon was not a choice for many and obvious reasons. Esther parked in front of the store, and hitched the horse to a post. Her mind suddenly went blank and numb, and she moved mechanically, standing up straight, and putting on dignity like makeup. She held her hands in front, and screwed a smile onto her mouth. She nodded to the men and women coming and going about the store.

"May I help you," someone asked, not unpleasantly.

Esther turned to see a woman coming towards her from a back room. "Oh," the woman exclaimed when she got a little closer. Esther drew back, feeling a shock, and wondering if it was over already.

"Oh, I'm sorry," the woman said, "I thought I recognized you for a moment, then I realized the woman I thought you were is dead. Dead a year or more. I didn't mean to scare you. Now, what can I do for your today?"

"I was wondering," Esther said slowly, carefully and with as little volume as she could, "if you might know the where-abouts of a plantation owned by an Osgood family?"

"Osgood?" the woman repeated. "Around here?"

"In these parts, I'm pretty sure."

"No."

"Osborne, maybe?"

The woman looked like someone had hit her with a board. The smile faded from her face. "There is an Osborne Plantation," she said, forcing the smile back to her face, "just down the road about ten or twelve miles."

"Wonderful," said Esther, "is this the right road, then?"

"Cuts the farm in two. No offense, madam, but I hope you have no business to conduct with them."

"No," Esther replied perhaps a bit too quickly, "my brother has a small farm near there. He merely mentioned it as a landmark in his letter."

"Oh, that is a good thing. No good ever came from that plantation, as they call it. Broken down dump for humanity's refuse is more like it. Steer clear of that place and those people."

The news was disturbing, but Esther tried to let little expression into her face. "I will surely avoid them. And thank you. I have traveled a long way to see my brother."

"And what is his name?"

Esther froze. Why had she not thought that someone would ask her that question? "Nathaniel," she blurted.

"Nathaniel?" the woman asked. "Comstock."

"Don't know the name. Guess he must shop elsewhere."

"Very possible," Esther said walking toward the door.

"That's a very pretty dress," woman remarked, "well made."

"Thank you, a slave woman made it for me. Very clever hands. Wasted," she added, and walked back to the wagon.

CHAPTER 25

Master Osborne grabbed Comfort's hand and raised it up close to his eyes so he could see it clearly. "Ain't much of a field hand if the hand's broken," he said with a smile. Comfort hung her head. "What's your name?"

Comfort hesitated.

Master's reaction was swift. The flat of his hand caught the side of her head in an instant. "What's your name?" he asked again without heat or volume.

"Com..." she never got to finish.

His hand struck quicker than a snake coiled and cocked. "You know very well you were born and raised here on Osborne Plantation. Emerged miraculously one day from the good brown earth to serve me and my wife and children. We've seen it again and again, the good Lord sends us brown servants to tend our land and cook our food and make our clothes. And you, Virginnie, are merely the latest. But you won't be the last. No, no," he said, taking the arm of the slave named Beck, who guided him through his myopic world, "you are but the latest. The last will spring from the earth to defend this land upon Armageddon." And he laughed a shrill laugh that cut to the heart of everyone in the field, a high-pitched womanly laugh that would have embarrassed any man among them.

Master swung around and stared at Comfort, inches from her face where all was clear and he could see the fear and hatred in her eyes. "Observe," he hissed. "See what the others do and do it likewise. My eyes are watching you," he said, jerking his thumb towards Beck. The man bowed quickly and slightly. Master pulled some jerky from his pocket and handed it to Beck who shoved it into his mouth and chewed.

He backed away from her and she swam into a pool of cluttered shapes and colors, fuzzy images and blurred lines. He, however, was clear to her, a lumpish little man going bald, hanging for dear life to the arm of a slave. He raised his hand and beckoned her forward. "Until you can use your right hand," he said, and raised it from her side, "you might need some assistance."

Beck took her hand from his Master. He placed her hand roughly on the haft of a hoe and lashed it in place so that the tool was an extension of her arm. A long, awkward extension she would have to maneuver with her wrist or forearm to make it perform in even the most rudimentary way. "Meet your new best friend," Master said. "Needle hand and shuttle hand meet Mr. Hoe. See how expert you get with that," he spat in her face. And again the shrill, girlish whine.

Isaac walked next to her when Master left the field for the shade at the verge of the woods. "I'll work with you. He'll give you a little time to get used to being strapped to the hoe, but not much." Isaac took a length of rope from his pocket and had a woman tie his hoe to his hand. "Let's figure this out," he said, trying to smile.

She was, always had been, a quick study, and soon found the rhythm of the work. She observed how others seemed to fight their tools or let their tools fight them. They were awkward and fought the dirt, they jerked and jabbed and wore themselves out. Her motions were smooth and metered, merely larger motions than she used when she was knotting. She eased herself into a flow and found it was like a dance with a long, skinny partner.

Deep in his own rhythm, Isaac watched her in side-glances. Looking to the shade he saw Master nodding approvingly as Beck described every motion the field hand made hobbled as she was with the tool lashed to her arm. As long as Beck and Master sat together, the conversation went on without pause. Beck was his master's eyes. Comfort cut her glance toward them from time to time, but mostly she stared ahead at the smooth, unbroken motion of the hoe tearing weeds away from full grown plants, smoothing out wrinkles in the earth, piling rocks and pebbles, making hours disappear as the sun spun another cycle across the warm blue sky.

Isaac untied the hoe from his arm. He had not needed to imitate for her sake. She had not watched the others, she had reached inside and found what she needed, borrowed from what she already knew. Expand and contract. Make it bigger, make it smaller. Take what your body knows and make it something new. Let what your fingers know teach your arms, picot and rings are stretch and drag, make a collar around the plant, make a cuff, knot a snood, watch the hoe shrink to a shuttle and knot the earth into a pure white design so delicate and fine it might reduce the world to tears.

Comfort danced with herself, found she could disappear into motion and the faint scraping of the blade across the land. Over and over and over. It was all the same no matter how large or small the motion was. Ride the motion. Move to the rhythm of your own making, the music of the work. And she was gone. There and not there. Not happy and not unhappy. Comfort and Virginnie, slave and free woman, mass and energy, motion and motion and motion.

CHAPTER 26

At its top speed, which they did not achieve often, the horse lumbered. Pompey, Esther and Rose grew accustomed to the pace as day in and day out they seemed to melt deeper into the upper edges of the South. They were below the Maryland state line, they surmised must be approaching the plantation Joe Johnson had spoken of. It was raggedy, mistreated land already over farmed, the soil depleted. But the farmers would not let it lay fallow for even a year and tried to force crops from soil meager and malnourished.

Slaves worked the fields, some in slow but steady motions that bespoke a life of husbanding energy. Some, perhaps those new to the work, hacked and chopped at the fields in anger and frustration and inexperience. Esther watched them as they passed, the pain of it settling on her like the dust kicked up by the almost constant peninsula winds.

Rose watched too, but did not understand. Her mother had been a domestic slave, and all she knew were houses and the clean, close handwork her mother did endlessly. Sometimes she waved, but no one waved back at the risk of a whip across the back, or a swift slap to the head for wasting time. The slow, constant forward drudge created a kind of trance that helped drag them through the days and smooth out some of the fear that followed them closely every minute.

Esther's plan was to find the plantation and then create an excuse to go to the house in hopes that Comfort might see her. It was not, in the broad scheme of things, a plan. It was a wish and a prayer and a miracle wrapped around crossed fingers.

Around noon the wagon passed a field where an overseer was seated on a fallen tree near the road. Esther looked at Pompey and said under her breath, "I have to ask directions again. For all we know we may have passed the place." The wagon slowed and Esther stepped down into the thick dust of the road.

The overseer eyed her suspiciously. "Can you tell me," she began, "where the Comstock place is?"

"Never heard of it," he spat back at her. "Sure you got the right part of the world?"

"Yes, I'm sure it's nearby."

"Well, I been here all my life and I ain't never heard of no Comstock. Why you ask?"

"He's my brother, and he's feeling poorly of late, and I'm hoping to help him some."

The man, medium height and nondescript, eyed her up and down. "Don't look like you got the back for farm work. No offense."

"I'll be helpin' my sister-in-law, my man will do the farmin'."

"Well. I can't help ya."

"It's supposed to be near the Osborne Plantation."

The overseer roared with laughter and took several seconds before he could speak. "Plantation?" He finally managed. "Plantation? That what the jackass calls his place?"

"That's what my brother told me in his letter."

"Well that sorry excuse for a stone pit's a ways farther down the road. Can't miss it. Look for the worst crops and the most bedraggled collection of field slaves, and you've found Osborne's place. I wouldn't ask anyone aroun' there where your brother might be. That is the palace of ignorance and stupidity. Plantation."

Esther returned to the wagon, and Pompey drove quickly away in case the overseer changed his mind and decided to grill him. Esther's confidence inched up with each encounter, but she talked to herself constantly about getting cocky and tipping her hand. But there was a certain amount of satisfaction in there being a disguise with no disguise.

They did not roll on through the nights anymore. Since the contact with the stranger in the mist, and the woman in the store, there seemed to be no hint of suspicion. And stopping in the woods to rest at night was better on all of them. Pompey slept lightly for fear that hunters of runaways might stumble on them, and there would be no explanation for their being in the woods. They took nothing for granted.

About four o'clock, the sun cocked slightly toward the west, they entered a section of road that bisected fields. This might be the place, she thought and nudged Pompey. "This it?" she whispered.

Pompey shrugged. He slowed the wagon further, but Esther dared make only furtive glances around the field. It was a poor excuse for a farm, let alone a plantation, which she understood to be beautiful and well kept, the envy of passersby, regardless of the truth on the inside. The house was in shambles and the cook shed listed to one side. The foundation had crumbled. Where other farms they had passed had used the fieldstone to make walls, here the stones were merely tossed to the side in heaps and mounds. Whereas tree stumps were dug up and dragged from the cultivated fields elsewhere, here they were left in place, and the slaves planted around them.

In one glance Esther spotted two men, one Negro, one white, seated in the shade just past the wagon wheel ruts that served as a driveway. The white man paid them no mind, but the Negro stared and spoke to the white man as he did.

In another glance she saw an old, white-haired Negro in the field who worked steadily but kept an eye on everyone else as they worked. A woman, about fifty yards from the road moved in a steady, smooth motion that rivaled the spastic, cut and pull of most of the others.

Finally, the Negro in the shade broke his stare and went back to watching the work in the field. The other man cut his eyes toward the wagon, Pompey and the man nodded ever so slightly to one another. A few moments later the wagon passed a stand of crepe myrtle and the fields were blocked from sight. That was the only pretty thing on that farm, Esther thought. But it was what flashed across her mind like a shooting star after the thought faded, nagged at her, rising now and again like a snatch of tune that won't go away.

CHAPTER 27

The Osborne "plantation" straddled the road. Sometimes they worked one side, sometimes the other. But Isaac was always where Comfort was, and she felt protected from the prying stare of Beck. Even when Master was not in the shadows, Beck was and his constant, hawk-eyed surveying of the fields was unsettling. Nothing that happened went unreported. If someone stopped for a drink of water, it went into Beck's mental tabulations of wasted time and wasted motion.

Comfort counted the number of wagons moving north and the number moving south along the road. The motion of the work let her daydream a plan of escape. She knew which was north, and that was the way to safety. Mistress had read her stories of escaped slaves and their journeys north, so she knew it could be done. She knew, too, that if caught, it would no doubt be the death of her. She was no more than property, and property could be replaced. It was, for the first week in the field, just that, a daydream.

Beck told Master he liked the fact that, even with the hoe tied to her arm, she had quickly discovered a rhythm that wasted neither time nor effort. "She worships de earth, Master. She strokes it like she might a baby's face," he said only a few days into her new job.

"'Bout time I got somethin' over on my wife. She's evil, Beck, but don't you never say I said nothin' like that 'bout her."

"Naw sir, never heard nothin'."

Late in the afternoons, early in the evening when work in the fields was winding down, Master would take Beck's arm and walk back to the house. In the shadows in the field the workers would slow and finally stop whatever flow of work they had kept up all day. The eyes were gone to deliver Master home. And Comfort knew this was the time when Mistress would begin to harrow the kitchen slaves for the second time of the day. She would yell, and threaten, brandish large spoons and use them frequently as weapons until the meal was on the table. Cold or hot, she wasn't happy until everyone was moving and all that could be heard was her own voice above every other sound.

Should something fall to the floor, no matter how insignificant, she flew into a rage fit for a threat of starvation. Her arms swung, her legs blundered about the shed followed by her enormous backside that shifted and bounced and seemed to have a life of its own. Oh, the women laughed at her, but she never knew why. And finally she forbade any laughing, any smiling, any but secret communication behind her back.

It was a cantankerous existence. But it was only as nasty

and disagreeable as she intended. She had no love for anyone, not even her children who learned early in life that they were to lead loveless lives among parents and siblings, and the sooner you accepted that, the better off you would be. Strike first, get the upper hand, and never surrender or admit to pain.

They watched their mother to learn how to act, and they watched their father to learn how not to. He was weak and dependent. He knew it and he exploited it. He found strength and power in his weakness, but only because he had been that way all his life. His children were not clever enough to watch manipulation and deception and raw underhandedness in business and life and learn to appropriate it to their own ends. They were dull and unimaginative and mistook the ranting of their mother for power and control, and the arm holding and small, careful step behind myopic eyes as weakness. He told each of his children in turn that he was glad he could not see beyond a hand span so he didn't have to look at them.

Meals were elaborate displays of ignorance and bad behavior. It was everyone for himself, and if the food was gone before you had some, you went hungry. No knives were used, or spoons. It was all hands and fingers grabbing and ripping and shoving. It was mouths ringed with grease, cheeks caked and smeared with whatever missed their mouths. And much did because eating was a frenzy to be survived, not a few moments to gather together and celebrate. No, this was survival of the most brutal sort.

And Mistress, served first before the melee began, watched from the far end of the table away from the whirlwind of food and water and slashing hands and teeth sinking in to whatever got between them, be it food or finger, their own or someone else's, for it was not beneath them to take food right out of a sibling's mouth.

Master was served, alone, in an outbuilding constructed just for his pleasure, so great was his hatred of his progeny. If fewer people knew of the children's existence, he might have drowned them himself.

SPRING 1816

❋

Chapter 28

A dim light seeped through the closed window and fell on Rachel Mifflin's shoulders like dust. It was not May light as May light should be. A gunmetal sky and a fire in the fireplace testified to the chill. Her gnarled hands, twisted and swollen to impossible shapes, gripped the newspaper. She was silent except for the thin column of air that would be a whistle.

"Comfort, this world's comin' crazy apart."

"Yes'm. I suppose it is if you say so."

"Not me saying so, it's this newspaper. Some expert at a university says he thinks the reason the sun doesn't shine and practically nothing but scraggy weeds come up in the gardens is because some mountain blew its top on the other side of the world. Imagine having the time to sit around and think up such notions, and then loosing them on the world."

"Where is the other side of the world? Do people live there? People like us?"

"Comfort, listen to you. You make me laugh, you've got more questions than a three year old."

"I suppose I do. But I want to know things for when I can go places someday. I don't want my mind to just sit here in Wilmington forever. I can see that mountain blowin' up, and rocks squirting into the air just as clear as I see you. But I wouldn't know how to get to the other side of the world, 'cause I don't know which way to go. Maybe that university man isn't so crazy at all."

"Well the paper says it's in the Dutch East Indies. Does that help?"

"No'm. But does the mountain have a name, maybe I'd know it that way."

"Tambora. Mount Tambora on the island of Sumbawa. Those are crazy names, probably made up by someone else at that university. They're all sitting around right now laughing at all of us taking their pap serious. Blew up April 10th last year—my hind foot."

"What's that got to do with us on this side of the world? But you're right, this world is crazy whether it's coming apart or not."

"Blew ashes into the sky twenty miles high some sea captain says. Ninety thousand people dead. People starvin' in Europe. Snow in Richmond last week. They're ash clouds, this reporter says, and they drift across the world and block the sun and make things cold and keep the plants down in the dirt. I know that last part's right, but the rest sounds like something out of a storybook. "

"Like a winter in summer."

"Like a new season, Comfort, wintersummer. We had a chill summer thirty, thirty-five years back, but not like this. The crops were spindly and puny, but they came up. We ate, but we chopped a lot of trees to stay warm."

Comfort set her hands in her lap. "Well, the light's going out of the day and I can't see to knot no more. Should I light the lamps?"

"Let me see what you've got first. Beautiful. I guess these'll be the last cuffs and collar you'll make for me."

"Maybe. I knotted them to match your snood. They'll look awful pretty when we get them attached to your new dress."

Rachel Mifflin touched the lacy cap on her head and smiled. "May be the only knotted snood in the world, Comfort. You have clever hands. Clever, clever hands. Mine used to be. But not now, they's twisted into claws. Your hands have to be my hands now, and I don't know what I'll do when you're gone."

"No'm. Comfort won't let you starve or do without anything. You deserve to rest, and read, and tell stories this time in your life. Everything'll be fine. You got a lot of stories left to tell me and Rose. I see the world clear as a sunny day when you hatch out a new story I ain't heard before."

"Well. It's fine work," she said, handing back the collar. "I am proud to be seen out when I'm wearing your knots.

Surely am."

"Yes'm. Miz McLane said some people's calling it tatting nowadays."

"They can't leave anything alone anymore, can they? New names for this and that; who knows what's next. Now you get home before it's full dark. Where's Rose?" she asked as if just now missing the child.

"She with Esther next door. She spoils that chile, I swear. Sometimes she even nicks some pennies from her freedom money and buys Rose candy. Ain't that somethin'?"

"Yes, yes. She's a good friend to you and Rose. I almost envy your friendship."

"Yes'm."

"Now, go get your daughter and go on home to your husband."

"Yes'm. But I need to give you this first. Two more dollars."

"My. You always surprise me, Comfort Mifflin. Did Cuff give you this?"

"No'm. I earned it myself on Saturdays. I knotted up a couple small things for Miz McLane. You said it was all right."

"Of course it is. Saturdays and Sundays are yours. But why is Cuff making you pay your own way? He knows how hard that is, he did it himself."

"He says I'll appreciate it more if I do it alone. Besides he's spending whatever he makes. Bought a load of old boards off of Pompey so he could build a shed in back of the house."

"For what?"

"Don't know, he won't say. But he's back there all the

time, bangin' and sawin'. He's most powerful energetic when he sets his mind to it."

Comfort gone, Rachel Mifflin lit the lamps and sat down at the table. In a minute, she thought, I'll take the chicken and cornbread Comfort made for dinner from the pie safe. After supper I'll finish reading about this world coming crazy apart.

She nodded and laid her head slowly on the table—just for a minute, she thought, just for a little minute.

CHAPTER 29

Cuff wiped sweat from his neck and broad forehead as Comfort came into the yard. She held her daughter's hand as she stood for a moment in the twilight and stared at her husband. At seventeen she first noticed he was looking at her in side glances as she rocked in the parlor opposite Mistress Mifflin learning to knot, or carried a basket to the garden for a meal's vegetables.

He was nearly six feet tall, muscled and ten years older than she. She had watched him too, from time to time, and she knew he liked to see himself in the hall mirror. His skin, she thought at the time, was the color and depth of midnight.

But he was always badly dressed. He wore his clothes to rags, or until Mistress forced him to put on something different. But Comfort knew that he had sold his new allotment of pants cut from Osnaburg, cotton shirt and shoes for freedom money—and Mistress knew it too, so she did not press him very hard. Next time they saw him he'd have on, perhaps, last year's rags—sometimes patched or sewn, sometimes just covered by a slightly less disgraceful jacket. He is a man to make his way in the world, she thought. And she dreamed she might go with him.

When he turned, he saw his wife and daughter, and the smile that finally snared Comfort's heart emerged like the Barley Moon, full and brilliant. Rose squealed, "Papa," and ran to him. He lifted her up and held her at arm's length as if to make sure she was whole and well and safe after a full day away from him.

He couldn't make that smile go away if he tried, Comfort thought. In two strides he had his arm around her shoulders and bent to kiss her.

"I missed my girls today," his voice was as big as his smile.

Rose wiggled to get to the ground, then scurried away toward the back door. He picked Comfort up and kissed her again, but longer and harder. Back on the ground, Comfort laughed. "A woman would have thought you'd be stove in by now working on your shed." "It's almost done. Put the roof on tomorrow, then see if I can't swap something to Pompey for a hasp and lock. Then I'm in business."

"And just what would that business be, Mr. Mifflin, sir?"

"Nothing for a lady to worry her head over," he said, the

smile waning to a half moon. "Nothing at all. You just think about getting yourself paid off."

She thought how he seemed to be hiding something, maybe something a man shouldn't do. But she blinked it from her mind and smiled.

"Bring some wood inside," she said, her smile waxing. "It's cold."

Over cold meat she told him about the mountain on the other side of the world that blew up and was now making them shiver in August. He chewed and listened, chewed and wrinkled his broad brow. She went on, seeing he was interested, and tried to remember all she could. It was important, she knew, because it was unusual, strange forces were at work from strange and faraway places.

Cuff was patient, like a parent with an imaginative child, and even cocked a curious ear toward her as her tale stumbled deeper into implausible territory. Finally, he pushed himself from the table, and wiped his mouth on the back of his hand. In one arcing movement he swept his drinking gourd toward himself and downed the last of the water. "I needed that to get the last of your talk down my throat. That is some story you and the Mistress has combobulated."

"We ain't combobulated anything, whatever that means. It was in the newspaper."

"Uh huh."

"Cuff Mifflin, what in the world do I have to gain, and what would the widow gain, by combobulating a made-up story to tell you? Can you answer me that?"

"Naw. So maybe you didn't make it up. So maybe somebody smarter than us made it up to pull the wool over our eyes..."

"Mistress said the same thing. She said maybe those university men make things up to make the rest of us look foolish when we fall for their tales."

"Well, then, Mistress ain't lost her senses after all. It's just you got dust in your brain."

"Ain't nice of you to say that. Sound like you don't trust me."

Cuff rose and walked toward her. Her arms dropped limp to her side as he hugged her. "I trust you," he told her quietly, "but you ought not to trust other people so much. What with mountains blowing up, and clouds stompin' down crops—ever think God might be mad at this country?"

"What's God got to be mad about, Cuff?"

"You think about it, woman. You think real hard. With your imagination you should know what I'm talking about before Rose falls asleep. Now I've got to go find Pompey. Don't wait up for me, don't know where I might find him."

She sat down at the table again and stared straight ahead. She knew these flashes of anger but never when or most times why.

When she felt Rose at her knee, she lifted the baby to her lap, stroked her hair and began a lullaby.

Sleep li'l child, sleep for a while,

While the world spins 'round and 'round.

CHAPTER 30

"He got mad when I told him what you read from the newspaper. He said I shouldn't trust anybody that makes up tall tales like that. First he said you and me combobulated that story..."

Mistress Mifflin and Comfort sat on either side of the chill gray window where unrealized sunlight mocked the air and filched even the green from the plants and trees outside.

"Comfort, did you say combobulated?"

"Yes'm. Cuff said that's what we done."

"What does it mean to combobulate?"

"I told him I didn't know what it meant. Do you know?"

"Well, I know discombobulated means something that's come apart or confused. Did he say we combobulated the story about the mountain?"

"Yes'm."

"Well, then, I guess he means we made it up. If you can discombobulate, I suppose you can combobulate. Funny. But you have to careful about using words you don't know. They can get you in a mess of trouble."

"Yes'm. I'm sorry."

"No need to be, but just because Cuff says it doesn't

mean you ought to repeat it. But you know you're safe saying most anything to me."

She smiled and blew a contented column of air. They rocked awhile, the only sound was a faint tick-tick-tick of the shuttle as Comfort deftly formed lacy picots and wheels from string. Rachel Mifflin watched her absently, remembering the bag her mother gave her before she left Ireland for America.

"I came here when I was fifteen, Comfort. I was indentured for five years to the Mifflins in this very house. I was a beauty then, the men all told me, and I could have been married no sooner than I'd stepped off the boat, if I had a mind to—which I didn't."

"No'm. You wanted to see the world, right? Like me. Except it's gonna be harder for me."

"The world is changing, Comfort. Maybe a day's coming when it won't be so hard. I think Rose will live in a different world soon."

"Yes'm. I suppose if you say so."

There was silence again nearly, just the creak of rocking chairs going about their business, and the shuttle going about its.

"The Master took a liking to me," she began suddenly. "He would buy me little things, hair combs and handkerchiefs sometimes, needles and string. Others because he knew how much my knotting meant to me. The Mistress was always owling me when he was around. I think she suspected he might have been sweet on me. When he was out of the house or out of town she would make my life mean and puny. I'd about starve when he went on long trips. It just made me hate that woman even though she had nothing to fear about me. I was just doing my time and waiting. This was a brand new country and I wanted to be a member of it."

"Tell me about mean ole Mistress Mifflin, she sounds like the stepmother in some of those fairy tales you taught me to read off of."

"I tried to like her because I knew she was sick. She already had consumption when I got here. She was always toting around a white hanky with little red hearts or strawberries on to it. But she didn't fool anybody. Even I knew those red embroideries were there to make people think we were seeing hearts and not specks of blood she coughed up. Master warned me."

Rachel Mifflin stared into the fire. She was years away, yet in the very room she was remembering. Beside her again was an angry Mistress Mifflin and she was young Rachel McArthur, head hung low and wishing she had never left Cork.

"You have designs on my husband, and don't deny it. I see it in the way you look at him, and I ain't so sure he isn't looking back at you the same way behind my back. You're two of the same, he's just had more practice."

"I don't have designs on anybody, Mistress. I just want to work my five years and get away. I don't want your husband, I want a young man with a strong back that can build us a life."

From out of her waking dream she said, "She beat me one time nearly to death when Master was away. I guess she figured the wounds would heal, and if they didn't she'd know something was up if he complained about them. She stripped the dress right off of me. Buttons popped and cotton ripped and

I was standing in this very parlor naked to the waist. I crossed my arms over my breasts, but she wasn't looking, she was too busy beating me with a carriage whip. The first lash sent me to my knees, after ten I couldn't count any more. When she finally tired out, I had already quit crying, because that's what she wanted to see, the servant girl beaten to a dog—yowling with each lash. And I wouldn't give it to her. I just made up my mind not to give her what she wanted, even if she didn't know that she wanted it."

"Mistress, did you ever beat your slaves like that, just because you could and not a soul could say you couldn't?"

"Never, ever laid a hand on anybody. When I stood up that day, I could see drops of blood on the walls of this room, my blood, spattered like the blood on her handkerchief. And seeing that was worse than the pain, and I vowed to God I'd never hit anyone, black or white, for any reason."

"What did Master say when he saw you?"

"What could he say? If he confronted Mistress, then he was admitting he'd seen me naked. Then everything she suspected would be true in her mind. It was a trap, and I was the bait. But what she didn't know is that when Master saw the lashes Mistress gave me it was the first he'd seen me undressed."

"Did she beat you again?"

"No, she never raised a hand to me, never threatened to again. I was a ghost to her. She spoke to me through Master, and wouldn't even let me tend to her on her deathbed two years later. I've never seen the life go out of anybody the way it did the day she beat me. She never apologized and never accused me of anything again. She even cleaned the blood from the walls herself. The last time she touched me was when she put a dressing on my back."

"Cuff says he thinks God is angry with this country. I been stewin' over that since last night. I couldn't sleep with Cuff gone out the house, so I just lay there thinking about what he said on his way out. Now I think maybe I understand what he meant. Do you think he meant we treat each other bad?"

"He just might, Comfort. Just might."

CHAPTER 31

Cuff stood with his back straight and breathed deeply several times. He knocked lightly on the door. Then again. And again until a large man in a dirty apron opened the door and peered into the morning brightness.

"That you, Cuff? Back so soon?"

"Yessir, it's Cuff all right."

"You must have one powerful thirst."

"I do indeed, but I'm fixin' to change that real soon."

"I'll bet you are. I've heard better men say they was going on the wagon, but I've never seen it happen. The last wagon they get on is on its way to graveyard. It gets like a devil in you and it's hellified agony trying to chase him out."

"I know that, too. Lord. But I got me a plan to run him

off."

"But in the mean time you mean for me to keep on filling your jug. That right?"

"Yessir. And here's the money up front."

The man in the dirty apron squinted hard at the coins dropping into his palm from Cuff's fingers. He grunted, turned and let the door slam. Minutes later he was back with Cuff's jug filled and stopped.

"Go easy on this stuff, it'll kill you before you have a chance to give it up."

Cuff nodded and backed slowly away from the tavern door. His big grin bloomed as he made his way home to the shed now roofed, hasped and locked.

When Cuff came through the gate into the back yard, he saw Pompey on his knees playing a solitary game of mumble-ty-pegs. The tip of the blade was balanced momentarily on Pompey's elbow, then somersaulted into the air expertly and came to rest an inch deep in the soft soil.

"Remind me not to play you anymore, you got too much free time to practice your silly game."

Pompey rose from the ground and smiled at the jug in Cuff's hand. He put the knife into his pocket and brought out a small crockery jar. He thrust the jar in Cuff's direction and made a gesture that said fill it up, I'm dry. Cuff laughed and pulled a key on dirty, unraveling string from his pocket. He unlocked the door and stepped into the darkness of the shed. Pompey followed and looked around at the small room. He nodded at Cuff and slapped him smartly on the back.

"Good job? Is that what you're sayin' to me?" Cuff asked.

"Well thank you, but it's still gonna cost you to get your jar filled up."

Pompey shrugged and thrust the jar at Cuff again. "Now don't go getting impatient on me. I'm a businessman and I've got to do things in my own time and style. Now take a look here at these."

Cuff took down a sack hanging from a nail on the wall. He opened it and pulled a dandy's suit of clothes from the bag. Pompey's eyes grew large and he made as if to whistle, but there was no more sound than there were words. It was a dumb show of delight as Pompey doubled over, slapped his knee and laughed silently.

"You think my customers would see me coming? You know they would, and that's why I won't wear these glad rags when I make my rounds. Customers see me coming, the law see me coming, Comfort see me going. No, sir. I wear these when I play, but not when I'm working."

Cuff noticed that Pompey was still holding his empty jar toward him and took it from the man's hand. "Show me your money 'fore I fill this up."

Pompey took a coin from his pocket and laid it on the shelf growing out of the back wall. "That's double what it costs, and I don't have any change yet."

Pompey shrugged, took the full jar and gulped it like a mug of pure stream water. When he swallowed the last of it, his eyes watered and he danced around like a snake-bit child. Cuff watched him, half expecting him to fall over in a faint. But Pompey just grabbed his throat and contorted his face beyond recognition. "Damn fool. I'd swear you never drank whiskey before. Some green boy might do like that, but you know better. Now, I'm gonna fill your jar again, but you've gotta take it with you. I'm not runnin' a tavern here. Comfort would have my hide she found out I'm sellin' whiskey and fixin' to set up a still."

Pompey took the filled jar and tipped an imaginary hat toward Cuff. "Pretty soon I'll have my own juice to sell, better than this swill, I swear. You come next week and Cuff'll have the best whiskey you ever tasted. And I just might try makin' some rum."

Pompey patted his stomach and smiled. He raised his jar as if to drink, but Cuff frowned at him. Pompey pointed to Cuff and pretended to drink. "Me?" Cuff asked. "I don't drink that stuff. Besides, I wouldn't be any kind of business man if I drank up the profits, would I?"

Pompey shook his head slowly no, and turned to the door. With a final shrug, he was gone.

From a nail keg in the corner Cuff pulled out an assortment of ceramic jars and odd-sized glass bottles. He lined them up on the shelf and carefully filled each one. Then he stopped them each with whittled stoppers or bits of rag.

When the jug was empty, he began stuffing the whiskey into pockets and the sides of his boots. When all were hidden away, he locked the shed and began his circuit through the back streets of Wilmington, searching out his customers who would trade their empties and coins for a refill. Cuff Mifflin was in business, and business was good. Thirst without bottom, he thought.

CHAPTER 32

Esther was sitting on the back steps of her master's house watching Rose chase a moth across the lawn. A stranger passing by might have mistaken her for the daughter of the house—tall, fair, one eye blue and the other brown. When she called to Rose, her voice broke like a delicate cup, and she cried. Rose lifted her hand to Esther's face and wiped the wetness away. Esther laughed and hugged the child close.

Comfort walked into Master Clendaniel's back yard a few minutes before the sun went down. She could see Esther and Rose on the porch laughing, but closer she could see Esther's face was wet.

"What's wrong? This is supposed to be a big day for you. Don't you have your bags packed and your walkin' shoes on?"

Esther began to cry again, and put her head on Comfort's shoulder. "He done it again," she whispered.

"He hurt you again?"

"No, no. Mistress is home. He's a monster, but he ain't stupid. He raised my price again. Like I told you yesterday, I paid him the last dollar on Wednesday, and today he told me I was too valuable to let go for that price and he raised it up fifty dollars more."

"Fifty dollars more? He did that to you last time you paid him off. He's never gonna let you go, I suppose."

The two women walked deeper into the back yard where the trees formed a natural curtain. "Why don't you run, Esther?" Comfort said quietly. "Won't anybody question you. You'd be just another white woman walkin' down the street, merry as you please."

"Because I'm scared, Comfort. If master rapes me now, what do you think he'd do if he caught me running away? He'd just add beating to his list of miseries, if he didn't kill me first. You know he sold my Mama and brother before I was a year. What kinda man would do that? Do you think he'd hesitate to kill me? I don't. Last time he said to me, 'you tell Mistress what I done to you and I will kill you.'"

Lights came on in the house and the two women walked slowly back across the garden. Rose sat on the steps chewing a small piece of sugar cane another of the house servants had brought out to her. "Do you think Mistress will do that to me, too, Esther? I'm so close I can smell freedom for me and Rose." Rose smiled at the sound of her name.

"She didn't change up her mind on Cuff, did she?"

"No. But he's a man. She said to me the other day that she don't know what she'll do when I'm gone because her hands so gnarled she can't barely put a shawl on by herself. Cuff never did for her what I do. She pays him to do man work from time to time. So it ain't like she lost him."

"I don' think Mistress Mifflin's got it in her soul to hold you back like Master is doing to me. She let you marry Cuff. She lets you sleep in his bed at night, lets you stay home with your family Saturday and Sunday. Master just wants to keep me here for his pleasure, keep me till he's too old to do it anymore. By then I'll be too dried up for any man."

Comfort put a hand on her shoulder and pulled a handkerchief from her sleeve. She patted Esther's face dry. "We got to think hard on this. We got to figure a way," she whispered.

"Esther," a man's voice boomed from the center of the house.

"Probably wants his whiskey. Least when he drinks he leaves me alone. I ought to poison him, but he makes me test it first. I hate the taste of whiskey because it tastes like his meanness." And she was gone into the house calling "Coming, Master," with no hint of the bitterness and darkness she carried like a tumor inside of her.

Comfort shook her head slowly and picked Rose up from the step. She kissed her on her cheek and said, "Let's go see Papa."

"Papa, Papa," Rose squealed, "Papa."

CHAPTER 33

Cuff listened to the music of the bottles tinkling against one another in his pockets. He smiled, and continued to turn the stack of coins over and over in his big left hand. Big coins and little coins stacked and restacked themselves as he turned them deftly over and over. It was a good day on Locust Street.

He reached his house and slipped into the back yard through the gate. He had to free the bottles from his pocket to find the key. There you are, he mumbled to himself as he forced the key into the rusted lock. There you are, he mumbled again as daylight brightened the interior of the shed.

He unloaded the bottles into the nail keg and surveyed the parts stacked along the walls of the crooked little room. But it made him smile again, for here were the pipes and kettles he needed for the still, the still that would make him a man to be reckoned with in the free black community growing ever larger in Wilmington. With Mingo, the architect of this strange machine, and Pompey, its principal scavenger of parts, he would begin tomorrow the job of building his future. And a future for Comfort and Rose.

As the door swung closed, the parts became dark and indistinct, a pile of uncertainty and deception. He flung the door open again, and the parts regained their shapes and sizes. He tried again, and the same blurred uneasiness came over him. He knew it was an illusion, but it unsettled him in an odd way.

He closed the door a third time without looking inside at the assembled pile of discarded things that would soon enough take on a new shape and hence begin their new life. Cuff was deep into this thought as he swung the hasp closed and locked the door. He did not hear Comfort come noiselessly behind him until her foot snapped a twig. In a nonce he turned, his fist balled and raised, and would have knocked his wife to the ground if she had not called his name with some frightened force.

Cuff stood, arm still cocked to punch, rigid, but his fist relaxed and the tense set of his eyes softened as he realized what had happened. He blinked and dropped his arm. "Didn't mean to scare you, Cuff. I thought for a second you were gonna lay me out." She laughed a nervous, relieved laugh.

Cuff allowed a half smile. "I wouldn't ever hit you if I knowed it was you. But you come up behind me like some dog in a dream. You've got a big yell for a little gal, I have to say."

"If you were about to get busted in the mouth, you'd have a yell too." They both laughed and hugged each other.

"Where's Rose?"

"She's taking a nap. She was so outta sorts today, Mistress said, 'Take that baby home, she'll make my ears bleed for sure.'"

"Is she sick?"

"No, just approachin' two. She'll be fine when she wakes up. Now what's in the shed that you're so intense about?"

Cuff's face tightened. "Why?"

"Why? Don't a wife have a right to know what's in her own back yard? What her husband is doing in a dark shed he combobulated and won't let her inside of?"

"Sometimes it's best to just leave it be. Trust me that I wouldn't do anything to hurt you or Rose or me."

"So if it isn't bad or dangerous or against the law, why can't I see inside? Or are you just funnin' with me?"

"I'm not funnin', woman. It's my business locked up in there. My business that makes the money to feed you and Rose and me. My business that's gonna get us to Pennsylvania or Massachusetts someday soon as you get out of bondage. The sooner you tend to your knots and sell some of those fancy collars and think about your business the sooner you can buy yourself free."

"And the sooner you loosen the grip you've got on your money and help me out, the sooner we can get to wherever we're going."

"I paid for my own self, and that freedom tastes sweeter than a cup a cold spring water. If I help you out, it'll taste like watery tea. You'll see." He hugged her, but her face hardened, and her back stiffened as she walked back to the house. Nothing else was spoken between them.

Cuff straightened an arm and leaned against the shed to watch her go. His head spun around the resolve to keep his business between he and his customers and the people he needed for help.

But she's grown suspicious of me, he said out loud. That ain't good.

In the kitchen, Comfort moved wordlessly through her cooking. She chopped and stirred and moved through steam and shadow, vague and distant and giving Cuff only a view of her back. He sat in the half-light and drummed his fingers on the table. "Guess I'll go check on Rose."

Comfort turned and glared at him, a look that said leave the child alone, you've got more important things to do. "How long are you gonna to stay mad at me, woman? It's not like I've got a passel of women in the shed. I got no stolen property. Nothin' like that. I'm makin' money for all of us. What have you got to go and worry yourself over every little thing for?"

"Cuff Mifflin, I don' give a rap what you've got in that lopsided little shed. You could have dead bodies stacked up in there and it wouldn't matter a jot to me."

"Then what's got you so cold? You're moving around here like I'm a ghost or part of the furniture, like I ain't Rose's Papa or your husband. Dirt gets more respect than me."

Comfort did not turn and look at him. "I don' give a rap for dirt or your shed or what's in it." She turned and firmly planted her hand on her hip. "I care that you don't trust me enough to tell me what you're doing to make all this money for me and Rose and your secret self. Trust, Cuff, that's what I care about. Trust between me and you, a wife and her husband."

Cuff sighed and slumped deeply into his chair.

"Whiskey," he said softly after a couple minutes of silence.

"Whiskey? We don't have any whiskey in this house. And you don't drink anyhow, at least that's what you told me before we were married."

"I don't drink the whiskey. I sell it."

"What? To who? Where do you get whiskey to sell?"

Comfort moved closer to Cuff. She was now standing over him, looming as much she could, though his seated self was nearly as tall as she was at full height. "Whiskey?"

"I buy it at the tavern. A jug. I fill small bottles and take them to my customers."

"That ain't illegal?"

"I don' think so, no. I'm just very quiet about it. I only sell to those I know. They know when I'm coming. I go there regular as sunrise. But I'm fixin' to build my own still. Got all the parts in the shed. When I make my still, then I'll make better whiskey, maybe some rum. And we'll be rich."

Comfort sat down in a chair across from him. She stared for a few minutes at his face. Then a laugh that was relief and humor all in one rolled up from her feet and stumbled across the table and yanked a smile from deep inside Cuff's soul. They laughed and laughed like a call and response until they woke up Rose and the sun set and the moon rose giddy with its own thin light.

CHAPTER 34

"Mistress died on a Sunday," Rachel said as she awkwardly folded the knotted cuffs for her new dress. "Master had her bed moved into this room. It sat right over there in the dark corner. He had a desk set up about here," she said pointing to the wall beside her. "He could work by the window light and still listen for her. She was all rattles and backwash toward the end. At times I thought I would go mad listening to her. Sometimes I even prayed that she would die."

"Did you hate her that much? I guess you did, she beat you so bad."

"Comfort, I don't know if it was because of the beating, or because I wanted her pain to end. Or mine. A long dying takes it out of the quick and the one preparing to go. Every day she'd say to Master, 'Today's the day, Thomas. Today I'm free.' Then she'd hold on. Her heart was strong. Her lungs were full, but her heart refused to give way to those lungs. It was a tug-o-war, I guess."

Rachel rose from her rocking chair and left the room. Comfort, alone, laid her hands in her lap and looked around the room. With her eyes half closed she could imagine the bed in the dim corner, the desk near the window and the faint shape of a man hunched over his work, papers neatly piled, ink bottle, blotter, a nib scratch-scratch scratching columns of names and numbers in a ledger. In the terrible mid-day light Comfort imagined this ghostly world, and behind it was the give and take of Mistress's failing breath like the swash on a beach she'd heard once as a girl. It was vivid and terrible, and Comfort could not separate her feelings about the going. On the one hand she felt like an evil was passing away, on the other she felt a twinge of pain of delusion. It was almost like Mistress had willed Thomas and Rachel together.

Comfort's rocking picked up speed. Could it have been, she wondered.

Rachel sat noiselessly back in her rocker. Comfort stared at her but did not see her return. "Comfort. Where are you?" Mistress smiled.

"Far back, I suppose," she said, startled. "Far back?"

"Yes'm. I was thinking about your mistress. When you were gone it was almost like she was in this room again, like she wanted to say something to me. All of a sudden I had this thought ... But you must think I'm about crazy, talkin' on like this."

Rachel sat quietly feeling the familiar knots in her hands, letting the wheels and picots pass between her fingers like beads. Her rocking was meditative, patient and slow as she waited for Comfort to go on.

"Mistress?"

"Yes?"

"Do you ... do you think maybe your Mistress put an idea in your head, or tried to anyway, and when it didn't seem to stick she beat it into you?"

"What idea would that be?"

"To go to Master's bed." Comfort sat completely still, fearing even to look anywhere but straight ahead. "I mean she knew she was dying, maybe she was just looking out for her Thomas."

Rachel Mifflin raised one gnarled hand to her eyes and wept.

Comfort sat still as the silence gathered. She dared not rock or knot or even breathe. Instead of the tick-tick of her shuttle now, it was the faintest suspirations of weeping breath. She took in what she could out of the corner of her eye. But it was mostly a gray assemblage of ordinary things disheveled and desperately seeking to re-form and re-establish the bliss of the everyday.

"I felt like I had my revenge," Rachel said vaguely, "when Master finally showed me his attentions. It was six months, maybe a year after her going that Sunday. Master took my hand all of a sudden and kissed it. He looked at me like a small boy who wondered if he'd done some terrible wrong. But he hadn't, of course. But I remember thinking that Mistress finally had her excuse to beat me—if she hadn't already drowned."

"Maybe it wasn't a trap, but a plan."

Rachel's crabbed hand slid from her eyes to her mouth and she took a deep, deep breath. "Things changed quick after that. Thomas manumitted most of the slaves—your mother and father and Cuff, the baby, were all that were left. And me. Five years came and went. I was emancipated, but I stayed on cooking and knotting. And somewhere, sometime Thomas stopped kissing my hand and instead asked for it. He was, I think, genuinely in love with me ... and I ... I loved him too. I no longer dreamed of a young man with strong back to build a life for two or more. But a man with a spine fell into my life."

Comfort rocked slowly, and the gray light and chill of a June afternoon rocked with her.

CHAPTER 35

Cuff slipped down Locust Street, a fresh supply of coins jangling in his hand. It was well before noon and he had finished his deliveries for the day. Now he had only to check his first batch of whiskey coming from the still, and the rest of the day was his—and he knew right where he would spend it and the coins going heavy, heavy in his fingers.

In the shed Cuff and Pompey drew off some of the brown

liquid. Cuff poured a small amount on a polished piece of stone, struck a match and drew it close to the stone. The liquid caught fire, flared and steadied into a blue flame. Pompey clapped and spun around on one leg. Cuff shook his hand and offered him the rest of the glass. Pompey wet his lips, ran his tongue over them, and smiled. After pouring the rest down his throat, he closed his eyes and gave a quick affirmative nod. It was good.

When Pompey left the shed, Cuff took the bag down from the wall and carefully pulled the clothing from it piece by piece. The suit was like no other he had ever laid eyes upon. It was bright yellow with a peacock embroidered on the back of the jacket. Each of Argus's eyes set in the tail was a slightly different hue. From a distance one might have imagined a constellation of brilliant stars fallen to earth and re-formed on this coat that might have rivaled Joseph's.

The buttons were glass. Lapels to tails were piped in black silk, and on each breast were griffins staring at their beholder with dark, menacing eyes. The suit had been crafted for someone passing through Wilmington who never returned for it. It hung in the tailor's window, subject to much abuse by passersby who would stop, gossip and laugh a while, then move on with wagging heads. Who might be so foolish? Who might be so brash?

Cuff had bought it for one tenth of what it had cost the tailor in material alone. This tailor vowed never again to make gaudy suits, or any other articles of men's clothing, for strangers. If they did not live in the neighborhood, or come with a letter of introduction, they could find someone else to make their trousers and coats. Had Cuff not made an offer, the tailor might have offered Cuff a small sum to carry the offending garment away. No matter, both men were happy with the transaction.

Except for trying on the suit when he first brought it home, he had not placed it on his back again. Now that was about to change. Cuff the honest, steady businessman who dealt in spirits, was now about to transform. There had been on the wind for about a week a mumbling about a cockfight on the fringes of the city. He had from time to time wagered on a dogfight and on horse races, but he was new to cock fights, and eager to see one.

Who but a betting man would have the confidence to wear such a suit among strangers, he thought. This is what money buys you without spending a dime.

Cuff lifted a cedar box down from the highest shelf in the shed. Inside was an immaculately clean white cloth folded deliberately and precisely. With great gentleness and care, he lifted the cloth from the box and laid it on the bench. He closed the lid on the box and replaced it on the upper shelf. He was wearing his suit now, and the newness of it lent an air of even greater formality and weight to the rareness of his taking this cloth from its box. He breathed easily and steadily as he unfolded the first part. He closed his eyes and said the remembered prayer. On the second fold, another prayer. When the cloth was lying stark and bright in the dim room, he said a fifth and final couplet of faith.

For a year when Cuff was very young, a slave named

Henri, from Saint Dominique, had lived in his neighborhood. He was a storyteller and a kind of shaman who knew powers and how to control them. He told Cuff he saw in the boy a rare faith and ability and slowly began initiating him into his secrets. The objects in the cloth were deceptively everyday things—and only to the knowledgeable and the skilled could they alter the flow of events. One by one Cuff lifted them from the cloth: a halfpenny, dull and worn; a dog's tooth; a nail from a church Henri said once stood near his Caribbean island home. It was, he said with awe still in his voice, the only building left standing after a fierce hurricane had all but destroyed the island when he was a boy.

Cuff put each object in a different pocket—in the cloth and box their powers relaxed, their vibrations stilled. But together in a human hand, a human hand knowing and skillful, they could stop a horse, put out a fire, or change the numbers on a pair of dice.

Cuff was warned not to use the power for frivolous things, and he had taken that advice to his young heart. Only rarely did he alter the flow, and only when it was for the best. Not even Comfort knew of the box and the cloth and the secrets kept wrapped inside.

Taking the power to a cockfight ain't frivolous, is it, he asked himself, and began to have second thoughts about this plan. If I can make some money to feed my baby, that would be a good thing. Maybe buy a bonnet for Comfort, he thought. I owe her that because it was the halfpenny, dog tooth and nail that had changed Comfort and sent her heart to him. I think I'll be okay with that. He rolled the white cloth up and put it in a fourth pocket.

No one waved to him as he made his way down the street and across town. No one could see tattered and patched Cuff beneath this outfit of a dandy. As he crossed town, many stopped and stared. Some, no doubt, had seen the suit in the tailor's window and wondered now how anyone had had the nerve to animate it. But block after block his confidence grew with this outlandish anonymity.

He walked quickly toward the location whispered by his customers, accompanied by winks and confidential tosses of heads. He wanted to roll all of the newness in his life into a ball and place it somewhere safe and clean and light. He touched the halfpenny, pinched it tightly and repeated the halfpenny prayer. The dogtooth stung his finger. "You're still bitin' me, even in death," he said aloud. "Old hound." And said the dogtooth prayer; held the church nail and said the church-nail prayer.

Cuff could not remember ever being happier. Maybe he'd been the day he bought himself into freedom from Mistress Mifflin, but that was a one time, magnificent happiness. But this, this feeling seemed like it could go on day after day almost forever, or at least until he could abide the happiness no longer.

CHAPTER 36

The livery stable delivered Master Clendaniel's horse and carriage at nine a.m. He kissed his wife gently and stared hard at the shrinking, bruised Esther, threatening her with his eyes into silence. The night before, while Mistress visited her sister elsewhere in the city, he had forced himself on her more brutally than ever before.

Now, she had stanched the blood but not the tears. She cowered in the dimmest corner of the hallway when he passed by. For years she had fancied his eyes were the eyes of the devil. But now she knew it to be true. He was on his way, she had overheard, to buy more slaves, more lives to decorate his little hell.

Mistress sat in the parlor crocheting. She was a handsome, but dimly aware old woman in her mid-fifties. She wore a crocheted bonnet of her own making. She had little to do with the house slaves except issuing orders each morning. Then they were expected to follow her demands if it took them all day and night. She was not the devil's paramour, she was too distant and dull for that role. She was merely an animated form for whom luck struck once in her youth when she happened to catch the eye of William Clendaniel. Had a year or two intervened before they met, he might have passed her by as just another fading beauty, past her blush and vegetatively crocheting a life for herself. She could have been happy with that life too. It was all the same. Neither father nor husband put any stress or demands on her. Were she to simply vanish one day, it would cause little fuss, except, perhaps, among the servants who would no doubt feel her absence like a tightening in the belly.

Esther had never resisted Master for fear of the consequences—he often threatened harm, but rarely delivered it. So it fell like a lightning bolt when he sneaked up behind her as she folded laundry, tore her dress, and forced her to the floor. There can be no satisfaction, she thought, it was over so soon. It was animal and painful and bloody. He nearly spat at her as he buttoned his trousers, walking away. "Say nothing!"

She pulled herself to her knees and gathered her torn dress around her, dazed and pained deep inside. She barely noticed when, in a minute, he returned and threw a new dress on the floor beside her. It was identical to the one he'd torn away.

But she was petrified to try to leave. She might well have convinced every other citizen of Wilmington that she was white and just passing through to who knew where. But she knew he would not kill her once he found her and forced her back into the house she rarely left—and never alone. But he would do harm. It would be swift and deep harm. She knew that pain would never heal.

So she had only one vaguely possible way to survive.

"Mistress. "Mistress?"

The voice startled Mary Clendaniel into another consciousness. She sat for several moments like one who was awakened suddenly. Her eyes blinked, she gathered in the room around her, and smiled finally, and vaguely up at Esther. "Yes?"

Although her face was bruised, Mistress seemed not to notice, or care. "Mistress, Master told me if I ... if I told you what he done, he'd kill me."

Mary Clendaniel's reaction was the same as if someone had offered her tea. "What Master does is his business. It is not yours or mine to question him."

"He raped me, not once but many times. Last night, when you were out, he hurt me so deep I bled."

Her countenance did not change. In fact, she seemed perturbed at the news. In one rusty, jagged move she stood and slapped Esther hard in the face. "Liar!"

CHAPTER 37

Comfort laid the shuttle on the table and held the knotted collar so she could examine it in the poor window light. Mrs. Townsend should be pleased with this, she thought.

Mrs. Sara Townsend did not own slaves, never had owned slaves, and was a member of the Abolition Society of Delaware. Knowing that Comfort was trying to earn her freedom price by taking in extra handwork, she occasionally ordered a collar or doily. "Comfort," she said after seeing her first knotting, "your frivolite outshines 'em all. Your work is even better than what Rachel used to do," she whispered, even though Rachel Mifflin was nowhere around.

"Frivolite?"

"It is the French term," said haughtily

"Oh." More new words for the old knots, she thought.

They had agreed on the price of one dollar for the collar. If Comfort attached the collar to the new dress Mrs. Townsend was expecting from France, then that would be fifty cents more. If she could find more rich customers like that, Comfort thought, she could make her freedom price in just a few more years. She decided to ask Mrs. Townsend to show her collar to friends and tell them who made it.

Cuff was standing in the backyard talking and gesturing to Pompey. "Cuff, I got to deliver this collar, so you need to listen for Rose if she wakes up, you hear?"

"I hear, it's not like Pompey'll chatter so I can't." Pompey put an exaggerated hurt look on his face. "So now your gonna act like a child. Go on with ya, I've got to listen for my daughter."

Comfort brushed by the two men. She carried her knotting bag, a handkerchief in her sleeve, and wore a new bonnet bought for her by Cuff—one of the few things he had ever given her besides his name. In a moment, she disappeared down Locust Street. A few minutes later Comfort turned with some trepidation onto Smyrna Street. She had written down the address and now quickly scanned the numbers. She had never been here before, had always met the woman elsewhere and turned over her handwork for coins. She spied the house three doors away. She tried to look straight ahead and simply go about her business, but she could see women looking out from between parted curtains, concerned to see an unfamiliar black face on their street.

She knocked on the door at number seven, and was surprised to be met by a black man in a very formal suit. "Yes," he said, sounding surprised to see her standing there as if she had some business in this neighborhood.

"I have some knotting for Miz Townsend. She hired me to make it for her." "Knotting? I don't understand."

"Frivolite?" Comfort said, lifting the delicate collar from her knotting bag and holding it up for him to examine.

"Very beautiful," he said coldly. "Just a moment." He left Comfort standing on the porch, the door ajar, and more curtains up and down the street parting around her.

She laughed a short, nervous laugh. Imagine me, she thought, stirring up so much curiosity in a white neighborhood. A moment later Mrs. Sara Townsend appeared at the door, her face screwed into scowl. "I suppose you'll want to come in," she barked.

"No'm," said Comfort, rattled and confused.

"Well come in anyway. The whole street knows you're here."

Inside she demanded to see the collar. She took it lightly in her fingers and held it to the window light. "I'll bet you wouldn't do work like this for Rachel Mifflin."

"Ma'am?"

"This is sloppy work, young woman."

"No'm. But I suppose it is if you say it is."

"I'll give you fifty cents, no more."

"Miz Townsend, we agreed on a dollar, and fifty cents for me to sew it on."

"Fifty cents. And I'll have my seamstress attach it if this is the kind of work you try to pass off on me. I thought I was helping you out. But now I see you're trying to take advantage of my generosity."

"No'm. This is the same work I do for Mistress Mifflin. I never tried to take advantage of anyone in my life." Her fragile features began to tremble. She did not want to cry in front of this stranger. But Sara Townsend had insulted the very skill that gave her pride. The only things that mattered more to her than her knotting were her daughter and her husband.

"Well?"

"Ma'am?"

"Fifty cents. That or nothing."

She thought "nothing," then quickly changed her mind. She dared not speak for fear of weeping openly. It was bad enough that tears inched down her cheeks. She could not risk her voice cracking. Her body shaking, she held her hand out toward the woman, her eyes down, her mind and body now just wanting to get out, to leave this street and all of its horrors behind.

꠸

On Monday Comfort sat knotting in light so dim and dirty that she had to squint. Rachel Mifflin rocked on the other side of the window, occasionally breaking the silence by reading snippets of news she thought might interest Comfort from the newspaper. She was convinced that the more stories she told, the more articles she shared with Comfort, the more the girl would want to go on reading after she paid her freedom price and went permanently away.

"Says here that Levin Thompson died."

"Who is that?" she asked distractedly.

"One very rich man down in Little Creek Hundred."

"A white man?"

"No, he was black. Owned hundreds of acres of land, timber, mills and spinning wheels. My, it must have kept him busy."

"Yes'm."

After a few minutes of quiet, Rachel Mifflin spoke again. "Down in Washington they've started a new Society—like we need another society in this country. Best I can make out in this puny light is it's called the American Colonization Society."

"What for?"

"Article says it's to help those who want to return to Africa."

"Return to Africa? Don't you have to be from somewhere to return there?"

"I suppose they mean ancestors came from Africa."

"Do you suppose we'd be better treated in a country of all black people than we are here?"

Rachel Mifflin let the newspaper fall to her lap as if someone had slapped at her. "Comfort," she said so loudly that the girl jumped in her chair. "Don't I always treat you right?"

"Yes'm."

"Then why in the world would you ask a question like that?"

"I didn't mean you treat me bad."

"Then what did you mean?"

Comfort sat quietly. She did not rock, and her shuttles were still. "Nothing. I'm sorry. I didn't mean anything by it."

"Comfort, I know you better than that. Why would you ask such a thing? Has Cuff been talking about taking you and Rose to Africa?"

"No'm. Never heard such a thing come out of his mouth."

"Well?"

Comfort was quiet. "Miz Townsend."

"Miz Townsend? Sara Townsend? What about her?"

"I knotted her a collar. That's all."

"That's all. Curious. What happened to the collar?"

"I took it to her."

"And?"

"She said it was shabby quality. But I done my best. She said I wouldn't make anything like that for you."

"Did she pay you?"

"Yes."

"How much?"

Comfort thought. She felt trapped, this was not a conversation she'd planned to have. "Fifty cents," she said finally.

"That's cheap. I thought you charged more for your work."

"I do. We agreed on one dollar for the collar, and fifty cents to sew it to a new dress she had coming from France."

"So she said it was inferior work and she'd only pay you fifty cents?"

"Yes'm."

"When did this happen?"

"Saturday. But I shouldn't have said anything to you. It's my business."

"And it's my business too. People can't get away with treating someone like that just because they're in bondage."

"No'm. I think that too."

Rachel Mifflin knocked on the door at number seven Smyrna Street. In a moment the same servant who had greeted Comfort opened the door. He seemed surprised as if a steady stream of strangers would not stop knocking on the door.

"Yes," he said. "May I help you?"

"I would like to see Sara Townsend."

"Whom shall I say is calling?" he inquired, ushering her into the foyer, and absently staring at her hands.

"Rachel Mifflin."

"I will see if Mistress is in."

"Rachel Mifflin, my word. I don't think you've ever been to my house before. What brings you here?"

"Oh, I think you can figure it out."

"Does it have anything to do with that girl of yours?"

"You know quite well it does. I have given her permission to earn extra money to pay her freedom price, and I don't appreciate your taking advantage of her."

"Taking advantage? That's strong language. The work was

not her usual quality."

"Is that so? Perhaps then you will let me buy it from you and you can have another made. By someone more clever than Comfort."

"Well, Rachel, I don't think..."

"Oh, I insist. Fifty cents is too much to pay for inferior knotting. Besides, there must be dozens of people around here could do better for you."

"Well."

"Please, Sara. I don't wish to take any more of your time."

Sara Townsend made an annoyed gesture toward the servant who disappeared into another room. After a few uncomfortable moments for both women, he returned followed by a short round woman holding a dress.

"I was having it attached," she said.

"But you must have paid a fortune for a dress from France. Why would you allow an inferior collar ..."

"Inferior?" blurted the seamstress. "This is the finest knotting work I have ever seen."

In a blurred, sudden gesture, Sara Townsend handed Rachel Mifflin a dollar. "Tell Comfort I said thank you," she whispered.

CHAPTER 38

Cuff heard the voices through the trees. Thin smoke rose above the stand of forest and the smell of game cooking drifted in it. It was rabbit or venison, and Cuff stopped to wonder if he had stumbled on someone's camp, or if some enterprising soul had set up a cooking pit to profit from the gamblers. He took a chance and entered the woods.

The underbrush was thick with holly saplings and brambles that he carefully pulled from his clothes. Nothing, he thought, would look worse than a powerful suit with rips and tears in it, or worse, patches. He worked his way slowly toward the voices— many voices he could tell now—that were sounding increasingly excited. And some were angry.

An old man with white hair and a large mustache sat on a three-legged stool on the outskirts of a rough circle inscribed in the dirt, he had a large wooden bowl on the ground in front of him and it was filled with coins. In a basket were thin sticks all cut to the same length. As men approached him to place bets on the next fight, the white-haired man would carve a series of notches on a stick and hand it to the bettor. The men would nod, yet not a word was spoken once the bet was in.

A large group of men milled around the roasting pit

where several animals were cooking. Those, presumably, who had won, were cheerfully gorging themselves on large portions of meat. The losers, on the other hand, merely looked on the feast, or walked away, or prayed, Cuff imagined, for better luck.

Two cocks were brought forward in primitive cages made of twigs and sticks. Both were frantically beating their wings, threatening to burst from their cages and disappear into the thick forest around them. Cuff stared at them for several minutes, but he was not trying to see the spirit that would force them to win the fight. He imagined instead that both birds only wanted to escape. There was not the hatred he'd seen in the eyes of men about to fight, not the blood thirst that kept bare-knuckle fighters standing long after the fog of loss had invited them to lie down and give up. There was just the resolve that they must fight or be killed instantly. In the end he didn't choose the cock by size or presumed strength or strutting bravado, but by color. He liked the burnt-orange color of autumn maple leaves. He handed over his bet to the white-haired odds man, received his stick with the strange notches, and tried to blend into the margins of the clearing. But no matter where he went, eyes turned toward him and for a moment he didn't know whether he was sorry he had worn the suit, or proud that he was the center of attention. No one else was dressed as he was, no one approached him, and no one wondered if he were the law. The law would never seek to be so singular.

After the dust and feathers, after shouts and curses, the manic gestures and the blood, Cuff stood on the cusp of the circle holding tightly his notched stick. In the center of the ring etched into the dirt and duff of the forest floor, one bird lay dead. Cuff felt as he had when a dog died in a fight, vaguely put off, mildly sympathetic. He preferred a victor and a vanquished rather than a victor and a victim. But he quickly roused himself and presented his stick for payment. The coins doubled in his pocket, and he could see years and miles ahead, the green and gold expanses of Pennsylvania or Massachusetts.

The used sticks were transferred to the roasting pit where a younger version of the white-haired man was turning chunks of meat above the flames. Cuff's stomach could not stop rumbling from the scent of rabbit, venison and dove cooking to black promises of flavor. He took a coin from his pocket and gave in.

As he chewed the meat from the skewer, he watched the two birds being readied for the next fight. This time one bird was larger and stronger and strutted outside its cage without his owner keeping a close eye on him. He was clearly a veteran. Scarred and showing signs of battle—missing feathers and healed wounds on his comb. The other bird was small and compact and seemed to nestle uneasily into his owner's arms. No experience there, Cuff thought. The bird seemed to stare at his opponent, seemed not to be able to do otherwise. The larger bird did not return the stare, but strutted, impatient to begin.

Cuff bet on the smaller bird. Instinct said he would lose, would probably die in the first few minutes of the fight. The larger bird would stroll back to its cage across a circle littered with feathers and blood. He took his stick and walked back to the lucky spot he had stood in for the first fight. He removed the halfpenny, the dogtooth and the nail from the different pockets and walked casually toward the small cock in the man's arms. With the three charms in his fist he quickly but gently passed his knuckles over the bird's head and down his back.

That should be enough, he thought, and took his place again away from the knot of men loudly cheering for the fight to commence. Cuff watched as a silent signal was sent from the white-haired bet taker to his younger look-alike at the pit to the man at the center of the circle. When he brought his raised hand down, the two cocks were released. Cuff watched only the smaller bird that had become brazen and bold once in the ring.

It was over in less than a minute. As Cuff made his way across the circle to collect his winnings, a tall white man with long dirty black hair and scar on his left cheek was coming from the other direction. He looked angry and fierce even though he too was going to collect. Cuff handed his stick to the white-haired man, but the white man thrust his ahead and pushed Cuff's hand aside. Cuff withdrew, but the white man stared at him, and then, as if seeing him for the first time, began to point at Cuff's suit, and laugh.

CHAPTER 39

Pompey straddled the nail keg and watched Cuff pour his home brew into glass bottles, crockery jars—anything that would hold liquid and not leak. "I'm makin' more money'n I can count, my friend. I've been to the cockfights five times, and the third time it struck me that these here gamblers seemed thirsty. I had figured out that the white haired man was in charge of the fights, so I approached him after a fight began, and the cussing and hollering was in full throat."

Pompey nodded as Cuff spoke. He watched carefully, in case one day he was asked to help—when Cuff got too rich to want to work for himself.

"Old Mustache is a foxy one, I'll give him that. He asked for a taste, then he said I could sell all the whiskey and rum I could if I would give him his for free. He didn't say anything about the other two, so we shook on it, and now I'm makin' money off of the whiskey and on my bets. I've lost only two fights so far." He nearly mentioned the charms above their heads in the cedar box, but he caught himself and stayed mum. "I think it must be my lucky suit," he added, and Pompey smiled and nodded.

When he had changed into his yellow suit, and filled

all of the pockets with the bottles and crocks, he turned to Pompey and said: "If I had more pockets I could make more money."

Pompey stood and pointed to his pockets with a smile.

"If you had some clothes, like me, to make you not look so much like you, then you could come with me, but I don't know where you are likely to find any." Pompey sat back down on the nail keg and looked beaten. "Don't take it so hard. I'll think on it and come up with something before the next fight."

Pompey brightened, and walked a ways with Cuff down Locust Street.

Before each fight Cuff placed a bet on, he transferred the half penny, the dogtooth and the nail into his right hand and passed it as close to the bird as possible without raising the owner's suspicions. The two times he had lost a bet, he told himself, he had not completed the pass before someone looked at him, so the charm was weakened and didn't cause the flow of power to embolden the bird. It was simple, if he couldn't get close enough, then he didn't bet on that fight.

And some fights he didn't bet on because he could see thirsty money standing around the circle. They seemed to get thirstier if they won. Cuff kept a careful eye on everyone who traded a carved stick for cash. Not too early, not too sudden, not too quickly after they had the cash in their pocket. He sidled up slowly, or those with a soul-deep thirst needing to be slaked, sought him out. And he was not hard to find. Like the mustache man, he was a kind of fixture. No one knew his name. No one could claim they'd seen him in Wilmington or anywhere else for that matter. Cuff liked this anonymity. He took so naturally to his outlandish costume that it seemed to make him invisible to all but the very thirsty.

The man with the dirty hair and the scarred cheek who had laughed at Cuff's suit was not a regular at the fights, but when he was there he kept a close eye on the man in the clown suit, as he called it to his wife and mother-in-law. "Damndest thing you ever see'd, a nigger in a suit brighter'n a buttercup." And when he bet, he bet big. Cuff watched him closely, but kept his distance. There was something about him that made Cuff curious and cautious. Maybe it was the scar, that had to be a story, or maybe it was the utter contempt he showed to everyone.

At times even the old bet taker was loath to take his money, and did so only by treating it as if it were diseased. It passed through his hands into the wooden bowl quickly, barely touching his fingers. No words were ever spoken between the two, but the old man's eyes said the other had no worth. And it appeared to be mutual.

It was a democratic gathering of thieves, and drunks, ne'er-do-wells and hucksters and would-be businessmen like Cuff. Except for the cussing and screaming when they lost their money and the hoots of delight when they won, it was a quiet crowd, at least in the beginning. Once the winners had appropriated some of Cuff's "blue flame" as they took to calling it, it could, and did, become somewhat more raucous, and unfriendliness cast a pall across the entire affair. That is generally when Mustache called it a day, sending the bird handlers home and selling what cooked meat remained for whatever he could get. Cuff sometimes took a hunk of venison or a dove or two home to Comfort and Rose as a special treat.

He had placed winning bets on four fights and was running low on whiskey. It was especially cold, the light particularly grainy and thin—even for a spring that always felt like early March or late October. Two or three unsold bottles tinkled in his pocket, and he decided to go home. Coins jangled in another pocket and the sound was pure happiness to Cuff.

He waved to the old bet taker and turned to leave. The dirty-haired, scar-faced man blocked the path to the woods. "What you want?" he asked.

"You sellin' whiskey?"

"I am."

"I want a taste."

"A dime to you like everybody else."

"A dime for nigger whiskey?"

Cuff turned to walk away. A hand came down on his shoulder and spun him around. His normal instinct would have been to raise his fist to defend himself, but the scar-faced man was not in a fighting attitude.

"I said I want to taste your whiskey, and I'm prepared to take it off you if I have to."

Cuff thought, there is too much at stake here to fight for myself, and too much at stake not to. I give in and every good-for-nothin' that hears about this will think he can take my whiskey for free."

"Well?"

"I told you it was a dime to you like to everybody else."

"And I told you there ain't no watered down slave liquor

worth two cents let alone no dime. Call it 'blue flame,' 'angel sweat' or 'Satan's swollop,' but you'll get no dime offa me. But I will have your whiskey."

He was very agitated and the scar on his cheek glowed black with his anger. He rocked from foot to foot and seethed, nearly spitting the words at Cuff who stood motionless trying to figure his next move. He couldn't run with bottles in his pockets. It would be hell to pay if he hit a white man, even one as onerous and intoxicated as this one. But he could see the whole encounter coming to an end soon, and he did not like where it was going.

"Not now, Johnson," a voice said calmly from behind. Johnson spun and stared into the eyes of the mustached man. "Not here, not now, not ever."

"Says who?"

"Says me, Johnson. You're a snake. I may be old ... I ought to beat you while you're a drunk snake, but I won't unless you force me to." His son walked up and stood shoulder to shoulder with his father. The two stood with arms across their chests and waited without saying any more. Johnson wavered and appeared to go for a knife in his pocket. Cuff jumped backward, and the two men dropped their arms anticipating his move. Unsteadily his hand pulled from his pocket, but he did not hold a knife. Between his fingers was a coin that he threw with some power at Cuff's chest.

"Here's for your nigger whiskey, whiskey man," he spat. Cuff picked the coin up from the dirt noticing it was more than what was owed, and carefully held a bottle out to the man. He thought for just a moment of dropping it, but chose not to. The two men watched Johnson as he took the bottle from Cuff. He sneered and drank it straight off.

Cuff turned and headed for home.

CHAPTER 40

Pompey was not tall, nor large, but he was stringy and quick. He'd had to be to defend himself against those who took the fact that he was mute to mean that he was also stupid or fey. His wiry response to their taunts and threats had changed more than a few minds—and lips.

With more pockets to fill now, Cuff sent his silent friend off to scrounge as many bottles and jars as he could find, paying him for each one, and a discount on his whiskey. While he was gone, Cuff made a quick trip to a shop three blocks away. Pompey would be very surprised. Very, very surprised.

Cuff felt the heft of his bag of coins, feeling a moment's guilt for not securing his wife and daughter's freedom right then. But it passed. Comfort would soon pay off her freedom price and she would thank him for letting her do it herself. That final payment to Mistress Mifflin would let Comfort feel a draft of pure exhilaration that freedom brings.

The look on Pompey's face was pure suspicion when

he held up the new clothes. The cloth was a large checkered pattern, black frames over a red background. He first held them at arm's length then looked from Cuff to Rose who sat quietly eyeing the jacket and trousers as if she were pleased that they were not for her. Pompey squinted and raised his eyebrows, looking for all the world like he was about to break his silence and complain about this offense that he still could not imagine climbing into. He could not have looked more wounded had Cuff come straight out and cold-cocked his dignity right there in front of the child.

"You don't want anyone to notice you going to the fights."

Pompey shot a shocked look at Cuff. He shrugged violently and shook the clothes. Not notice me, he seemed to shout.

"I didn't mean notice, my friend, I meant recognize."

Pompey was indignant. He shook the clothes at Cuff, asking in his silent fashion how Cuff had come into possession of this insult.

"Where did I get them, is that what you're askin' me? Don't see where it matters much, just got to have luck and timing. Got my suit from a tailor that used to work on unsecured orders. Notice I said used to."

Pompey shook the clothes more violently. "All right. Different tailor, same bad deal."

CHAPTER 41

It was nearly full dark when Comfort left Mistress Mifflin's house. She had been instructed to light only the lamps in the kitchen, so the parlor was deep in shadows from the faint light in the next room. It was colder than most nights in this colder than ever spring. Rachel pulled her shawl tighter around her, shut her eyes and rocked.

Images of Cork rolled like waves in and out of her interior field of vision. Buildings, perhaps long ago torn down, or burned down stood as they had in 1775 when she had walked out of town for the last time. Her eyes moved behind their lids as she saw again the colors and shapes of her hometown. People came and went. Her mother and father, both dead, seemed to step from shadows to greet her. They smiled and reached out their arms to embrace her. As the rocking chair glided back and forth, she reached as well. Then there seemed to be an odd or unremembered glint in her father's eyes, it jolted her for it seemed he beckoned his runaway daughter to the other side. In the scene playing out in her head, she backed away realizing he had never forgiven her, even from the grave. To a watcher, her expressions were kaleidoscopic, joy and disappointment flashing, colliding, melding one into the other.

A waking dream she thought. A sometimes restless, sometimes serene but strange place between sleep and wakefulness—yet not fully either. Rachel Mifflin was tired and knew she needed to feed herself before bed, but she could only rock and flatly, tunelessly whistle airs she remembered from her girlhood. Soon the soft, hollow column of air that just failed to form itself into a whistle, soothed her.

She felt a yearning for her birthplace, something she had not felt in many years. Or perhaps, she thought, she yearned instead for the youth it represented. Suddenly there was a pang of regret for all of her years of servitude, then a quick blossoming joy for the life she had gained in its stead.

For a long while she let the images stand just out of her inward vision. She rocked, feeling whatever the moment gave her. She had not felt this much pure peace in a long time and she was content to forget small stirrings of hunger, the absence of light or the presence of cold and just feel her life wrap around her. The fire stirred in the grate, dropped its ashes silently upon the hearth and glowed as Rachel felt herself glow from within.

Little everyday pains and annoyances seemed to wink out while she failed to notice them. It would be nice to sleep like this, she thought. She was aware of the soft, feminine world around her, warming her, keeping her safe, delivering up forgotten images and scenes decades out of mind. In a state restful as sleep, she was unaware if she wanted to be, traveling if she wanted, right here and now if she chose.

If death is anything like this, she thought, I would be glad to go. Suddenly she thought how odd it was to think of her own death, something she never did. Perhaps it was the images of my mother and father, she thought sadly, remembering the letter that brought the news of their dying—together, at least. The flames of their death leapt before her, but she quickly willed rain on them, and in a moment peace returned.

This must be where only old men and old women go for comfort. This is like no state I remember as a girl, she thought, so there is a benefit to growing old. She had drunk a little wine at her wedding, and she remembered the feeling in her head was like this. Only now her brain did not swirl and dance, but hung like a cloud between earth and heaven.

She was rocking and not rocking, she was whistling and not whistling, her hair rose in electric bolts toward the sky, her feet were rooted to the cold ground. Somewhere between earth and the universe, between waking and sleeping, between life and death, between her lungs and her heart, she felt, for the first time, the faintest welling up of pain.

CHAPTER 42

Despite the strange cold that gripped this spring, Esther sweated in the kitchen shed. No one came to bother her there. Meals were always prepared and brought into the main house on time. She was a good cook and needed no supervision, so it was with impunity that she practiced Roots there, a potent magic divined from plants and the tinctures, potions, infusions and lotions she concocted. She had learned it practically at the breast of Namby who took over raising her when Esther's mother was sold.

Namby had come from Africa on a slave ship. She had instinctively hidden away seeds from the plants she would need to carry on. It was Namby who taught Esther the fine art of blending the herbs into the garden among look-alike plants, or deep in back corners where no one ever went except her.

As the keeper of the garden, Esther's job was far easier that Namby's had been. As long as the food was hot and nicely flavored, the meat not too old or discolored, the wine bottles never showing signs of pilfering, no one seemed to care what she did there. She might sleep or hang squirrels from a gallows as long as she had meals cooked and brought in on time. Even Master honored that space. Why, Esther had never figured out—it was safer than the main house if he planned to rape her. But perhaps he reasoned that his coming and going to the shed might raise too many questions—not that Mary would question him or even suspect him of anything sinful, she hadn't it in her to doubt. And that, he concluded, is because she cared for little but herself and the cocoon she had constructed around herself.

Esther had practiced Roots secretly for some time. Then one day it dawned on her that it had been perhaps as much as years since anyone at all, except Comfort from time to time, and Cuff rarely, stepped into the kitchen. Soon she began hanging bundles of herbs to dry from the beams, kept her infusion jars on the table. Should anyone ask, they were the secret flavors of her most secret dishes.

Namby had taught her the nine sacred herbs of the ancients. The herbs of Africa, and those of this new place: root, seed, leaf and bark. Namby taught her: herbs are the friend of physician and the pride of cooks. Something she had heard and memorized. Probably the words of some old, dead white man, Esther thought. On these cold spring days she put cayenne in her shoes, and the herbs warmed her when she went to the garden. Not that much grew there this year, a few puny stalks here and there. But the year before—what was it, 1815—had been a bountiful year and she had bound bunches left over, and strings of peppers, and bags stuffed with the plants she loved the names of: purple coneflower, fennel, dill, calendula, catnip and feverfew.

Had Clendaniel known of her powers with herbs and spells, he would have banished her from the kitchen forever, for he lived in constant fear that one of his slaves would try to kill him with poison. He had adopted the practice of kings and princes of having every meal he ate tasted by the maker of the meal. He rarely ate food prepared outside of his own house. When he traveled, he took Jonas with him, a twelve-year-old slave who served as taster and scapegoat for all of the many things that snarled and bedeviled travelers. Clendaniel devised ever harsher punishments for the boy whenever he convinced himself that Jonas was responsible—however absurd the notion. And Jonas endured, plotted Clendaniel's death, tasted the food—always far better than he was given in appreciation for his risky services—and knew that one day he would see a space between wall and window, carriage and horse, house and barn, and slip quietly and forever away.

Such thinking kept many slaves alive through such heart-less treatment. The very notion of living to spit on Master Clen-daniel's grave hardened him against every stroke of the lash, every foul bite of week old food, every swallow of rancid water. Esther listened to his stories when they had rare moments to themselves. She cringed and told him of her own mistreatment and pain. And there was a quiet conspiracy between them—unspoken, conveyed through a private language of the eyes. This was, along with herbs and magic spells, her only defense against a world that wanted to make her see herself as some-thing less than human, something to use and discard, hurt and humiliate, abuse for its own pleasure.

Esther sat down hard on a chair. Her infusions were making, her tinctures reducing, and a tea steeping. She grew sad when she thought of Jonas, sad when she thought of herself and the miserable life she had been given. She cursed William and Mary Clendaniel, casting a long, slow curse that she could only hope would see the years deliver—a curse of pain and decay and finally madness.

Next door, Rachel Mifflin rocked. She heard in the air that passed between her lips, a simple air she'd known as a girl, "The Lass of Kilgary", she remembered as the name of it. She heard it clear as if it tweedled from a proper pipe. The notes were sweet, yet mournful. She yearned for the sweetness of the song that turned melancholy for the mournful part that finally drove her from Cork. Drove her ultimately from Ireland. The British systematically drove the Catholics into absolute poverty and ruin, stole the land and passed laws that would keep them tenth-class citizens forever.

In her reverie she fought the demon images that even still visited her in dreams, tried to force them out and resurrect the beauty of village and sea, heath and house. But there was an ache—for herself, her family, her people—that would only go with her own passing. It was a scar healed badly, a birthmark that every window and mirror forced her to recall. So she imagined that she whistled the air from her childhood perfectly, made beautiful the squalid pictures that came into her head, and twisted distractedly the wedding ring she had refused to remove ever since Thomas died. It had grown tight, then tighter in the last few weeks. And she wondered if she would have to take it off, or risk her flesh swelling around the ring. For now it spun tightly and she stopped wondering.

Comfort moved her chair closer to the fire, knotted almost silently and looked at her Mistress from time to time. "Tell me more about Cork, please. You haven't told me stories or read to me from the newspaper in a terrible long time."

But the voice came to Rachel as if from way far away. You simply must not respond to voices on every distant wind, she thought. You never know who you might be speaking to. There are some things in this world that we can't know—and should not want to.

CHAPTER 43

Cuff was flush. His whiskey fueled the cockfights, and the halfpenny, dog's tooth and nail insured win after win. He unhappily paid Pompey at the end of each day. Even though Pompey's assistance brought in twice the money, Cuff was sorry he had promised him so much, and the man could drink, stand up, walk and for all the world appear he'd imbibed nothing stronger than milk. With each gulp he'd wipe his mouth with the back of his hand and stick his glass out toward Cuff until Cuff put an end to it and sent him home.

"You gonna drink me into the poor house, you know that. You can drink more than that Johnson fella, and hold it better, too. He's big and tall and you's sawed off. You must have a hollow leg."

With that Pompey doubled over and shook with delight. He took a kind of pride in being able to hold his whiskey among men, and Cuff's despair at having to keep his glass full made him twice as tickled. When Cuff finally ran him off and closed up the shed for the day, Pompey merely shrugged, waved and walked away in his big absurd suit. But true to Cuff's prediction, no one ever recognized either one of them.

It was still hours until Comfort and Rose would be

home. Cuff removed his suit and put it back it its secret place. His moneybag had grown to two bags, both pregnant with coins collected from his regular customers, the clientele at the cockfights and his own wagers. Sometimes he just stood in the dark of the shed and hefted the bags until arms could not lift anymore. How easy, he would think to himself, it would be to march right up to Mistress and buy his wife and daughter into freedom. He would buy Rose, he thought, but she was whatever her mother was, not her father—free or in bondage. He clung to the notion that Comfort would one day thank him for the joy of freeing herself and feeling no obligation to anyone else—husband or not.

So he took some coins out of a bag and placed them in his pocket, carefully checking that there were no holes there for the coins to escape. He quickly hatched a plan and set off to see it through before he changed his mind and put the coins back where they belonged.

Cuff knew that slave clothes would no longer do for his wife once she was free, and from what she said that day was coming sooner than later for she had been knotting like a mad woman every weekend, and there seemed an endless line of customers wanting her handiwork. Comfort spent nothing on herself and left it to Cuff to feed them—though there was little this summer that would grow. Days when he was not selling whiskey, he fished or hunted. Some scraggly vegetable plants slowly hoisted themselves out of the ground, but their fruits were few and puny. Occasionally on the way to a cockfight he and Pompey would find wild berries to pick, or wild apples. Sometimes there would be meat left over and he would buy what he could and take it home to his wife and daughter. All in all they got by. But something tugged at him deep inside, and to make it subside he would buy Comfort little things to make her happy—or was it to make him feel less guilty?

Either way, coins in pocket he found himself on the way to the milliners shop to buy some cloth and notions. Whenever Comfort might find a break from knotting for others, she could work for herself and make some freedom clothes, clothes fit for a free woman. She was a fine seamstress, and Cuff liked to daydream of the day they'd both be free. He saw it all: the whiskey business growing, his gambling become almost a profession, and Comfort taking in sewing and knotting, Rose at her knee and one day being as quick and nimble as her mother—her hands in demand—and her daughter's hands, and her daughter's hands. And so on 'til Cuff could not see that far into the future. He smiled a lot while he lived in that future a few moments.

He found himself blocks past the milliner's before the reverie broke and he had to turn around and walk back. This is good, he thought, this is good.

Comfort opened the paper package Cuff handed her and hugged the cloth to her. She held the cloth out for Rose to see and touch. "Rose, your Papa got me a dress to wear one day real soon. And I bet there'll be enough so's you can have one to match." Rose clapped, then lifted the corner of the cloth and looked up inside. "Oh, Rose, it's not dresses yet, but one day I get through making things for everybody else, you'll see how I'll find the dress in that pretty cloth."

Cuff sat at the table sipping from a water gourd as Comfort went on about finding dresses in cloth as if they were hidden in there and she had to go like with a map to find them. Comfort held the cloth in front of her as if it were already cut and sewed and hanging on her like fur on an otter—sleek and slim and seamless. Comfort kissed him on the forehead and thanked him.

"It makes you that happy, I'll just have to get you more." It was out of his mouth before he could stop it. He couldn't take it back because she was smiling like he'd promised her a ruby or something. Maybe she'll forget, he reasoned, but felt not even a little hope that she would—ever. Cuff helped her fold the cloth and put it back in its wrappings. The notions she put into a small knotting and sewing bag Mistress had given her.

Comfort determined that that very night she would dream a dress, and that she would make that dress even if she had to stay up nights and risk falling asleep in front of Mistress's fire the next day. What a fine dress to walk into freedom in.

CHAPTER 44

At least for a few days it felt a bit like spring, Comfort thought. She had removed her shawl, but there was still a fire in the grate and mistress dozed wrapped in hers. She awoke with a sputter, and for a moment she seemed not to know where she was or why a young black woman was sitting next to her. Comfort smiled at her. "Finally seems to be warming up. Would you like to go outside for a walk?"

Rachel did not respond right away. The residue of a dream settled like ash on her consciousness, and she was having a hard time placing herself in time and space. Only a moment ago she was walking away from Clonakilty toward Cork with no idea in her head what she would do, or where she would ultimately end up. And now she sat in a small parlor that was overly hot and stuffy. "Let's walk," she said as her head cleared.

"Are you all right, Mistress?"

"Yes, I suppose. It's funny, I've been havin' memories of the old country lately. Things I'd forgotten. Places I never thought I could remember. I guess that's age. Can't sometimes tell where you are, but can recall initials carved in a tree fifty years ago."

"My memory ain't that good," said Comfort.

"Well, right now you don't need memory. All you need to remember is to take care of your husband and your baby girl. And me for a little while more."

"Yes'm. I guess there's plenty ahead, plenty that ain't happened yet, that's just waitin' on me to get there. Though I 'spect I'll remember this summer, and that mountain that blew its top around the world. I guess Rose won't remember; she's too young."

"Can't tell with children. Sometimes they remember the strangest things."

"What's the oldest thing you remember?"

"My mother crying. She was walking and crying. Everything we owned was piled in a cart, and father was driving. We were leaving the farm in Lismore, County Waterford."

"Why? Did they buy a better farm?"

"Buy? Irish Catholics didn't buy land. They rented it. The owners lived in England. Farmers barely scraped by after the heavy rents—two thirds of the land's value every year my father later told me. My grandfather rented that farm, and my father stayed after he died."

"Then why were you leaving if it made your Mama cry?"

"We couldn't rent land for more than thirty one years, and our time ran out when I was four years old. Landlord none of us had ever seen sent word that we were to get out."

The two walked about the small back yard in silence. There was little green to break the monotony of brown earth, brown trunks and stalks. The sky was a gray monotony.

"Father was very angry. It took much and a long time to get him there, but when he angered he was capable of deviltry. He whipped the worthless little horse like he was the landlord himself. Poor thing. I think Father felt bad later, but that horse paid the price for the bad luck of being in front of him.

"I don't remember, of course, how long it took us to get to Clonakilty, and don't even know why we headed that way except there was good farm land down there. I guess Father figured eventually we'd run into a farm for rent and start another thirty one year race against hunger and empty pockets."

"Did you ride in the cart?" asked Comfort, unsure what

to pursue and what to leave be.

"I remember riding some of the time. But mostly I think I walked and held my mother's hand. I think that was the closest we ever were. Once we got to Clonakilty she worked with my father to get the farm going so we wouldn't starve. I was four so I could fend for myself while she worked."

Her voice trailed off. She was again a fifty-eight year old woman whose ankles were swelling from the stroll around the yard. If this is what fifty-eight feels like, I don't want to know about seventy. With a hand on her elbow, Comfort helped her up the back stairs. In the parlor she dropped a log on the fire.

"Mary Clendaniel sent over some stew last evening, so you won't have to cook today. My, my—cooking, eating, sleeping, it's all become such a bother."

"Yes'm, I suppose it is." Comfort held the final lace cuff up for Rachel to inspect. "You like it?"

"Beautiful, as always." But there was sadness in her voice and Comfort couldn't tell if it was the Ireland of long ago that saddened her, or the old farm lost, or those who were dead and gone. So she said nothing. She sat and listened and let her hands relax a moment. A tuneless song of Rachel's making filled the room.

CHAPTER 45

Rachel was jolted awake by a hand swinging toward her in a dream. She was gasping for breath and terrified. The dream was of long ago. Her father stood with his hand roofed above his eyes and staring toward the horizon. Little puffs of dust could be seen, and Michael McArthur was not happy. The overseer was coming, and it was no social visit. They hated one another with the passions of Catholic and Protestant. He did not even dignify the man with a name. He called him simply Overseer, and out of earshot, the Landlord's Whore.

The horse stopped a few feet from Michael, and the man on his back spit. It landed nearly on Michael's brogans. He looked down, then up at the rider but said nothing. "You've overstayed your welcome, McArthur. You've got 'til tomorrow night to clear out. I catch you taking anything not yours and you'll deal with a lot more authority than me."

Michael McArthur stared up at the Overseer, squinting. "Not much time to pack up a household."

"You've had thirty one years to get ready. Now it's time."

"And you've had thirty one years of rent paid in my sweat."

"Catholic sweat."

"Irish sweat to bathe the British bastards that never set foot on this sod."

"If you owned property you could bathe in sweat too. I work for my wages. I do what I have to do. And today I have to tell you to clear out. You've stayed as long as the law allows. Day after tomorrow some new Catholics'll be sleeping in your shack and tilling the Landlord's earth. And you, McArthur, will be gone from my sight."

Rachel moved cautiously behind her father and hugged his leg. One eye peeked out at the man casting a shadow on the ground around her. She had only seen him a few times, but she did not like when he came to their house. He did not smile, and she sensed he would hurt her if her father didn't stand between them. He sneered when he saw her and shot his hand out like a snake as if to harm her.

"You'll be leavin' my daughter alone, Overseer. She's no part of this. She's just a child."

"She's more Catholic deadbeat scum who'll just bring more into a world that can't feed the beggars it's already got." He spat again and Rachel felt sure he meant to spit on her. She trembled and held tighter to her father's leg. What had she done, she wondered. What had her father or mother done?

"Tomorrow night," the rider repeated, "and I'll be here to watch your back hump down the road." He snarled out a laugh and circled his horse behind McArthur. Before Michael could turn, the overseer leaned far out of his saddle and swung his arm to her. He missed and nearly fell from the saddle. Michael grabbed him by the chin and balled his other hand into a fist. The overseer was hanging from the saddle. Rachel thought the moment would go on forever; her father would punch the man, or choke him or let him fall in the dust.

That was the swing that had wakened her and quickened her breathing. It brought back the sorrow and confusion of more than five decades. She could not recall what her father had finally done. He was not given to violence unless provoked. And he had been provoked. But she could not recall. Finally, to still her breathing she imagined he simply swatted the horse on the rump and sent them both away. Victor and vanquished. But which was which?

❧

False dawn brightened the horizon, then settled back into full darkness while Rachel lay in bed remembering. They had left the farm, as commanded; everything they owned piled in or tied to the little horse-drawn cart. She wore no shoes, she remembered. Her mother's hand was warm and reassuring. It seemed to Rachel that her mother cried every time she looked at her. An orphan, it was the only home her mother ever had, and none of them knew where they would end up, or even if they would end up anywhere at all that they could call home.

Quilts were piled over her against the odd cold of May. She tried to think about that for a while, because sleep would not come back and she was afraid to enter it anyway. It was a place of fat, soulless landlords and overseers stuffed with their own self-importance. She preferred the strange world where spring never came. At least once it was established that spring and maybe summer weren't coming, you could count on it and pray for their return next year—then throw another log on the fire.

It was warm under all of those covers, even if her breath fogged the brightening air. Once the fire, banked against a long, cold night, flickered back to life, it would warm her bones. Until then, she would have to wrap up against the cold for a while, or wait for Comfort to arrive. She swung her legs over the side of the bed and placed her swollen feet and ankles on the floor. The pain shot up her legs and she swung them back into the warmth. What is this now, she wondered, fighting the urgings of the warm to go back to sleep.

CHAPTER 46

Cuff was putting bags in the back of a wagon when Comfort and Rose walked into the little back yard. The shed door was locked, as usual, and Pompey was sitting on a nail keg watching Cuff work.

"Where'd you get the wagon?" Comfort asked. Cuff, deep in concentration was startled.

"You always comin' up behind and scarin' a year off my life, woman." He reached for Rose and swung her up onto his arm. She squealed and wriggled until Cuff put her carefully back on the ground. She ran to Comfort, who raised her eyebrows, but did not ask the question again.

"It's Caesar's," he said, finally. "Me and Pompey's going

down to Smyrna tonight. We'll be back late tomorrow I 'spect."

"What's in Smyrna that ain't in Wilmington?"

Cuff turned slowly toward her and put his hand on his hip. He smiled the smile that nearly always got him out of trouble, the smile that got him married. He said nothing. But Comfort's face did not unfrown, and soon enough his smile relaxed. He looked nervously at Pompey, who shrugged and looked the other way.

"Honey, my empire is enlarging, you might say, and I have to go tend to some things down state. Now, I'll only be gone over night. Should be here by the time you get home tomorrow. One day this is all going to make sense to you, but right now I just got to do what I got to do."

Comfort's eyes arched higher. "Humph," she muttered and turned toward the house.

"Don't be like that, Comfort. I told you before I ain't doin' nothin' illegal."

"You're willin' to take a chance and a wagon load of your whiskey all the way to Smyrna? Have you got wood in that skull of yours? I swear, Cuff, sometimes you act like you're ten years old." Pompey shook with his silent laughter.

"Ain't funny, Pompey." His jaw slowly dropped as he looked back toward his wife. "You see, that's what gets me into trouble. You assume I'm taking whiskey to Smyrna, but I ain't, only what Pompey takes to drink himself. You see, you get het up about somethin' you don't know gnats about."

Comfort's face slackened. "If you ain't going to sell whiskey, what are going to do?"

"I just told you my empire is expanding and me and my

business partner have to attend to some business. That's all."

A world of suspicion swam in Comfort's eyes, but she decided to drop it. "Maybe it's better I don't know what you two fools is up to. Might make me lose sleep." She reached up and kissed Cuff on the cheek.

In the wagon, heading south, Cuff told Pompey about the horse race he learned about at the last cockfight. "Just north of Smyrna, if I understand right, there's a big patch of woods where some enterprising gentlemen have carved out a little race track. So far the authorities have let them be. Or maybe they don't care. But I hear of large money changing hands."

Pompey nodded his approval, then ran his thumb back and forth across the rest of his fingers.

"That's what I'm hoping, my friend. The cock fights might be boys' games to the ones these men play." Pompey winked and nodded again.

Cuff said nothing of the charms he carried in his pockets. He had never tried them on horses before, but they worked almost every time on those chickens.

They smelled the campfires from some distance. The orange light said that these were white men gathered in the woods. Cuff thought it a good idea to make their camp for the night in another part of the woods, someplace where someone wouldn't stumble over them and get the wrong idea. Cuff and Pompey both had their papers where they could get to them in a hurry, but there was no point in looking for trouble. Cuff had brought along some ripped up feed sacks and some apples. They would be warm enough, and fed.

A lone man stood guard at the entrance to the makeshift track. When Cuff and Pompey approached the next morning, the man didn't even need to speak. Both black men produced their papers and waited. He took a long time, occasionally looking up at the two. Cuff looked down, and noticed that Pompey's papers were upside down. The man could not read.

"Stay away from the white men wagering in there. You want entertainment, you stand away. Keep clear. We don't fancy you coloreds being here, but I got no orders to keep you out. Someone comes up and tells you to get out, you git."

"Yessir," Cuff said, bending slightly toward the man. His years of enslavement had taught him the subtle body language that seemed to reinforce the authority and superiority of whites. There was no hint of irony or sarcasm in the gesture. But not too deeply, Cuff knew it was part of the game.

They passed through the woods. A few white men looked up, but no one approached them. They stayed clear of the white men until it appeared the races would begin. The horses were corralled near them. Cuff took the nail, the half-penny and the dogtooth from their separate pockets and put them in his right hand. He casually walked toward the corral and tried to look innocent as he passed his hand near each one. As he approached the only sorrel colored horse in the pen, the dogtooth pressed itself into his palm to the point of pain. "Ow," he said.

Pompey looked at him as if to ask, what was that about? Cuff shrugged it off. Charms were nothing to fool with, Henri had taught him that. Everything the black Frenchman had taught him had stood him well for a long time. A shrug and flap of his head was all he would say.

As the horses were led to the starting line, Cuff wandered toward the clot of men exchanging money. The bet taker hesitated when Cuff put forth his hand with a sizable pile of cash in it. The white man's eyes grew large and round. "Which horse you want to bet that on? Do you know how much money that is?"

"Yessir," he said, "to both questions." He made his little subservient bow, and said, "The sorrel."

The man's eyes grew large again. "That horse is racing at 20 to one. He's never raced before and doesn't stand a chance. I know. He's mine. Just giving him some experience here in the sticks before I take 'im down to Dover. Still want to throw your money away? I'll bet it took you years to come up with that."

Cuff shrugged and kept his hand outstretched.

"Okay," the man said. "You've been warned." He handed Cuff a small slip of paper with some strange letters and figures jotted on it. Cuff stared at it.

"Don't worry about it," the man said offhandedly. "I know what it means." Cuff nodded and walked away. "Hey," the man called after him. "Your friend got any money he wants me to have?"

Pompey shook his head no. "Shame," the man said. "Damn shame."

The sorrel won.

On his way into Wilmington later that day, Cuff stopped and bought Comfort an entire bolt of the finest cloth the milliner had.

CHAPTER 47

"You are dying, Rachel," the voice said with absolute clarity and authority. "It is your heart, and it is coming on a time when it must stop serving you."

The voice stopped her right in the middle of a tune she was struggling to remember. It was her own voice when she finally recognized it. It was without pity or agony or any emotion. It was squarely matter of fact. "Oh," she said in response.

Her breath had come harder and harder in recent weeks, and more shallow. She sat still and bid the voice to speak again. But there was only a silence and a curious peace within her. Well, I guess it is better that I know, she thought. She sat a long time letting herself accept and grow accustomed to the idea of her own passing. She was not frightened, and that surprised her. I'm tired and I haven't felt well in a long time.

Her muscles relaxed, but she could almost hear the throbbing in her ankles. She closed her eyes and willed there to be only darkness, no images from the old life or this one. There were no images of Cork. She was not walking again beside her mother from Lismore to Clonakilty. The darkness lay like a shroud over all she imagined. It would not occur to most people to bring it up in everyday thought. She rested until she began to wonder what people did who were given warnings about their own death. She could not recall ever hearing of such a warning before in conversation. It was, she thought, the most intimate topic one could imagine. She had not been blessed in her life with relationships that would allow such talk.

She waited for her voice, somewhere deep in her mind or soul to speak again. How long would she live? How long and how deep would she suffer? She would like to prepare herself. But the voice did not return and she grew impatient with waiting.

"Fine," she said, rising from the chair. "I'll go it alone. Can't take anybody with me anyways—not that I'd want to." She thought grimly that her grave could not be any colder than this summer. A small smile came to her lips when she thought how, years from now, when she flitted mysteriously across someone's mind, and they tried to remember when Rachel Mifflin died, they would remember this strange year, 1816 when spring did not arrive. Fitting, she thought, to die when mountains blew up, and dust blotted out the sun, and washed-out light barely had the power to make shadows.

She shivered, and tried to make the thoughts go away. They didn't scare her, in fact she found it all a bit amusing. But she had little time left to her, she didn't wish to use it up on such thinking. There must be things she had to do. But what, she couldn't say.

It came to her as she was taking her shawl down from its hook the next morning. Someone will eventually have to go through my things, she thought, so it might as well be me.

She had no closets, closets were taxed. Thomas had been scrupulous when plans were drawn up for the house. There should be space left for chests and cabinets, but no closets were to be built, and the carpenter agreed. Of course, that was long before Rachel arrived in the house. He had talked about it near the end of his life, wanting her to share as much as she could of his. They would sit in that very room where Rachel rocked her life away, and he would strain to recall everything he could. And he was meticulous about details. His business ran on small details, and the habit found a niche in every other facet of his life.

Just as neatly as the pens and ink and ledgers were lined up on Thomas Mifflin's desk, his memories were stored away— neatly folded, he liked to imagine them. In the failing light of evenings, in the last moments of sunlight before the lamps were lit, he would rise and pace the room and begin another story, another day in an orderly life that had produced prosperity for two wives, and a very high standing in the community.

Taking Thomas's coat from a chest, or a hat of his from a drawer, Rachel would enter a reverie so profound that at times she stood a full half hour or more listening to the echoing voices of the dead as their lives unfolded again. The coat clutched to her chest, the hat hanging by her side, she stood still far, far away.

After several days she realized why the living usually gathered the possessions of the dead. It was going to take a very long time at that rate to go through all of the things of the house and the memories that clung to them like a shine on silver.

Perhaps it will keep the vultures from the door, she thought, and turned again to the objects that had built a life, precious to her as relics, and useless to anyone else. She hadn't looked at these things in years, and now she understood why. Some instinct had told her to let them lie undisturbed—the little knotting bag brought from Clonakilty, the button hook Thomas kept on his chest of drawers, the small Bible her father had hurled at her when she left the farm for America.

All came from their resting places and were placed together to be sent ... where? Who would want such things? She could not think, but somehow it seemed right to be doing it. Though the voice had not told her to do that peculiar job of sorting and remembering, the notion to do it had come just as clearly.

CHAPTER 48

Namby had taught Esther more than Roots—more than potions, decoctions, salves, teas and poultices—she taught her spells and curses. At twelve years of age Esther had watched in awe and horror as Namby raised a rabbit from the dead. Her heart knocked powerfully against her rib cage, her mouth went dry, and everything she had ever believed was changed in the moment the rabbit's heart beat again. She went blind and deaf and dumb for fourteen hours.

Namby stripped the young Esther's clothes from her and placed her in an herb bath. The old herbalist stroked the girl's arm and head, and Esther soon lost her fear. But she never once wondered during that half a day of darkness and silence whether she would ever see or hear or speak again. A small voice far off said she would be made whole. So she sat in the bath or lay on a straw mat and watched that rabbit open its eyes, stumble to its feet and then run a zigzag course across the field. Over and over she watched it, always wondering how something dead could live again. It was no trick, she knew, but a kind of power she feared to possess.

Slowly her vision lightened from black to gray to colors. Voice and hearing came back suddenly and simultaneously. It was like, she thought, the suddenness of the sun rising over water. It just appeared. She gasped when she heard Namby's low chuckle. "How?" she asked

Namby closed her swollen eyes and slowly shook her head. "There will be time, child. You are not ready yet. But there will be time. Life is no game to amuse your friends."

It was not spoken of again. It was a glimpse into another world. A frightening inkling of what lay beyond the everyday, the ordinary, and the way the world appeared to be. Sometimes, over the years, Esther would convince herself that it had been a dream, a vivid dream brought on when she heard a wolf howl in her sleep, or the wind knocked against the house. At other times she blamed it on her imagination that often got her into trouble with Master and Mistress. But there was something about Namby after that day that was different. Esther saw her in a light that had shifted. She did not move through the world as others did. There was a faint glow around her that Esther saw from time to time, not directly—no not ever directly, but in a mirror half glimpsed, or out of the corner of her eye. Namby was sometimes just there, without having seemed to arrive.

Over the years Esther learned in small lessons the wisdom of the herbalists and healers that went before her, knowledge and secrets taught to Namby and then to her. Her decoctions gradually began to help others, her salves and lotions mended wounds, her teas and silent spells cured diseases. She learned from Namby the art of calming body and mind and spirit with spells and prayers repeated until they became the natural rhythm of the brain and heart. As words disappeared, her life swayed and danced to the cadence and pulsation she herself had created.

She thought often of poisoning Master Clendaniel. He had deeply wounded her soul and her body. Mistress had no spine, nor did she want one. But as official taster of the Master's food, Esther dared not even try to kill him, though she knew she could. Since she was fifteen, when he had raped her the first time, and threatened to kill her if she spoke of it to anyone, she had secretly consumed minute portions of herbs for constipation. When she felt they were no longer a danger to her, she had mixed dogbane and spurge and mallow into Master's gravies. She felt no effect. He could not eat or sit comfortably for a week.

She immediately began taking a grain of arsenic a day. One day, she knew, she would have to eat a lot of it—just once— but a killing dose.

Namby died suddenly. Crossing the parlor where Master and Mistress kept each other company evenings when both were at home, and where each maintained a personal chair that no one else ever sat in but them (thrones, the house slaves joked behind their owners' backs, for the King of Asses and the Queen of Useless Lives). Namby slumped into Master's chair, and her massive head dropped to her chest. Master mourned for his chair, which he had to replace. Namby insulted him in death, as she never could in life.

Upon Namby's death Esther was sent out to the kitchen shed to take an inventory of all that was there, as if a dead woman might have taken things with her. Esther wrote down all that Master needed to know about, but declined to list the herbs, flowers, roots, barks and other ingredients she would need to carry on Namby's work. The poisons she kept in a place known only to she and Namby, a place that would not be found until the building fell down someday. By then there would be no need to fear anyone finding what had been secreted away for so long. All involved would be dead.

Esther had learned to cook from Namby as well as make remedies, and she welcomed the privacy of the cook shed. She spent all her time there unless summoned to the house to serve or pour spirits for Master. She began meals early, and spent the rest of her time listening to ailments and making the cures she was becoming famous for among the local slaves and freedmen in the community. She charged a little and squirreled it away until she had enough to make another payment on her freedom price. Namby had always warned against greed. "These is poor people," she counseled, "and the herbs come like a present from God. Greed and Roots and spells make a poor medicine. I ain't taught you this to make you rich, I taught you to save your life."

And that was all she said on the matter. So Esther served her apprenticeship and grew almost as talented as her teacher. Now Comfort was urging her to run. With her fair skin she might pass for white outside the neighborhood. Her clothes might have given her away, but Comfort had seen to that detail as well. When Cuff bought her cloth with his whiskey money, she would make a dress for Rose and one for Esther. If there was material left she made one for herself. Esther now had three dresses fit for a white woman. They were hidden in the cook shed along with the snood Comfort knotted for her without Esther ever knowing. It was, except for Mistress Mifflin's, the only knotted snood she'd ever seen and she dreamed of the day she could wear it. If she were caught with it, she would be assumed a thief—wherever would a slave get the money to buy such a thing?—and lashed severely for it. She kept it with the dresses and wore it only in her imagination.

While everyone else continued to wear heavy clothes against the strange summer cold, Esther sweated in the heat of the shed, swinging pots over the fire and stirring the stingy ingredients Master provided—even for himself. As long as he had strong drink in his belly, and Mistress let him be, which she nearly always did, he was content with small meals. They never entertained, yet went to other wealthy homes to dine.

Esther thought it an odd convention among whites to enter-
tain those who did not return the favor. But then there was
little in white society that she had observed that made much
sense at all.

Except for her clothes, Esther owned virtually nothing,
and except for her freedom she could think of nothing she
desired to make her own. On the other hand, Mistress accu-
mulated French figurines and fancy wine glasses as if she were
building a dowry. How odd, Esther thought.

CHAPTER 49

The fourth time Cuff and Pompey went to the horse
track outside of Smyrna, Cuff took a small amount of his blue-
flame whiskey with him. Once all the bets were placed on the
third race, Cuff approached the bet taker. He held his hand
out toward the man who was busy counting money. The man
looked up briefly, then said, "You're too late." Cuff kept his
hand out.

A moment later, annoyed at the hand so close to his face,
he looked Cuff in the eye. "I said you're too late." Then he
focused on the small bottle in Cuff's hand.

"What's that?" he asked.

"You a drinkin' man?"

"I imbibe on occasion."

"Try this." He was smiling his broad smile. Pompey stood next to him nodding furiously.

The white man, a plump local named Ross, eyed the bottle suspiciously. Finally he said, "Ah, what the hell," and threw back the contents. When he stopped shivering, he looked up at Cuff whose eyes were arched into a question.

"Damn," was all he said.

"Well?" Cuff asked.

"Got a kick like a three-legged jackass."

"So I've heard," he said, smiling even more broadly.

"So," Ross said, "people don't give away good whiskey unless they got a scheme in mind."

"Yessir, that's true. I been selling a lot of whiskey at the cockfights outside Wilmington. Man there lets me sell if he gets his for free."

Ross narrowed his eyes. "Don't say."

Pompey was nodding again, a smile as wide as Cuff's.

"Looks like your friend's a big fan of the stuff."

"He is at that. Ever since he seen it burn bluer'n June sky."

"Hard to remember what color that was," he said looking up and feeling the chill gray air around them.

"Then this might just help," Cuff said handing the man another bottle.

"Just might at that," he smiled, taking it in his pudgy hand, "just might."

Cuff watched as his whiskey disappeared. Ross wiped his mouth with the back of his hand. "You got a deal, boy. But you keep it to yourself. I guess there ain't no worry your friend'll say anything," he laughed. The smile drained from Pompey's face, and for a moment Cuff was afraid he was going to attack the man. But Pompey merely turned his back and walked away to watch the race. His glance chilled Cuff, and did not go unnoticed by Ross.

"Your little sorrel running today?" Cuff asked quickly.

"Last race."

"He done right by me," Cuff laughed.

"I guess he did," Ross turned and walked away.

As the cart rounded a curve in the road, a large crowd was gathered. Many were loud and not a few were obviously drunk. A rope had been thrown across the limb of a tree and several men and a woman were standing in the back of a wagon. Beside the wagon was a large pile of dead brush and logs leaning teepee style. The woman's hands were tied behind her back, but she faced the crowd defiantly.

"Cowardly bastards," she said. Many in the crowd laughed at her and taunted her, "drunken cowardly bastards," she roared. It only urged them to laugh and point even more.

Cuff and Pompey stopped to watch as a noose was placed around the woman's neck. "To show how humane and civ'lized we are," one of the men in wagon said, "we're gonna hang you dead before we burn you, and it's a lot more kindness than you showed my brother Tom." She turned and spit in his face. Another man cuffed her on the ear.

"Mind your manners."

The crowd laughed. Cuff looked at the spectacle and shook his head sadly. "We best be going, these folk out for blood." Pompey nodded and the cart pulled away. Few noticed the two black men passing by. Someone set fire to the teepee of logs. The men jumped out of the wagon, and one slapped the horse on his hindquarters. The wagon moved and the woman dangled above the flames. Her feet kicked violently and the crowd cheered. Then, to everyone's surprise, the rope burned through and the woman dropped into the flames. Screams caused Cuff and Pompey both to look over their shoulders at the sight.

Pompey's eyes grew large as he watched sparks scatter from the center of the fire, kicked outward toward the crowd— orange-red-yellow tongues of flame and spark forced the horde away. A woman yelled, "Kill your husband? You're getting better than you deserve."

The crowd hushed as the burning woman sat up, silenced now, and seemed to stare at them, her face scorched to bone, her eyes melted.

"I've seen death herself," Cuff said out loud and urged the mule into a canter.

CHAPTER 50

The sign read R. Baxter, Scrivener. Rachel stood outside for a few minutes thinking over what she was about to do. She had slept better since she decided, but who would care for her when Comfort was gone? You owe it to her mother to finally let her go. She's grown up, married, has a child of her own. Comfort doesn't need you to watch over her any longer, and she hasn't for a long time. Rachel gave the doorknob a painful twist and walked inside.

The office of R. Baxter—she never did learn his first name, they kept it to Mr. and Mrs.—was dark and cramped. It was not just the lack of sunlight, but the furniture was old and dark, the few books lying about all had dark covers. Mr. Baxter wore a dark suit that had been in fashion in the decades after the revolution with a dark scarf encircling his neck. His hands were stained black with ink. Even his teeth, the few he showed when he opened his mouth to greet her, were blackened. If she had not already committed herself by coming through the door she would have left this hovel to seek out another, brighter room. This was a good and proper thing I am about to do, she thought, and it should be accomplished in the light, not this dim, hellish place.

But Mr. Baxter had fairly leapt from his stool when she entered, and stood in front of her being most accommodating. He offered her a chair, turned the wick up on the lamp a bit, "My name is Baxter, third generation scrivener." He held up his dark hands, "Born with these," he said, and smiled. "Even me blood's part ink." Rachel thought him an odd little man, but harmless, and a little engaging.

"What can I do for you today, Madam? A will mayhap, a letter home to the old sod, Mrs...?"

"Mifflin, Mr. Baxter."

"Ah," he said quickly, "a name well known in these parts,

no?"

"Yes, I suppose," she replied. "My husband's family is well dispersed in Delaware."

"Indeed," said the little man who could not hide the fact that he was very pleased to have made her acquaintance. "I believe you are the first Mifflin to seek my services."

"Yes," said Rachel wanting to move on. "I want to manumit a young slave girl of mine. My last. To be honest with you, Mr. Baxter, I'm dying, and I want her freed as soon as possible."

"My condolences, Madam." He could hear her labored breathing now and saw how she fought to speak more than a few words. "Madam, are you aware that all you have to do is tell the girl she is free. It is legal."

"But nearly impossible to prove once I'm gone. Husband dead, no children. Who would protect her?"

"True enough, Madam. Patty Cannon and her son-in-law come up here from time to time, steal free blacks without papers, and sometimes some with."

"So I've read. Papers'll protect her a little bit."

"Right and heaven, Madam. I can have the document to you tomorrow, deliver it right to your door if you wish." ·

"Thank you, that would be most helpful."

"Madam, may I inquire? You seem a woman most at home with words, why do you not save two dollars and write it out yourself? Then you would only need to file it with the courts and supply witnesses."

Rachel slowly removed her hands from inside the shawl where they were warming. She held them in front of him. "It is not the words I lack, Mr. Baxter, or the will, but as you see it is all in ability, or lack of it."

"Sorry, Mrs. Mifflin, I should not have asked. I am here to serve."

"May we begin?"

"Of course."

"Is there a standard form you follow?"

"Yes, I will read it aloud to you as I write. 'To all whom it may concern, be it known that I, Rachel Mifflin, of the Borough of Wilmington in the county of New Castle and State of Delaware, for diverse good causes and considerations me thereunto moving, as also in consideration of...'" he broke off, "Did she pay a freedom price?"

"Yes. One hundred fifty dollars."

"One hundred fifty dollars lawful money," he resumed writing and talking, "to me in hand paid have released from slavery liberated manumitted and set free and by these presents do hereby release from slavery liberate manumit and set free from and after the thirteenth day of September in the year of our Lord one thousand eight hundred and sixteen my Negro woman Comfort Mifflin being of the age of twenty one years..."

Rachel stopped listening. She saw only the hand of R. Baxter moving deftly across the page. She was at once glad to finally set Comfort free and anxious for her life, what was left of it. She might starve, or freeze ... She forced herself to stop thinking of those things. Her shallow breath whispered to her that whatever she had to endure, it would not be for long.

R. Baxter's voice broke through her thoughts. "In testimony whereof I have here unto set my hand and seal this thirteenth day of September in the year of our Lord one thousand eight hundred and sixteen. Signed in the presence of us."

"So."

R. Baxter looked up. "Yes?" he said.

"I have waited a long time for this. Perhaps too long. And now it is done."

"Not quite, Madam. You must sign before a judge or a Justice of the Peace. Then you must file the papers and they be recorded in the office for recording of deeds. Two witnesses sign here," he pointed at the last line of the document. "And you sign here. Then the young woman will be free. This is a good thing you have done, Madam, if I may express myself. Human bondage may be the ruination of this country someday."

"I have done what heart and soul have commanded. I can only hope that releasing she and her daughter to her husband is the right thing to do. He's not much of a husband. Offered not one cent toward her freedom price. Imagine."

R. Baxter shook his head. "I will make a fair copy of the document and deliver it to your door tomorrow morning. Or I can take it to your attorney's office if you please, they can execute the filing for you."

Rachel stood up and pulled her shawl around her shoulders. "How soon will it all be finalized?"

"Tomorrow, perhaps, day after at the latest. I will bring you her papers on my way home tomorrow night. Those, for now, she must carry with her."

"And the child?"

"Her mother's status is hers as well. Let us just hope that

this peculiar institution is long in our past before she grows up."

"Thank you for your services, Mr. Baxter. I look forward to seeing you tomorrow evening."

"Good day, Madam."

Rachel was glad to be out of the dark little room that smelled of ink, and oil, and old books, and of the man who'd spent his life there writing other people's words. She wondered how someone could aspire to follow a father into such a trade.

Walking slowly home, trying to save her breath, she remembered her own day of liberation. Master took out his copy of her indenture, and she produced hers. Her heart raced as he laid both parts on the table. Thomas Mifflin carefully lined up the bottom of his copy and the top of the bottom copy Rachel had kept in a chest for seven years. They of course fit together perfectly.

"Your obligation is fulfilled," he said to her. Both were smiling. It was, perhaps, the first genuine smile she had seen on his face since Mistress died. She hoped her face revealed as much when she handed Comfort freedom from further obligation.

CHAPTER 51

Namby had planted the quassia tree well beyond the garden where it would be lost among the native maples and poplars. She had told Esther to walk ten paces east of the locust tree and she would find it. She had brought the root-stock from the West Indies where she awaited the slave ship that would bring her, finally, to America. It had come in handy for treating fevers more than once.

Esther gouged a small amount of wood from the trunk and placed it in her pocket. Then she sought out the mother of thyme she herself had planted and cultivated far from the bitter wood tree. Namby had always said, "Spread the plants around. Grow 'em together and somebody might 'spect, 'specially the ones ain't from here. Master ain't too keen on plants, but can't never tell when someone else might walk down in here and figger out this ain't no accident, somebody knows Roots."

So Esther kept the plant map in her head and knew without consulting it where every plant and tree grew on Master's land. She found the mother of thyme and pulled a handful of leaves from a stem, she sniffed them and smiled at the scent. These will do nicely, she said to herself.

In the cooking shed she brought one cup of water to a

boil and added a teaspoon of quassia wood and let it steep. In another pot she brought a gallon of water to a boil and threw in a handful of mother of thyme. She covered the pot and let it steep. Good and evil, she thought to herself. One bring Cuff back from his bad habit, the other make a monster too sick to want to live.

When the infusions were done, she let them cool and put them up in jars, but not before she sipped, ever so slightly, the mother of thyme water. Take a little every day, she thought, ever so little. It had worked before.

CHAPTER 52

Comfort, bent at the waist, rubbed two ends of a piece of cloth together over a tub of water. Beside her, Rose played with a doll Comfort had made for her from a few sticks, a chestnut and some scrap cloth.

"You should get that child a real doll," Rachel said from under the Mulberry tree.

"Yes'm, someday. Right now I got to save every penny."

"What about Cuff? You said he was making some money doing something I don't want to know about."

"He's got secrets, and don't talk about money. We have food and candles and lamp oil when we need it. So I quit asking."

"You'd think a father'd want to buy his daughter things."

Comfort stood up from the tub. "Yes'm," she said, lowering her eyes.

"Oh, Comfort, I'm sorry for interfering in your private life."

"It's all right, Mistress. It's just a sore spot 'tween Cuff and me. He'd skin me if he knowed I said anything about him or his money."

"Ummm. Do you remember your mama and daddy, Comfort?"

Comfort laid the cloth down in the soapy water. "I do and I don't."

"You were very young when she died. Caught fever and didn't live two days. I've told you all this before. But it was such a shame, she was one week and a day from freedom. After Thomas died I promised to let all three of you go, and Cuff too. But she died and your father wasted away from mourning her. He was a good man and she was a good woman. I loved them, in a way."

"Daddy wandered off."

"That he did, and I never looked for him. I hope he made it north and found something to make him happy."

"Yes'm, I pray for as much. But I suspect he got caught by slave traders and sold into the South."

"Well, he wouldn't have survived long there. He was frail, built a lot like you, Comfort. Talking about Cuff reminded me of him. How good your father was to you. Cuff's a good man, but he's got a ways to go to learn how to be a good husband and father."

"Yes'm. I suppose if you say it's so."

"Your mother was a big woman, always singing. And I let her. One week and one day to freedom." She shook her head. "Now you're getting close to what your Mama never had."

"Yes'm. Cuff tells me what it's like. He says when I take the first drink from the cup of freedom, it'll be sweet like spring water, so cold it burns your throat, so rich you'd think it was French wine, so intoxicating you'd think you were drunk."

Rachel Mifflin leaned against the tree and watched Comfort and her daughter for a long while. Comfort returned to the wash, and Rose, far away in some imaginary place, talked to her stick doll in a language only those two knew. Rachel made up her mind.

The next day Comfort put her hands in her lap, in them was the completed collar for Rachel's dress. "Mistress, collar's done."

It struck Rachel like a blow. "Done?"

"Yes'm, done."

"Well. I knew you would finish one day, one day very soon, but I didn't think it would be today. Or even tomorrow or next week. It always seemed just beyond the next sunset."

Comfort smiled. "It's done."

"Would you sew the cuffs and collar to my new dress?"

"Yes'm, it'll look real pretty on you, I know it."

Rachel rocked quietly. No whistling, no airs played in her head. She was calm and empty.

"I'll get that dress and start on it right now."

Rachel nodded her head and watched her slave go out

of the room. Her breath came in shallow, painful sips. Even rocking sometimes tired her, and it grew worse day by day.

When Comfort returned with the dress, she looked squarely at Mistress Mifflin. "You're feeling poorly."

There was silence. Rachel looked straight ahead, each halation rattled in her chest, a froth, just visible, gathered at the corners of her mouth.

"Very poorly," she agreed.

"Can I make you tea?"

"No, no. I just need to rest. I am very happy you have finished the collar. It's beautiful. You were a good student. Your knotting is the best I have ever seen."

"Thank you," Comfort said very softly.

"I'm dying," she said in a quiet, yet matter-of-fact voice.

"Hasn't anything Esther's made you done any good?"

"I don't know how I'd be without her concoctions, but I don't feel any better."

"I'm sorry. I thought maybe it was helping a little."

CHAPTER 53

R. Baxter rapped smartly on Rachel's front door at ten minutes past six o'clock the next day. When she did not come right away, he waited, then knocked again. Her countenance, when she did make it to the door, was one of a woman perturbed, as if roused from a slumber or reverie. But when she looked at the man's face, which had gone quite pale, she smiled.

"I had quite forgotten you would be stopping by, Mr. Baxter. I was just rocking and reminiscing by the fire."

"Yes, Mrs. Mifflin, it is good for the soul," he said as the color trotted back into his face. "I often spend entire evenings imagining long ago events playing out in the flames like actors in a stage play. It is not at all unpleasant, Madam."

Rachel smiled again, nodding in agreement with the scrivener. He handed her the papers. "All is in order, Madam. Now I bid you a good evening." He turned quickly and was gone into the chilly, dim sunlight.

Rachel returned to her rocking chair and placed the papers gently on Comfort's chair. She had been gone nearly an hour, so, Rachel reckoned she had been day dreaming for that length of time, or perhaps longer for she only dimly remembered Comfort leaving for the day. She thought briefly of leaving the papers there for Comfort to find in the morning, but she decided that would be a cold and empty surprise, not one suited to the gravity of the gesture.

She rocked and imagined one scenario after another. It was not until she remembered the simple dignity of her own freedom from indenture, that she knew precisely how she would see Comfort and Rose into their new life.

Comfort unlocked Rachel's back door at six a.m. and quickly stoked the fire. She put the teakettle on top of the woodstove—Rachel did not have a kitchen shed like the Clen-daniels—and took out flour and lard to make biscuits. This was her routine five days a week and had been since Comfort was old enough to be trusted in the kitchen. And she went through it without thinking or making undue noise. At eight Mistress would rise and Cuff would drop Rose off at the back door. That is when the thinking part of the day began.

But Mistress was already up—or perhaps still up, since she slept in her chair more and more often. The fire had been stoked and, it seemed to Comfort, she rocked a little more vigorously than on recent days.

"Been readin' some more about that Mount Tambora," said Rachel from behind the newspaper. "Seems some of them university men been calculatin' in their free time."

"Yes'm. But calculatin' what?" It vaguely seemed to her that they ought to be figuring out how to get the sun back up to its proper heat rather that playing games with numbers."

Rachel lowered the newspaper. "Well, sit you down and I'll tell you."

"But the tea and biscuits ain't made yet," Comfort protested. She wondered what the interruption would do to her routine.

"They can wait, can't they?" Rachel asked.

Comfort sat to the front of her chair. "Yes'm," she said softly, rattled by the change.

"They's calculatin' how many's died from that blow'd up mountain all around the world. 'Cause it ain't just here, it's pretty near everywhere."

"That what they do at universities?"

"I guess, but I ain't never been. But they figure it must be ten to twelve thousand people's already starved or froze to death, and they think maybe another ten to twenty thousand might die before the skies clear. A foot of snow in Boston earlier this month. That is a long time between crops."

"That's a powerful lot of folk, Mistress," she said, thinking instead of what still needed doing in the kitchen.

"Think you'll ever forget this summer, Comfort?"

"No'm, don't 'spect I will, though Rose might. But maybe it's just froze into her memory."

"Go on to the kitchen, I know you's only half listenin' to me ramble on."

"Yes'm," Comfort jumped up smiling. "I'll bring your tea directly. And the biscuits won't be far behind."

Rachel raised the newspaper up and went back to reading. When her tea arrived, Rachel asked without lowering it, "Do I recall you telling me a while back that Cuff bought you some cloth?"

"Yes'm."

"You had any time to make a dress?"

"Yes'm."

"Since tomorrow's Friday, and we walk down town, do you think you could wear it for me to see?"

Comfort felt her body go cold. For years she imagined that dress. Then, thanks to Cuff, she had the dress. And for all those years she imagined her first day as a freewoman wearing the dress like a badge of victory. She could not speak.

"Comfort?"

"Yes'm," she said finally. "Did you hear me?"

"Yes'm, I heard you."

"Well, it would be a nice thing to do."

"Yes'm. Must be if you say so."

"Good. And does Rose have a dress too?"

"Yes'm."

"Then have her wear hers, too."

"Yes'm." But her heart felt like it was about to burst, her dream blowing up like Mount Tambora and scatter all its tiny fragments into the air, blocking her sun and making her world a very cold place. She moved slowly and mindlessly through the rest of the day.

Cuff watched Comfort in the dim morning light remove the dress from its paper wrapping. When she slipped it over her head, Cuff was fully awake.

"Comfort, what you doin'? Tha's your freedom dress, ain't it?" She turned to him, tears in her eyes.

"It is," she mumbled.

"Well why you wearin' it today? You ain't paid your price, have you?"

"No. I'm wearin' it 'cause Mistress asked me to wear it, tha's why. I been dreamin' of my freedom day so long, and wearin' this here dress. Now Mistress wants me and Rose to parade downtown with her today so she can show off her slaves. I ain't never seen her act like that before. She just want to have a looksee, and don't care what her wantin' does to my dream. Didn't even ask was it all right. Just said dress Rose up, too."

She put her hand to her eyes and sobbed. Cuff stood and hugged her. "Tha's just mean," he said. "Mistress never been mean to you before, neither. But she been lookin' sickly lately. I wonder if she got sickness in her head."

"Oh, Cuff, she got a cough and some swole up ankles. Ain't nothin' in her head ain't been there all along. She gets lost in her memories sometimes, but old people do that. Ain't nothin' strange there."

"I guess," he said, letting her go.

"You don't have to guess, I just tole you."

"Now don't go takin' your sadness out on me, I ain't brought it on."

"I'm sorry, Cuff. It's cause of you I got this dress. I jus' hope I don't spoil it. I'm even gonna try not to sweat today."

"That should be pretty easy seein' there's ice on the water bucket pretty near every mornin'. This here's a cold May."

Comfort put her oldest tattered coat on over her new dress so no one would see she was dressed like a freewoman. When she went through the back door, thoughtlessly left unlocked, Mistress was struggling to get the teakettle filled with water, her hands being nearly useless.

"Mistress, what you doin'? I always make the tea for you. And what you doin' up this time two days in a row. You ain't been feelin' good, why don't you go back to bed and I'll bring your tea quick."

"Comfort, I've got to do things for ..." She looked at the tattered old coat on Comfort's back, and the smile went off her face.

Comfort turned to see why she had stopped speaking. "Mistress?"

"Hmmm."

"Wha's the matter. You done stopped talkin' right in the middle of your sentence. You all right?"

"I'm fine. Just a tired old lady."

"Well, I'll get this water boilin' for ya."

"Yes, thank you."

As kindly as Mistress was to her, she could not recall ever having those words directed at her. She stood in silence and watched Rachel leave the room. She hung her coat on the hook and readied the tea and prepared to make biscuits.

When Comfort delivered the tea, Mistress sat behind her newspaper. On hearing footsteps, she said, "Got a drawing in here of the new bridge outside Philadelphia. Writer says it's a first in the world, a wire suspension bridge. Crosses the Schuylkill. Would you want to cross a wire ...?" She began, dropping the newspaper from in front of her eyes, then sucked in a quick, loud breath. "Oh, Comfort, your dress is lovely. I thought you hadn't worn it when I saw the coat."

"Yes'm, I'm wearin' it. And Rose be here directly wearin' hers, too."

"Oh, you have such talented hands. You should start a business some day."

"Yes'm. I think about it. I do. Someday." She turned to go to the kitchen.

"Comfort. No biscuits today."

"Ma'am?"

"Not today. If you got anything on that dress I'd never forgive myself."

"But what you gonna eat?"

"There's some chicken left from last night. Some potatoes."

"But?"

Cuff brought Rose to the back door and left immediately to run his errands around Wilmington. Rachel fussed over Rose until the child fell down giggling over so much attention.

"Don't you look the pair," Rachel said.

Comfort sat, almost in a panic. Her hands were quiet and she did not know what to do with them. She put them in her lap, but they were unhappy. She put them on the arms of the rocking chair, but they betrayed their uncomfortable idleness there, too.

"You're fidgety today, Comfort."

"Mistress I ain't got nothin' to keep my fingers occupied. Won't let me cook. Don't have my knotting bag, seein' it's walk-to-town day."

Rachel pulled the envelope from the drawer in the table between the two rockers. "Open that and see if it's enough to keep your hands and your eyes busy a few minutes." She turned up the lamp.

Comfort opened the envelope, her heart and mind racing. Before she started, she glanced at Rose playing with a doll on the floor near the fireplace. Only a few moments after she began to read, her eyes filled for the second time that morning. But these were tears of joy, not anger and frustration. This was the day she would walk into freedom, and Mistress had made sure she wore the dress.

"But I ain't paid it all," was all she could think to say.

"You paid enough. I've been selfish. I wanted to keep you around to help me, to be my hands. But there's no need for that anymore. As of this moment you are free. Free to go. Free to travel. Free to start your own business. Free to raise your child out of bondage. I want you to have what your mother never got."

Now both were crying. Rose looked up, then went to her mother. Comfort hugged her tighter than anyone she'd ever hugged in her life. For a while only sobs filled the room from two women and a girl. Then Rachel pulled a second envelope from the drawer. "Here," she said, "open it."

Comfort pulled the money from the tattered envelope, and her mouth hung open. She looked from the money to Rachel and back again. "Your husband is a good man in the making, but I don't trust him so much just yet. You take that and hide it in case you ever need it. It's your freedom money. You earned it, you deserve every penny of it."

Comfort sat a long, long time rocking. In none of her dreams did it end like this, free and rich in the same day. One hundred and thirty six dollars, fourteen shy of her freedom price, but all hers again. But she was too confused by the quickness and finality of the gestures to think clearly. She rocked and sobbed, and Rachel watched her already slowly, oh so slowly, fading from her life. And she thought, for one lucid moment, that what she had done had outdone her own emancipation, and she knew it was good and right.

CHAPTER 54

He had clutched the trio of magic charms in his right hand and swept it across the sorrel's head, back and tail. Cuff was thorough because a lot of money was riding on this race, enough, if he won, perhaps to break down and buy Comfort's freedom—maybe without her knowing it, a little business behind her back with Mistress Mifflin.

Joe Johnson stood on the verge of the woods surrounding the little racetrack and watched Cuff's motions. At that remove he might have been doing something to hobble the horse so he could bet against it. Hatred for the Negro burned in him like cheap whiskey, and he could not spit enough to cleanse his mouth of the taste of hatred. He wanted only to see him lose, and lose big.

Cuff finished his ritual and stuffed the charms back in his pockets and casually as possible ambled away. Pompey leaned on the rough fence rails that surrounded the track and watched Cuff approach. Cuff nodded slightly when he passed and went directly to place his bet.

"Your horse gonna win," Cuff said with a spreading smile.

"I hope you're right," Ross said.

"You can bet on it," he said with a laugh and handed Ross two small bottles of blue flame. "See you after the race." Cuff turned to walk away.

"Boy."

Cuff turned and stared at the man.

"Thank you. And watch your back."

Cuff walked closer. "My back? Why?"

Ross cocked his head toward the woods. Cuff narrowed his eyes. "Oh, that fellow. See him at the cockfights sometimes. Mean and surly."

"Worse. That's Joe Johnson."

"Patty Cannon's Joe Johnson?"

"The same."

"I knew he was a mean drunk, but I didn't know he was an inf'mous mean drunk."

"The devil's sidekick. Paper or no paper's all the same to him. He decides to rope you up and drag you back to hell with him, there's few men ready or able to stop him. Few worse in this world."

"I'll steer clear. Yessir, I will and let me go tell Pompey too." Ross nodded.

The last race was just going off when Cuff reached Pompey at the fence. They were at the first turn and the horses were coming toward them fast. Pompey was jumping like a child. The sorrel had a large lead and looked strong and confident. Suddenly something caught the little horse's eye—could it have been his, or Pompey's clothes, Cuff wondered later—but he broke stride and nearly fell. He recovered and ran strong, but Cuff's money was gone. He held onto the fence tightly and fought off the numbness of loss. Over his shoulder he could hear laughter. He didn't even need to turn to know where it came from.

Cuff sat on a log with his head down. Pompey tried to console him by slapping him on the back. But that might have been my wife's freedom, was all that ran through his mind.

"Tough loss, boy."

Cuff knew the voice, and there was not an ounce of sympathy in it. He didn't even look up.

"What say I buy what whiskey you got left for say a penny on the dime."

"I'd rather give it to the dirt."

"Give the grass a drink or drag it back to niggertown, all the same to me, there's plenty of whiskey in this world. But two dollar's got to be better than a complete loss."

Cuff stood up and stared Johnson in the eye. "I'd prefer not to contribute to more meanness in the world. You're a skunk sober and a mad dog drunk." He nudged the remaining jug toward the white man whose scar was black and pulsing. Cuff could see the thirst in his face.

Johnson reached into his pocket and pulled out several coins. He tossed them at Cuff and bent to grab the jug. Cuff's foot darted forward and knocked the jug sideways, the contents pouring into the dirt. Cuff quickly put his boot on the side of the jug so Johnson couldn't lift it from the ground.

Joe Johnson rose up to his full height and snarled. Cuff looked at him calmly.

"I told you I'd rather my friends have it than you," he said, and sent the jug tumbling end over end into the field.

Pompey and Cuff walked slowly away.

CHAPTER 55

Cuff lay sprawled on the floor of the shed. His head rested against the wall. He snored loudly. There were leaves in his hair. His yellow suit was stained and there was a tear on the left knee. Around him lay empty jars and an open jug of blue flame.

It was ten o'clock in the morning. Earlier Comfort had taken some beans and cornbread to Rachel Mifflin's house. She could no longer get out of bed, and what Comfort took her to eat, she barely touched. Esther came almost daily with another herbal treatment, but nothing worked. Each breath came to Rachel with great difficulty, and some days she did not even open her eyes. Her arms, legs and feet were grossly swollen. Like her hands years before, the rest of her body revolted against her.

The only things that remained pleasant to her were the warmth of the blankets against the strange cold summer, and her memories that marched in and out of her head unbidden but gratefully welcomed.

Comfort spoke to her, but she no longer replied. Even if she had the strength, what was there left to say? News would come and go, and Rachel made sure Comfort could read. All of the stories had been told, some of them many times. That she was dying, it was certain, it was just a matter of how stubborn her life would be, even though she was ready and willing to let go. She had granted it the right to cease its ebb and flow, its surge and sway. She had willed silence, but heard her breath sizzle and sputter like swash on the beach, pebble on pebble, rock on rock it rattled her lungs and ground her mind to disquietude. If only, she thought over and over, only to hear further proof that she was still relentlessly heaving air in and out of her exhausted body.

Passed out, but dreaming, Cuff chose winning horses and spotted shy cocks that became emboldened when his magic charm was waved across its head. There were again two moneybags stuffed to overflowing in the rafters of the shed. The charm was again complete, the dogtooth returned to the magical triune. And the world was warm and customers thirsty and the blue flame winning more fans than before. Yes, Cuff dreamed, perhaps saw his daughter grow up straight and beautiful, his young wife mold to her freedom as flawlessly as her body molded to the dresses she fashioned with clever hands from the cloth Cuff delighted in bringing her.

Yes, for a few hours each day Cuff dreamed himself out of the nightmare he had shaped and pieced his life into. He no longer walked the streets of Wilmington without exciting the stares and laughter of nearly everyone. His suit was soiled and fit poorly now. He was disheveled and unclean much of the time. Comfort scolded him, threatened him if he did not stop drinking that she would take Rose and go. But that drove him to drink more. Then he hid his drinking and tried to keep his breath to himself. But Comfort knew where he was going, and she cried. She complained to Esther, to Rachel. But where was there, really, to go? She kept Rose away from her father during the worst of it, but she could see him stumble, she was perplexed by the new, unpleasant smell on his breath. She could see he did not wash his hands and face, carried lint and leaves and grass in his hair at times. She would pick it out for him sometimes, but the next day it was back, perhaps worse. So she stopped.

Rachel crossed easily back and forth from America to Ireland, spoke as comfortably with the living as with the dead, saw with equal clarity the past and the present. Since her body would not let her die, then the company she kept was fine enough. She listened to the stories, told by those from her childhood, and long forgotten. The images she saw and tasted were vivid, they were full of color and piquancy they may have never had in reality. She lay in her warm bed, waiting.

Cuff snuffled awake around noon and stared at the vague outlines of things in the crooked little shed. It was dark and spiders had begun their web work in corners and under the shelves. What he could not see, he could feel. He felt pain in his knee, touching it he discovered the hole in his pant leg and cursed his clumsy self. A thin shaft of light fell on the floor from the narrow opening between the door and the frame. It lay across the jug of blue flame and a scattering of smaller jars and bottles. He had only begun drinking some weeks ago, but it already felt like years. He shook his head and stumbled to his feet. He held on to the shelf until he felt stable. In the dark he tripped over something left on the floor. He stopped himself from falling, but went unsteadily out of the door into the sunlight, but the world was foggy and cold.

CHAPTER 56

"Dog tooth done chewed a hole right in my pocket," Cuff said out loud, even though he was in the shed alone. He got down on hands and knees and examined every board and every darkened corner, but the tooth was not there. The nail and the half-penny lay side by side on the shelf next to the cedar box, but the dog tooth with the power was gone somewhere into the road from Smyrna to Wilmington.

Cuff put the balls of his hands to eyes and pressed hard until lights began shooting inside his head. Henri had taught him this too, said it would activate his third eye and might someday come in handy for finding lost things. If there was ever something lost that needed finding, it was the dogtooth, and quickly.

The lights fired, and Cuff pressed harder, but he could not locate the tooth in his head or in the world. Somewhere it might be scratching "HELP" in the dust, but he'd be damned if he could find it. Once his eyes began to ache, he stopped and sat down hard on the nail keg. "Oh, lordy, what I'm gonna do now?" He stood once again and thrust his hand into the deep yellow pocket. The hole was still there, and the tooth was still gone. "You been protectin' me most of my life." He thrust his hands into every other pocket in the suit. "Gone. Gone is gone." If I was a woman, I'd cry right now, he thought. But he had never cried, and probably wouldn't know how, or how to stop.

Maybe I'll find it next race. I know every place I went there today. Nobody would even bend over to pick up no dog's tooth. Tha's it, it'll be right there where I stood next to Pompey, or where I clumb up into the wagon, or where Joe Johnson tried to steal my blue flame for two dollars. Maybe the nail and coin will start rattlin' in their pockets whenst I get close to the tooth.

Calm down, he said to himself a dozen times. Worryin' ain't gonna make it appear, and it probably misses me as much as I miss it. If we work together maybe we'll get back together. But I know that a lucky charm ain't worth a bucket of stank if parts is missin'. Ole Henri would not be happy with me now if he know'd what I done. I got to just think good thoughts and everything'll be all right.

But he couldn't keep the worry off his face when he saw Comfort.

"Cuff, wha's wrong with you? You look like somebody stole yer brother."

"Nah, I just loss somethin' I had fo' a long time. I'll find it. It's just lost, it ain't gone."

"What is it, maybe I can help ya find it."

"Naw, tha's all right." He dared not tell her about either the tooth or the money he'd lost—nearly enough to pay her freedom price. Then she'd know he was crazy, and a fool.

Maybe about the biggest fool there ever was, but he didn't want to prove it to anyone else.

He held Rose on his knee, but there was no spark in it, and she soon climbed down and walked away. "That must be somethin' real important you lost, won't even be a father to your child."

CHAPTER 57

Comfort strode from Rachel Mifflin's house through the front door. She held Rose's hand tightly as she always had done in the dream. She kept blinking her eyes to assure herself that this time it was real. Looking down she realized she had forgotten her coat, but she would not go back for it. It would be there when she returned—and she had promised Rachel she would. No, those were the trappings of her old life, the one she left behind only hours before. She shed it like an old skin, and what appeared beneath glistered in the chill sunlight. This was the new life and she entered it in a brand new dress of her own making out of material fit for a white woman, a free woman, a woman.

There was a confused look of worry that crossed Rose's face, she had never used the front door before, and she somehow sensed she was not supposed to. But her mother was marching her out that way. And she followed, though not without some resistance.

"Oh, Rose," she said softly, "it's all right. We can go this way now. You won't understand this, but you is free, because I is free. And now we all free, you and me and your Papa. This paper in my pocket says so. We don't belong to nobody now but ourselves."

Rose looked up at her intently, but only giggled over the sudden attention she was getting. "I don' think you'll remember this day, Rose, but I'll remember for both of us. I'll write it down for you so's if I dies before you gets old enough to understand, then you'll know how we both walked into freedom in our new dresses. I'll write down how your Papa said the air would taste like a draft of fresh spring water, and how it does. It does, Rose. It's like I never tasted anything before in my life until right now, like my taste has been dead and now it's up like Lazarus. My mouth is full, full of milk and honey, full of strawberries."

She stopped walking. "This is real, isn't it, Rose. If it's not, please lie to me 'cause I don't want no more dreams, no more flitter-flatter in my sleeping head." Then the tears came, and Comfort did not think she would cry in her sleep.

Cuff was gone when Comfort got home. She left her new dress on, but covered it with an apron. She took her papers from her pocket and sat in the dim light by the window and read them through again. Unless some cruel god put a storm in her brain, she thought (and any god who can blow up mountains and take summer away half way around the world, could without breaking a sweat) then she was indeed a free woman, and she hadn't even seen it coming. This mornin' I was a slave, she said to herself, and tonight I'm free.

She placed the papers, carefully folded, on the table where Cuff would have to see them. Then she set about making dinner. Fortunately, she had put by tomatoes and corn and beans last fall, so there was always food—she had burned her fingers so badly doing so that she had not been able to knot for weeks. It was one of the few times Mistress had scolded her, but she knew she deserved it for being careless. Now, she thought, if I wants to cut my fingers off ain't nobody can say a thing about it.

She took cornbread out of the crude pie safe Cuff had fashioned from some salvaged lumber he got from Pompey, and set it near the papers. She put tomatoes in a pot. She sliced salt pork to season the beans. And she whistled. Real, melodic tunes, unlike the thin column of air that was strangled and punished from Mistress's lips. Comfort stopped dead in her work and laughed out loud remembering. Oh, how she tortures the poor air when she blows, she thought and laughed again. And she could not remember ever laughing out of the sheer joy of living before, the unbelievable humor of just being human.

Comfort did not turn when Cuff opened the kitchen door. She said hello to him over her shoulder, and kept on with the knife and corn bread and the little tunes that kept rising in her brain and swirling sweetly out into the room.

CHAPTER 58

Cuff slammed down his jug of blue flame and hurled his betting sticks into the fire where birds and venison roasted. The man tending the meat looked at him and shook his head. "Yer havin' a bad streak. I ain't seen you pick a winning cock in weeks. Somebody musta put a spell on ya."

His look was pure disgust because it was true. He was losing money on the cocks and the horses, and since Pompey no longer worked with him, his income went way down on the sale of blue flame. He lifted the jug and poured a swig and shot it back. Smooth, he thought, but it still burned in the belly.

"Mifflin, gimme a shot of that elixir of life you got there," a man said to him handing him a coin. He took it in one gulp and set the glass down, then he walked away, eyes watering.

"Mister," a boy of maybe thirteen said to Cuff. "My daddy says you make the best rum on the Eastern Shore. Gimme a taste and let me know that for myself."

Cuff eyed the boy. "You go along. I ain't sellin' you no blue flame. Yo' daddy come after me for sure."

The boy laughed. "He sent me over here, says I got to know what the best tastes like."

"How come you got to know?"

"He makes his own 'shine, and I'm his taster."

Cuff poured, the boy paid and sipped the flame. He smiled, "Damn that goes down easy. Stuff my old man makes taste like swamp gas mixed with hog swill next to this."

Cuff laughed out loud and pocketed another coin.

Changed out of his suit, the clothes returned to their bag in the shed, Cuff sat down hard on the chair. Rose came to him, but he shooed her away. "Go play with your doll," he whispered roughly. His elbow rested on Comfort's papers, but he did not look at them, did not seem to know they were even there. He put his thumb and pointer finger to his eyes and squeezed. Stars shot through his head, and then a bright orange light washed everything away.

Even with her back turned to him, she could smell the moonshine on his breath. She shook her head and kept working away at dinner. "Hard day, Cuff?" she asked.

"Miserable," he said.

"You want to talk about it?"

"Naw," he mumbled.

"Gonna ask me 'bout my day?"

"Slave days is slave days, Comfort, I knows what they's like. Yes, Mistress. Naw, Mistress. Kin I git you some tea, Mistress. I don't need to hear about it, wife. I said I had a bad day, le's jus' leave it there."

Then there was a moment when it seemed his eyes came on and was seeing what he hadn't seen. "Woman, why you still got your freedom dress on." He swung around and looked at Rose. "And the little one, too. You don' want to get too close to them rags till you got the price and privilege."

Comfort turned to him. "And how you know I don't—got both?"

"You twenty, thirty dollars shy, least tha's what you said."

"Well, maybe things is changed, and maybe yo wife and daughter ain't spent another slave day. Maybe both of them is free women now, and maybe yo ought to look under yo elbow fo' the proof, 'cause, Cuff Mifflin, yo's a blind and ignorant man who don't have no feelin's or sympathy for nobody but himself. Tha's a hard thing to see in a man who's becomin' nothin' but a scarecrow of himself."

Tears ran down her face and she tried not to wipe them on her sleeve. Cuff looked out of the window at the fading light, a ghost of himself flickered across his mind, but did not stay or materialize, it merely shot like a fall leaf across a spent garden and was gone, as distant as culls from fruit.

CHAPTER 59

Cuff parked the wagon as near as he could remember to where he parked the last time. He scanned the ground for the dogtooth, but it was not there. At the fence, as the crowd cheered for the first race of the day, Cuff's eyes moved methodically back and forth across the ground hoping light would glint off the polished tooth and give itself away. But nothing shone there. Every pebble and chip of quartz gave him a start, but after a closer look, it was nothing. Cuff's heart sank.

He tried the charm on a black gelding, then placed a small wager—so small Ross asked him if he thought he could spare it. But Cuff ignored him, took his stick and walked away. The horse ran dead last. Cuff stood with arms folded over his chest and spoke to no one, even the customers who eagerly thrust money at him for a taste of blue flame. He poured and made change. Several men suggested that perhaps Pompey was rubbing off on him, but he didn't laugh, and they walked away shaking their heads.

Pompey made his rounds and returned every hour or so to give Cuff money and refill the bottles and jugs. Cuff stood silently watching him work. And a strange idea came into his head. He thought: Pompey is a pack rat. He picks up everything he finds and puts it in his pocket thinking someday someone might could use this. A dog tooth is a rare enough sight, outside of a dog's mouth, that Pompey would, no doubt, pick it up and figure out later what someone might use it for. That's why he hadn't been able to find the tooth. Pompey had it, he was sure of it. And he would give it back when Cuff asked.

Cuff smiled. Mystery solved, he assured himself. He uncrossed his arms and quickly returned to the garrulous Cuff everyone expected. Business was brisk and they sold out before the last race. They headed home early to protect the profits from slow horses and bad luck from damaged charms.

It was a long ride back to Wilmington. Cuff felt cheered by what he knew was the answer to his problem. Lost dogtooth and pack rat friend added up in his mind. Cuff thought he might have some fun teasing the answer out of Pompey.

"Pompey, you a collectin' man, right?'

Pompey grinned. "You found all them parts for the still, or I suppose you found 'em and didn't steal 'em."

Pompey shook his head furiously. "All right, you found them.'

Pompey nodded agreement, but the smile did not return. Pompey's life had always been a serious matter of survival, from his size to his questionable status as a freeman. He scavenged to survive. No one would hire a mute ex-slave. They thought him stupid or deranged. And that suited him. It meant they left him alone. He trusted few, and Cuff was one of them. So when Cuff began his cat and mouse games, seemingly just to get Pompey's hackles up, he was quick to take umbrage at the suggestions Cuff made—even though he could see a poorly concealed smile start in the corner of Cuff's mouth.

"So you figger out a use for just about everything, don't ya?"

He nodded once forcefully, with a thoughtful look on his face. He couldn't figure out where this was going.

"Let's say you found a feather, a red bird feather, would you pick that up?"

He hesitated, then nodded, having thought of a time when a feather might have served him.

"A cat's skull?"

He grimaced and shook his head no.

"A turtle shell?"

He squinted one eye and shrugged.

"A nail?"

A perturbed yes.

"Pebbles and bird bones?"

No.

"An unraveled carriage whip?"

Yes.

"A broken plate?"

Yes.

"A dog tooth?"

Yes.

"A butterfly wing?"

Nod and shrug—maybe.

"A broken mirror?"

He shook his head disgustedly, growing tired of the game.

"So have you found anything interesting lately?"

Pompey screwed up his brow and sat still for several moments. He pressed his lips together and gave a thoughtful, slow shake of his head.

"Nothin'? That what you tellin' me?"

A tight, quick nod of the head. Then he leaned into the wagon and brought up a nearly empty jug of blue flame. He pointed to the jug and widened his eyes into a question.

Cuff laughed. "Go ahead. You must have squirreled that away. I thought we was dead empty."

Pompey smiled, the trickster letting his guard down.

Cuff guided the mules. Pompey drank blue flame—much more blue flame than Cuff could have imagined was left. In fact it angered him more each sip or gulp that went down Pompey's throat. But he said nothing more until the outskirts of Wilmington.

Cuff stopped the wagon and watched Pompey take yet another drink. "I asked you a while back if you had found anything lately. You didn't answer me."

Pompey smiled.

"What did you find? I lost something and I think you found it."

Perplexed, he shook his head slowly and shrugged.

"You found my dog tooth, didn't you?"

Pompey shook as if laughing. The game was over. The joke came to an end.

Cuff swung full force and drove the jug from Pompey's hands. It shattered in the road, its contents instantly darkening the dirt. Pompey jumped back into the bed of the wagon.

"You think it's funny I lost my dog tooth? Why you think I ain't won no races? Why you think I ain't been bettin'"?

Pompey jumped from the wagon and walked away. Cuff sat feeling his anger turn to panic. His magic and his power were gone. Not lost, gone. Gone.

CHAPTER 60

Rachel had been fatigued for months. She rarely had the energy to leave her bed, and the cold dug deeper into her bones. Although free, Comfort came every day still to see if Esther's potions might help her breathing or calm the coughs that often times racked her entire body for hours at a time.

The day before she had begun a coughing fit in the late morning, and it did not end until the pale gray sun was well westward. Comfort had become so alarmed she had called for Mary Clendaniel. Esther had come also with a tea that sometimes helped her when she had a cold. But Rachel was too weak to drink the alfalfa tea. Her breath was so shallow Mary leaned close to listen for breath, then placed her hand on Rachel's neck.

"She's alive," Mary announced, as if the fact perturbed her. She turned and left the room. As an afterthought, she returned. "You might as well stay here," she said to Esther. "You'll probably be needed before long. A body can't last any time at all on breath like that."

And she was gone. "Ain't you got anything else in your

magic might make her better?" asked Comfort, a look of near terror in her eyes.

"I couldn't sleep last night for thinkin' about what I had missed. Everything Namby taught me came to mind: Pipsissewa, skunk cabbage, clover, devil's bit, squaw root and squaw vine, sassafras and peach. Every one of them should have helped her. I didn't tell you, but I even tried deadly nightshade a few weeks back. Remember when she couldn't lift her left arm for a day or two? Scared me, but she got better—if you call this better." She looked sympathetically at the woman lying on the bed, eyes closed from exhaustion, a froth of spittle erupting from her mouth.

Esther motioned Comfort from the room. "She's dying, you know that, right?"

"I could have guessed as much. What do I do?"

"What you think you can do?"

"Just be here. Hold her hand. That's about as far as we can go with anybody into death, I s'pose."

Esther nodded. "This is the place potions and charms and teas and decoctions won't go."

Rachel heard the voices but was too weak to open her eyes. She watched a long parade of familiar faces pass her bed. Some stopped and nodded, some spoke. She thought it very odd that even through her eyelids she could see perfectly well, and none of her visitors seemed to notice or care that her eyes were closed. Thomas came and smiled calmly and sweetly down at her. "I'll see you again soon," he told her. Won't that be grand, she thought, to be with Thomas again?

Her parents came and passed on. But others followed, many she had not seen in years, many she had not thought of in decades. Now here they all were come just to see her. Isn't it odd, she thought. Yes, odd. That is the word for it, then instantly forgot why it was the word for it.

It wasn't sleep, she knew that. It wasn't death for she could still hear the voices of Comfort and the slave from the Clendaniel household. What was her name, the pale Negro who would look white in the proper dress and bonnet? No matter, Rachel decided. She made me teas, and tinctures and all variety of bitter stuff in teaspoons. She was trying to help me, I am sure.

She could feel someone take her hand. The touch was cold and she wanted to pull away. But it felt comforting to know someone was there when she hadn't even the strength to open her eyes. Breath grew even more shallow, the air colder. She wished someone would throw a log on the fire, or throw another blanket over her. But no matter, she was mostly warm. And she hadn't very much time to think about such things. The parade continued, the faces familiar or forgotten. She liked to see the smiling ones. Those crying confused her. Why would someone come all that time and distance to cry over me, she wondered, annoyed by what she perceived to be an insult. "We are, after all, together again," she tried to say out loud, but she could only think it. They wouldn't understand anyway, she thought. I'll just move them right along and spend more time with the smiling people.

Esther made tea. She added deadwood to the low burning

fire, and moved the kettle over the grate. The water heated slowly. The grayness of the day had given way to a strange yellowness in the air. Esther stood and watched through the window. What an odd summer this is, she thought.

❧

It seemed like everyone Rachel had ever known or met paraded through some sunny place in mind or memory. She felt a kind of contentment. It was then that she saw it, the end of the scene with the overseer so many years and miles ago.

Her father's strong left hand held the overseer's jaw. The man hung from his saddle, kept from falling only by Michael McArthur's grip. Then Rachel could see her father letting go, the man falling and the sputtering up of dust around him as he writhed in the dirt. She smiled.

It was the last thing in her mind's eye—ever.

CHAPTER 61

Joe Johnson had bought a whole jug of blue flame from Cuff. No more kicking jugs over and letting the whiskey get the grass drunk. Cuff needed the money, and for now he didn't care where it came from.

Johnson poured a cup and handed it to his mother-in-law, Patty Cannon. She knocked it back and a smile spread over her face. "May be the best damned rum I ever tasted. And you say some nigger made that?"

"Yes, ma'am. Boy by the name a Cuff up to Wilmington. Comes down to the races." He laughed. "Used to be a month or two ago he'd dump a whole jug out 'fore he'd let me have a taste. Thought I was gonna hafta beat him, but he's warmin' up lately."

"This the nigger in the clown suit you tole me 'bout?"

"The same. Still wears that damned suit, too. Used to get me hoppin' mad, don't know why, but now I just laugh. He was on a tear for a while, couldn't seem to lose races or cockfights or nothin'. Sellin' gulps of whiskey. I mean he was flush."

"And now?" she asked, a business opportunity blooming in her brain.

"Somethin's got your interest, Maw?"

"Maybe. Maybe not."

"Well, that clown suit's pretty well torn up. Boy looks dirty, lint and grass all the time in his hair. Ain't seen him win nothin' in weeks. And he warmed to me 'bout the same time."

"Ain't you figgered this out yet, son?"

"Figger'd out that the nigger's on a losin' streak? That I have. Started drinkin' too, never did before to my knowledge."

"Even better," she said, "even better." She knew her son-in-law well. He was big, and even stronger than his size suggested. He might even have been good looking before he took to knife fights and the skin trade. Running slaves had left him scarred and mean as hell, precisely what she wanted in a man who worked for her. He was wily, and quick for a man his size. Faced with a dilemma, he chose to attack it directly.

Abolitionist, preacher, freemen, slave were all the same to him. No point in sorting them out, he'd say. Hit 'em. Hit 'em hard. Hit 'em where it will do the most damage. Then get away. Big. Strong. Quick. And dim. She liked that in a man that worked for her.

"What's a man in his position gonna do, boy?"

"Whatever it takes to git back in the money? That right?"

"Yep."

"But how's he do that losin' his money all the time?"

"Think."

Joe Johnson, sitting on the steps of Patty Cannon's house, sipping blue flame, felt trapped. "Seems to me," he began, "'bout the only thing he can do is what he does so good—make and sell more whiskey." He gulped down another dram.

"Ain't that about what he's doin' now?"

"Yes, Ma'am."

"How's he look when the cocks start to fight, or the horses take off?"

"He looks most pow'fully sick. Now's I think about it, he starts to sweat. Most times has to turn away. Can't even watch no mo'."

"What you figger that boy wants more 'an anythin' in the world?"

"He wants to bet."

"Sure does."

"Well then?"

"Well, they don't let nobody bet with a pocket full of air, and they ain't takin' no I.O.U's, I 'spect."

"Then give him the money."

"Ma'am?"

"Give him the money. Let him lose it."

"I don't follow. Why'd I want to give some nigger my money to lose?"

"Give him some money. Let him lose it. Keep an account."

Joe Johnson stared intently at the jug as if it were suddenly animated. He could not look Patty Cannon in the eye. She was goading him, prompting him, but he could not put the pieces together.

"Someday, Joe, the debt comes due." She was smiling. "What's he got to pay you back with?"

Johnson hesitated. "Yellow clown suit. A still that makes damn fine whiskey."

"And?"

"Maw, I ain't cut out for all this thinkin'. Tha's why I work for you. You think it up and I'll go do it."

"Got a young wife just bought her freedom, didn't you tell me?"

"Yep."

She said no more, just let the last syllable out of his mouth hang in the air in front of him until a grin broke out. Then she was reasonably certain he understood.

CHAPTER 62

Cuff stood outside the back door of the tavern wiping away a white, chalky substance that had dried in the corners of his mouth. He tried to straighten out his clothes and knock away the grass and pieces of leaves he knew must be in his hair. He held a jug in his left hand and trembled slightly. Back to the beginning, he thought vaguely. He knocked on the door. Nothing. He knocked louder the second time, and in short order the tavern keeper opened the door.

The rotund man smiled when he saw Cuff, not because he had missed him—though he probably had missed the business—but because Cuff had become precisely what he had predicted. Oh, he wished Cuff no ill will, it was just predictable. He had observed many in his days. Now here Cuff stood looking like something that had washed up in the harbor, or blown up the peninsula by the ever-present wind.

"Where you been?" he asked.

"I been goin' to the races down to Smyrna and the cockfights here and there."

"Don't say?"

"I do."

"Well, you musta been winnin' cause you ain't been

sellin' none of my whiskey."

"I was winnin'. And I was sellin' my own whiskey. It was so pure dey called it 'blue flame' 'cause that's the color it burned when I lit it up to test."

"Don't say."

"I do."

"Competition, eh? You here to offer me some o' that blue flame of yours?"

"No, sir. I ain't got any more."

"How come, sounds like you had a good business among the scoundrels in these places."

"I did 'til I los' my dogtooth."

"Dog tooth didja say?"

"Uh huh. Dogtooth. Creole man give it to me when I was a boy. Taught me how to make a charm and use it."

The tavern keeper was entertained. He could see by looking at Cuff that he had stopped taking care of himself. He was dirty and disheveled and reeked of some kind of drink. "So you charmed the cocks and horses and they won for you, that about right?"

"'Bout right. The charm's in three parts and it changes the flow of energy. It's pow'ful strong when the parts is all together."

"Don't say."

"I do."

"Hmmm. What else was in your charm?"

"Naw, can't say. Henri tole me never to tell a soul, not even my wife knows. But I los' the dogtooth down to Smyrna and my luck turned sourer than three-day milk. Hain't won a race or a fight since. I started to drink a bit to take my mind off it, so my wife stole the key to my shed and still and won't let me make no more. She hid it."

The tavern keeper looked at him suspiciously. Started drinkin' a little, I'll bet, he thought to himself. Already today might be more like it. "That's a pretty strange story you're tellin' me."

"Yessir, does indeed seem strange now that I tell it all bunched up like that. But it's the truth, I swear to that."

The tavern keeper nodded. "So what is it I can do for you?"

Cuff held up the jug "Can't make your own so you'll drink mine again." He would have some fun with Cuff for a little while to repay the story he'd been told. Too, he sometimes liked to see the wild look come to a drunkard's eyes when he withheld whiskey, even for a short time. He didn't do it to be completely cruel, but to remind himself why he never took to the spirits he served. Then he would give in and see the relief that would come over their faces. Sad, he thought.

"I don't know if I can help you out," he said rubbing the stubble on his chin.

Cuff looked at him, but the desperation was not there. Disappointment, perhaps, but the wildness he expected to see was softer, a resolve rather than the gut-tightening, eye-bulging fear.

"But maybe I can," he recanted and disappeared quickly behind the slammed door, jug in hand and total confusion in his head. He couldn't figure the man out, never could. And all that other improbable mumbo jumbo, Cajun and charms and dogteeth and lord knows what all, might very well be true. He filled the jug while he thought it over. Back outside he handed Cuff the jug, and Cuff reached toward him with a small stack of coins.

"No," he said. "This one's free. Keep you comin' back," he joked. "Buy somethin' for your missus."

Cuff bowed the old almost unperceivable bow of servitude and thanked the man cordially. When he turned, he did not stumble, did not lurch. The tavern keeper watched him a few seconds, shook his head and closed the door.

CHAPTER 63

Cuff came to looking up at the sky, at least the part of it that wasn't blotted out. The sun was only an aura around the dark object that cast its shadow over him. He tried to rise, but there was a tremendous pressure on his chest. He tried again, but this time rather than merely resist him, whatever was on his chest pushed back with great force.

Then it laughed. "Goin' somewhere?" It was Joe Johnson's voice, and it was Joe Johnson's body that eclipsed the sun.

"Guess not," Cuff answered, and with those words discovered the pain in his jaw. "Damn," he muttered.

"I let you up, you don't back sass me no more."

"I s'pose."

"Then git up."

Cuff rose slowly. He was unsteady on his feet, and only part of it was due to the acid-like rum boiling in his stomach. He couldn't remember where it had come from, and for a moment he was uncertain where he was.

"Yo're a mess, boy."

Cuff squinted at the man, then turned away. He had no idea what he was in the midst of, but it felt wrong, and looked for a way out.

"Can't run, nigger. Not in the middle of negotiations."

Cuff thought hard. What in the hell was goin' on? His brain refused to yield a context, a meaning or purpose. Slowly he gathered the pieces: knocked down, apparently from a shot to the jaw, held down by boot and foot and leg and man, refused his dignity, if in fact there was any left to be refused. He closed his eyes and let his throbbing head loll back.

"Let me restate the conditions of our agreement," Johnson spoke slowly as if to a child. "I loan you money to bet with. When you win, you pay it back. When you lose, it goes on account. With me so far?"

Cuff nodded. It was coming back.

"But there ain't been no winning, has there?"

He could only shake his head from side to sorry side. There had been no winning since the dogtooth was lost. The bags of money in the shed had all shrunk to nothing, and the bags lay on the shelf deflated as a life come to nothing. Like his, he thought.

"I ain't got nothin' to pay you back with, Mars Johnson."

Cuff hoped the humility would count for something.

"No money? After all those cockfight wins? No money after all those horse races you picked like you could see the future?"

"No money," Cuff said and hung his head. His temples were pounding now, and when he shut his eyes lights sprayed in all directions like stars exploding. "No money."

"Well, tha's not what I said when you came to me. No money. I gave you, loaned you, what I could just so you could start winning again."

"That you did, sir."

"On good faith."

"Good faith, 'deed."

Cuff squatted down and stared at the grass, he could not foresee the tail end of this discussion and he could feel himself start to tremble.

"A deal's a deal, boy. The debt's come due."

"I ain't got nothin' to give ya, Mars Johnson. Ain't got nothing worth a blade a grass in this worl'."

"That ain't so."

"I tell ya I los' it all, every penny I earned from cocks and horses and blue flame."

"That ain't so."

"I tell ya it is. Broke. Can't even afford to feed my family. Don't wanna go home and face 'em."

"That ain't so."

"It is," he said with some force. "You got a free wife."

The words hung heavy in the air, their full weight not enough to keep him crouched down. Cuff reared up and the power and the roar that issued from him knocked Joe Johnson backward.

CHAPTER 64

Cuff's ferocious upward blast was met by the equal force of Joe Johnson's hands, clasped together, driving down. The hands caught Cuff's shoulder at about mid-crouch. Something cracked and the pain shot immediately into every district of his body. He went to his knees. Behind his eyelids showers of sparks flared and hissed, tumbled and exploded. He could hear Johnson and some other men laughing. He could feel his left arm drooping from its shoulder socket.

"Now you wanna tell me 'bout that wife you won't cover your debt with?"

Cuff said nothing. The money, the winning bets, the still, the customers, blue flame, Rose and Comfort all ran through his brain as the tall white man hovered over him taunting, goading another attack. But he didn't have it in him. He had nothing left and he wished Johnson would simply finish him and call it a fine day to be alive and white. But Johnson was hauling him to his feet. He awaited another blow, more pain, more humiliation. He stood a man before men about to give up his wife for a gambling debt. There was no shame greater, and all he could do now was give in to the inevitable. He stood before a raging runaway horse, and he could do nothing about it but absorb the blow and hope it killed him.

For a moment Cuff stepped out of himself and looked himself over. He looked absurd in the yellow suit with the garish peacock embroidered on it. Johnson had been right to call him a clown, a fool made more so by his clothes. His corporeal body hung its head, his ghostly body cried.

AUTUMN 1816

Chapter 65

The horse plodded on without any goading from Pompey. Miles slipped away under wheel and hoof, earth softened by heavy hooves and flattened again by wheels relentlessly turning. They passed few other wagons, or horses or people on foot. And they passed few other farms, and none that resembled the ramshackle place they had passed earlier. Something nagged at Esther, something other than the broken down buildings and tree stumps growing like crops in the fields. Something about the woman with the hoe, whose face was too far away to see, haunted her.

"Pompey," she blurted out, "we passed the farm. I know we did. We have to turn around." Nothing could have made

Pompey happier, he wanted nothing more than to head north. "Remember that horrible looking farm we passed a few hours ago?"

He nodded, it had made an impression on him as well. "That was it, I'm sure of it. There are a lot of poor farms, but that one was the worst. So far everyone has said no farm that looked like that should ever be called a farm, let alone a plantation."

He agreed, and prodded the horse. He looked down the road, then straight ahead before facing Esther head on. His eyes asked the question, did she see Comfort.

She looked back at him. "Yes, I think I may have seen her. There was something about a woman way off in the field that's been naggin' me. Way she moved, maybe. Her profile, though it was pretty much lost in the sun. I don't know for sure, but she keeps comin' into my head when I ain't invited her."

The horse's pace seemed to pick up a bit, and the trance-inducing motion was broken. They craned their necks to see into the distance. But what would she do if it was Comfort? She couldn't just walk into the field and take her home. She had Comfort's papers. Would they honor them? Give up a slave they'd bought and paid for? She knew about papers, and freedom, and the hopeless side of being owned.

She thought about going to the local authorities. But she had no idea where they might be, or if written proof of someone's freedom amounted to anything here. Manumission papers? What of it, they might ask and jail her too, white or not. Her mind clouded over, and she wanted someone to talk to, someone to give her ideas, solutions. Hope.

Pompey slapped the reins against the horse's rump and minded the road ahead in a way he hadn't before. She knew he was thinking it over too, but what good would it do either one of them?

She wanted to cry, to cry herself to sleep and wake with the answers that eluded her now. She wanted to wake with it all behind them, Comfort safe, Rose with her mother again, and all of them magicked north onto safe ground. She closed her eyes and tried to make it so, but she opened them only watch the rolling gait of the horse's behind.

She wished the stupor of steady, uneventful travel to descend on them again. But the horse was animated and seemed to sense the changes of direction and purpose, and threw himself into it with vigor, or at least as much vigor as this horse could muster.

CHAPTER 66

Sunlight was draining from the sky as Pompey and Esther passed the clump of crepe myrtle they had noticed earlier. The field slaves had quit after a fourteen-hour day and were gathering at the edges of the fields, talking. There was no sign of the white man or the Negro who sat next to him in the shadows.

Why don't they just run away, Esther thought. They

would be miles away by morning. But then again, why had she never run away, with the added advantage of being fair with one blue eye? She knew the answer all too well, and with it came the image of Master Clendaniel doubled over on the porch racked with jarring attacks of diarrhea and vomiting. What awaited her, she could not even imagine, if she were ever caught.

But that was far from here.

"Pompey," she said softly and watched him jerk to as if from a trance, or extraordinary concentration. "We're gonna stop at this farm. We have to know if this is the place."

Sweat beaded on his forehead, and the reins trembled in his hands. "Pull up close to that white-haired man, and stop the wagon." Her heart pounded and her palms began to sweat at the thought of it. She began talking to herself inside her head. Give yourself away for sure if you go actin' nervous 'round those folk. They slaves jest like you, ain't no white man there to question you. Act natural—whatever that is.

She stepped down from the wagon and began an unsteady walk up one of the wheel ruts. It was part out of fear and part out of the uneven ground she walked on. The white-haired man spotted her coming up from the road. When she drew near, he did the slight bow of slave to white that was trained into him from birth. A group of women stood beyond him talking.

"Good evening," Esther began, uncertain what to say next. "Can you tell me if this is the place they call the Osborne Plantation?"

Before Isaac could speak, Comfort twirled and looked

Esther in the eye. Comfort's hand shot to her mouth, but she quickly feigned a cough. Esther's eyes said, say nothing. We're here for you. Comfort looked beyond Esther before she turned back to the other women, and saw the wagon with Pompey at the reins and Rose's head peering over the side of the wagon. Rose could not recognize her mother a few dozen yards away in the dying light, though the people in the fields had caught her attention. The child had spent the better part of the day staring either at the puffs of dust coming from the horse's feet, or the long stretches of woods and the occasional farm.

Pompey stared straight ahead, the sweat now even more profuse than before. It was as close to panic as he had ever come, and it was not a place he would choose ever to revisit. If it were not for Esther being out of the wagon, he would prod the horse as if the devil himself was after him.

"Yes, Ma'am, it is," Isaac said to her. "Do you need to see Master or Mistress? This would not be a good time. They's havin' supper 'bout now I 'spect, and that ain't no good time in that house."

Some of the women behind him nodded in agreement. Comfort stood stock still, in shock and bewildered by what to do next.

"I guess I'll come back tomorrow. I ain't seen neither of them in a good many years. Just wanted to pay my regards."

"Shall I tell..."

"No, no," Esther said. "No need to say a thing. I'd like to surprise them," she said with a tiny smile. As she turned she pretended to stumble in the rut. "Oh," she said, "I can't see so good."

Comfort took the cue and rushed to her elbow. "Let me help you," she said, "It's dark and dangerous out here this time of day. I often stumbles myself."

They began a slow walk to the wagon. When they were beyond Isaac's eyeshot, Esther whispered, "We come to git you. I poisoned master and run away. Don't git too close to the wagon, Rose sees you and we're done for.

"Now we found you, now we got to make a plan. How close you watched?"

"Not very," Comfort said. "Nobody takes chances 'cause they know they'll git beat, then killed. I got to go 'fore Isaac gets suspicious."

"He a good man?"

"Yes."

"We may need his help. You gather here every ev'nin'?"

"Most."

"Look for me tomorra, at dusk."

Comfort turned. The conversation had gone on too long already. And Isaac was staring down the ruts through the gathering dark. Passing him on her way to the cabin, he looked hard at her until she felt the look and stopped.

"Chatting like old friends," he remarked.

"I warned her about the Osbornes. They ain't the way they used to be I'm told."

"Uh huh," Isaac said, "Kind of ya."

Comfort walked away still stunned, and more fearful than ever of what might happen to Rose.

CHAPTER 67

Isaac watched Comfort inch closer to the road throughout the afternoon. Something was going to happen, he could feel it in the pit of his stomach. And he could see it in the uncharacteristic tics and jerks as she hoed the rows. It was not her normal flow, the natural give and take with the earth that she had discovered in the first hours of the work. She was, he knew, distracted.

Comfort spoke to Fillis about the pain of abandonment, how she so missed her child, and the bitterness of bondage after tasting freedom, even if had only been a few weeks. And Fillis spoke with Isaac who kept an even closer eye on the girl just in case she decided to do something foolish, like run away. He'd seen it before, and the outcome was never pretty. Master was very, very nearsighted, but run from him and it was like sight came to him from some supernatural place. He could whip a slave to within a moment before death. Vicious, controlled, every lash calculated to flay strips of skin from the naked back of man, woman or child.

And the rest were forced to watch, then carry the unconscious, bloody hulk away and tend to the wounds. Then Master would take Beck's arm and stroll from the whipping post as casually as if he had just fed a lamb.

Isaac bent to the work, always with his eyes raised and squinting into the sun. It had to do with the white woman and the wagon that had come by the day before, he had felt the connection immediately when Comfort came to the woman's aid, took her arm in such a familiar way, a way no slave would touch a white woman she did not know intimately. And this was a stranger. Or so everyone thought. But not Isaac. He had studied nuances and subtleties of movement his whole adult life, had stopped countless slaves from bolting with just a well-placed word or two, or a look that counseled more thought before the deed was too hastily done.

Beck caught every detail of what transpired in the fields, but he was not one to perceive minute changes in action and concentration. He might have seen that Comfort's rhythm was not her normal smooth dance with the hoe, but he would have taken it no further, perhaps blaming the roughness on a lack of sleep or an upset stomach, but it would not have gone beyond that, and he would have turned his attentions to larger concerns, trouble that might build to something greater.

Comfort glanced constantly at the road that bisected the farm, and then cut her gaze toward Isaac, more often than not he was looking back with a stern look on his face, a look she chose not to interpret beyond bending harder into the work at hand. But the afternoon plodded in a way she had not experienced before, and the specter of Esther shimmered before her like an oasis in a desert. It had not occurred to Comfort how they had found her, she was still reliving every moment of their encounter the day before. She felt a joy that was instantly tempered by fear. Her heart pounded and she tried to see herself far from this place and safe with her child in her lap. But Isaac and Fillis had told her tales of runaways, and the images they created as the three sat on the steps to one of the cabins in the darkness, were vivid and bloody and horrible. But now she was contemplating just the kind of act that had gotten others beaten to just short of death. But she had known freedom, and it was worth the risk.

She glanced at Isaac and inched closer to the road. She thought she saw his great white head shaking, almost as if he knew what she was thinking. She wondered if she should seek his advice.

CHAPTER 68

A few miles north of "the plantation" was a large patch of woods where they had stayed the night before. It seemed safe, at least they had seen no one in the vicinity. So Pompey drove the wagon back there.

Esther did not speak during the trip. She was concentrating on Comfort and how they might get her out and north without all of them winding up in jail, or worse. She stared straight ahead and tried to envision the escape, the slow, careful trek north to Delaware, then into Pennsylvania, but her thoughts scared her, and all she could imagine was the darkness of uncertainty.

In the woods, Esther took the basket of blackberries they had picked in the morning. They ate, again, in silence. Rose would occasionally ask for her Mama, and Esther would stroke her hair and say, "Soon, baby, soon." And smile at her, and feel glad that she did not know what danger they were in, or that her mother was so close by. Rose had become so entranced by the slow pace of travel that she took every opportunity to sleep. And fortunately, Esther thought, it did not stop her from sleeping through the night as well.

The berries gone, and some spring water they had found, Esther began to pace, and Pompey knew full well what was on her mind, it was the same thing on his. How can you hide a full-grown black woman in an open wagon? The answer was, and always would be, that they couldn't. That was the problem, Pompey worried as he paced the little open space around the wagon.

Esther sat with her back against a tree and her eyes closed. Rose lay on the ground with her head in Esther's lap. They dared not light a fire, but the moon threw some light on them through the treetops. Esther dozed, and Rose fell into a deep sleep. When Esther hadn't woken in a few minutes, Pompey left the two of them, and slipped off into the dark. There was something he'd seen that afternoon that he wanted to get back to, something only his eyes would have been drawn to from a lifetime of scavenging and bringing back to life the dead things of this world.

⁂

Esther woke as the sun lit her face. She felt the weight

of Rose's head on her leg. Her leg was numb, but she didn't want to wake the child. Today was going to be difficult, at best, their last day in freedom if things went wrong. She wanted it to be tomorrow. But, she realized, she'd spent most of her life wishing for tomorrow or tomorrow's tomorrow. She tried to imagine what it would be like if they ever made it into Pennsylvania, as they had talked about, and melted into anonymity and freedom. Would she always walk around with one eye over her shoulder? Could she pass an entire life? Wouldn't the mask get cumbersome and heavy after a while? She had this same reverie almost every morning since they began traveling and looking for Comfort. Now the danger they had been in seemed minor compared to what they were about to encounter.

It was at that moment that Esther realized Pompey was nowhere to be seen. She wondered if he had climbed into the back of the wagon and fallen asleep. But he was always awake well before she and Rose. She relaxed figuring he might have gone off into the woods for a few moments. She waited but heard nothing.

"Pompey," she said in loud whisper. And with that a grinning Pompey dropped to the ground from under the wagon. He stood before her and made a large gesture that suggested that he had materialized out of thin air, magicked himself out of invisibility. "Where did you come from?"

He made a twirling gesture with his hand.

"Oh, stop it," she said, "we have to be serious today. And careful." The moment of levity broke, and Pompey gestured her toward the wagon. He got on his knees and motioned her to do likewise. She looked up, and there on the underbelly of the wagon, was a sling, or a web of bedding ropes, where a body might lie and be undetected by anyone except those lying in the road on their back.

Esther smiled. Where the rope had come from or where the idea had come from, Esther did not know, nor did she care. She remembered now that this little man had a reputation for finding what people needed when they needed it. She shook her head in wonder.

"Gonna be dusty under there. Think she might choke to death?" A new worry, not to be outdone by the old worries took up lodging in her head.

Pompey half closed his eyes and shook his head from side to side. He held out a few long scraps of fabric toward Esther. He took one and tied it so it covered his mouth, the other crossed his eyes.

"Thought of everything, haven't you?"

He smiled. "Well, if you could figure out how we could fly Comfort outta here, that would be even better." It was the last thing she said for hours, except some cooing to Rose when the baby awoke.

CHAPTER 69

William Clendaniel held the handbill at arm's length. It read: "$200 REWARD," in large, bold typeface. Then:

"ABSCONDED from the subscriber, on the evening of Wednesday, the 12th instant, a Negro woman, named ESTHER. She is 24 years old, five feet three inches high. Approximately 120 pounds. Appears to be white. One blue eye, one brown. Light skinned with thin lips and narrow nose."

The printer leaned against his press and waited.

"This will do," Clendaniel told him.

"How many?"

"A hundred. And I want them distributed all over the county, and down into Kent."

"And Pennsylvania?"

"Of course. Make it two hundred."

"And you'll send someone for them?"

"Don't you have a boy to do that?"

"No."

"Then get one. I want these handbills in every hamlet from Odessa to Philadelphia—tomorrow."

"Then I'll need two boys."

"Get a dozen if you have to. I want this girl back. She is going to pay for running. A nigger girl'll not make me a fool in my own town. She'll know what it feels like to be exposed when I flay her naked back on Market Street." He flung the bill at the printer. "Two hundred. By tomorrow."

CHAPTER 70

Again Comfort worked her way toward the road as the afternoon crept toward evening and the shadows lengthened and Master and his crutch, Beck, dissolved into the ramshackle cluster of buildings that were the diseased heart of the plantation. One minute there, Beck describing everyone's whereabouts and movements, the next, gone, swallowed up in the gloaming.

Moments after seeing that Master was gone, Comfort looked up the road and saw the wagon coming slowly toward her. She feared Isaac might see her staring and come to investigate once and for all what was happening. But he didn't seem to notice. When she shot a glance at him, he didn't look back, just kept to the rhythm he'd built all day long. But when she wasn't looking toward him, he watched.

Let not my heart be troubled, he thought to himself, fearful that Comfort would wind up with worse than a broken finger if Master even suspected she was up to something. Or worse, that Mistress found out. Hell itself would vomit forth a fury without bounds if that happened. Isaac had seen it unleashed on his own son, and he feared for Comfort.

It seemed an eternity for the wagon to get close to

Comfort. But when it did, Esther held a finger to her lips. Pompey slowed the horse to a crawl.

"Listen," Esther said in a whisper that she feared might drift across the evening calm to other ears. "Chew these hack-wood leaves." She threw a bundle to the side of the road. "They'll give you hives and a fever. Won't hurt you but you'll look mighty puny. Scares some people when they see a body under a hackwood spell."

Comfort motioned to speak, but Esther silenced her. "We'll drive by each evening. Stay here as near to dark as possible. When we don't see you here, we'll know you chewed the hackwood leaves. Two days later, come to the road when it is full dark. The wagon will be hid behin' that clump o' crepe myrtle."

And then the wagon rolled into the dark and out of sight. Comfort stood still and let the tears come. She had hoped for just a glimpse of Rose. So close, she thought, I could smell her.

In the nightly gathering, before the return to solitude and loneliness and the conquest of fatigue, they stood in groups and talked despite the sameness of the days, the eventless grinding of hour upon hour and year upon year. Only Sunday told them that another week had passed, but then, as harvest approached, even that would not be a marker. But what differ-ence, they were merely moving earth and stone, pebble and clod from one place to another, loosening the soil for the rain to soak in, to dislodge an occasional weed.

They gathered, the new and those who had been there for years, Isaac had long thought, because that's what people do. Some animals pack to hunt and survive, protect the young.

But people gather to share themselves, to share among themselves what little strength they had, what little hope each may have found in the nurturing of crops that their bodies would convert to energy, when the cold came, and get them through the winter. Surely there was a grain of hope for all in that, Isaac thought.

CHAPTER 71

Dusk seemed to descend like a shroud. One minute the sun lay in streaks on the tilled earth, the next it was a shadowless monotone of gray with brown humps and splashes of green on top of it all. Comfort hardly noticed, her heart thumped and raced. She glanced more and more frequently up the northbound road. But nothing came.

She could sense Isaac watching her, but she'd ceased to care. With his blessings or without, she was going to run. But where was Esther? She had promised to return, hadn't she? Or did she only imagine the whole encounter.

All of the other field slaves had quit work for the day and were standing around as they usually did talking, letting the fatigue drain away before the loneliness of cold food and dreamless sleep. Comfort kept on, needing an excuse to remain near the road. But it was too late. They were not coming today, maybe never. And her heart, yet again, broke.

Fillis sat on the step below Comfort and lay a hand softly on her knee. Comfort was glad for the contact. Isaac, uncharacteristically, paced in the dust, barely visible in the moonless dark. He tugged on a corncob pipe, and the glow let the women know where he was.

"Isaac, sit down," Fillis said, "You're makin' us nervous." He merely grunted and circled past them once more.

"Comfort," he said at last, but she would not look at him, she was afraid what she would see when he got close enough. "Comfort," he said again, without heat.

"Yes, Isaac."

"You're gonna get mightily sick."

"Sir?"

"Sick. It's the only way. Only Fillis will dare come in this cabin. It might fetch you a week's time."

"Yessir, if'n you say it's so."

"Go to the field tomorrow as always. Give Beck a good show in the morning, then slow down in the afternoon. Then collapse. Go down hard. I'll get Fillis."

Comfort listened, and nodded a nod he could not see. "Your friend come, I'll talk to her. It'll be moonless a few more nights."

"But Master'll be fit to kill when he finds out I'm gone."

"That he will."

"But I can't let you take no beatin' for me."

"You got your own troubles to worry about. I been beat before. 'Sides, even Master ain't fool enough ..." He trailed off.

"Ain't fool enough for what?" Fillis asked. But he did not answer. He couldn't worry about a beating that hadn't begun yet. And if he got beat bad enough, and died, would it be any worse than what he had now? He wondered, but refused to give voice to the thought. Crippled only? He was old and ready to slow down. No, no outcome seemed worse than bondage itself. Someone else's freedom seemed worth it.

They spoke no more, just sat in the dark and listened to the frogs and crickets and Clancy huffing as he dreamed. Little puffs of dust swirled up, then settled.

In the clearing a fire flickered. Esther and Rose sat with their backs to the tree, Pompey next to a wagon wheel. A white man stood over them with rifle cocked and loaded. He had stumbled on them in the afternoon just before they were to leave to see Comfort again. It struck him as very odd that a Negro child would be sleeping with her head in the lap of a white woman, and that the three of them would be hidden in the woods if they had a legitimate story. Hers sounded unlikely. He knew of no Comstock farm in the region, and he roamed much of it searching for game.

It had been hours like this, silence as the man just stood, saying and doing nothing. He was not a deep thinker, and depended for inspiration on tiny notions that slipped into his head unbidden. But no ideas seemed to be seeking a home. So he stood and stared into the woods. Except for the loaded rifle he did not seem a threat.

Pompey stared at Esther until she began to feel uncomfortable and looked back at him. From the few things the man had said over the past few hours, they figured out he was not plotting anything, probably only trying to figure out if this odd trio was worth anything. Pompey cut his eyes to the underside of the wagon. Esther furrowed her brow. What could he be thinking now, she wondered. Then she thought of the morning when he had essentially hidden in front of their eyes.

Pompey slipped quietly under the wagon and into the web. He was gone. When the man looked to him to say something, there was nothing but wagon wheel, and empty space where a man had been. "What?" he said, glaring at Esther.

"He does that," she said.

"Runs away?"

"Disappears."

"Nobody can do that."

She pointed to the empty space.

"Just 'cause he ain't there don't mean he disappeared."

"Didja hear him go? Hear him now?"

The man shook his head slowly. What might have looked thoughtful was only confusion.

"Roots," she said, adding deliberately to the jumble of thoughts going through his head.

"Roots?" he repeated.

"Voodoo," she said. He narrowed his eyes, the words failing to register.

"Magic," she said, "black magic. Right now he's off in the woods collecting roots and leaves and berries to make you somethin'. Saw a man after Pompey give him the elixir once. It wasn't pretty to see a grown man turned back into a baby. A sick baby, if you know what I mean."

"I won't take nothin' from him. Nothin'."

"You won't have to," she said, shaking her head slowly and with no hint of compassion.

CHAPTER 72

"She ain't white," Comfort said with her head down. "She a Negro."

"She passin' for white."

"Yessir, so far she say it workin'."

"And these leaves?"

Comfort hesitated. Esther let her knowledge of Roots be known to few people, and she did not feel comfortable telling Isaac. Though she could not see how she could avoid it, since he now held the leaves in his hand and looked like he wanted answers.

"Comfort, I just want to make sure she can be trusted."

"She has my child and risks gettin' killed if she get caught. Do I trust her? With my life."

"The leaves?"

"Hackwood," she said.

"To make you sick?"

"Only 'pear so. Give me hives and a fever, keep me outta the fields."

"How does she know it will work, Comfort?" Fillis asked.
"Esther knows Roots."
Isaac and Fillis looked at one another and smiled.

CHAPTER 73

The sun screamed into the field all afternoon. It was relentless and drove Master Osborne and Beck deeper into the shadows for relief. But not so deep that they couldn't see every field slave and what they were or were not doing. Isaac mumbled more than once that it was the hottest day of the year.

Esther had not told her, so Comfort was unsure how many leaves to chew, or how long they would take to bring results. For several hours she chewed small pieces tentatively with no effect. Suddenly, and with no warning at all, she felt her forehead burning and large boils appeared on her arms. She spun once where she stood, as if looking for someone, and fell unconscious into the dirt.

Beck assumed it was the heat and motioned Isaac to attend to her. He dropped the hoe and walked toward her. She was not moving. She must have chewed those leaves she told us about, he thought as he approached her. She looked dead, but sweat poured out of her, her face glistened and her dress was quickly darkening. He knelt beside her and placed his hand on her forehead. She was on fire.

Isaac stood and motioned for two slaves to help him. He and one of the men lifted her from the ground, the other was sent to tell Master what had happened. Comfort hung, as if lifeless, between them. She roused once on their way to her cabin, but she did not recognize anyone or anything, and fainted again.

When she came to in the evening, Fillis hovered over her with rags soaked in cold water, and a tincture Comfort did not recognize dabbed on the sore on her arms, chest, back and stomach. She was stripped to the waist, and Isaac was embarrassed and kept his eyes averted. "How'd I get here?" she asked Fillis.

"Isaac and another man brung ya."

"Like this?" she asked looking down at her nakedness. She crossed her arms across her chest.

"Naw. You was in your field dress."

Comfort looked down and saw the raggedy blanket that covered her from waist to toes. "I got sores down there too?"

"Not as bad," Fillis said. "Seems they's worst nearest your heart."

"Anybody else seen me?"

"Isaac say Beck come by 'fore I got here. Scared him pretty good. He run off to tell Master like a good little rat." She laughed for the first time since Comfort had known her. "Your friend knows her Roots, I'll say that."

Isaac stood by the open door peering into the night. "You got anymore them leaves, Comfort?"

"I do."

"Good," he said. "Good. I seen a boy with pox once, dead from it."

"You can turn around now."

Isaac turned and saw that Fillis had covered Comfort. "You look like he looked," he said. "I'll talk to Master in the morning. He may come have a look at you, or send his Beck again. I'll suggest Fillis stay with you till you're better." There was a glint in his eyes.

The wagon plodded past the field some time later. A small group of field slaves were gathered, but neither Comfort nor the white-haired Negro was among them. A shiver ran down Esther's spine. Pompey sweated. Rose moaned in the back of the wagon.

Two days, Esther thought.

CHAPTER 74

The handbill swam in and out of Cuff's vision. There was something vaguely familiar to the message, to the words that would, for just a moment, untangle themselves and sit still.

"Esther," he slurred. But there was no use. He leaned against the wall to steady it, but his elbow gave out and his shoulder slammed into the boards. He caught himself before he went to his knees.

"Esther," he repeated, and for an instant an image flitted across his brain, then, with hummingbird speed, darted off. Cuff slipped the cork out of a bottle and took a short pull. It was early in the day, and he could feel the hours calling him toward dark and sleep. He had nowhere to go, and most people had stopped talking to him, but the quotidian regularity of darkness and sleep gave his days some sense of shape, a goal to reach just one more time.

All of this bubbled to the surface of his brain from time to time with no particular clarity or form. But it came nevertheless along with the countless plans, schemes, and regrets that haggled for their moment in consciousness.

"Esther," he repeated.

CHAPTER 75

Fillis was leaning over Comfort when she woke. Sweat still poured from her, and the boils were alarming. Esther had called them hives, but these were large and angry and oozed, and Fillis was sure Esther had miscalculated, or at least failed to give proper guidance in their use.

"How you feel?" she asked.

Comfort hesitated while she let the regions of her body report in. Head? No headache. Stomach? No stomachache.

Body? No body ache. Fever? Yes. Hives? No, boils. "I's all right, I 'spect."

"You look awful," Fillis told her.

"I s'pose tha's Esther's plan."

"I s'pose it is," Fillis repeated, and allowed a little smile.

"Anybody been here to see if'n I died?" Comfort asked.

"Not a soul."

"You mean Beck ain't been stirrin' the dust up out there to see if Master's investment still able to drag a hoe across the dirt?"

Fillis shook her head. Clancy walked out of the shadows and licked Comfort's hand. "You thought to feed that old hound?" she asked.

"He finds food. Don't know how, but he always got som'fin in his mouf. Half the time's so mangled can't tell what it was in life. But he seem pleased with hisself. God love'im, don't never complain."

"Gonna miss 'im, too, when I goes."

"Just a ole dog."

"Yeah, but sometimes he's all I got."

"You got Isaac and me."

"In the night," Comfort said. "When loneliness come on pow'ful, the onliest warm thing in the world is him. Tha's a burden to put on a dog, but he carry it, and me."

Fillis shook her head and dabbed at Comfort's brow. "You got to drink somethin', girl. You keep sweatin' like this, you gonna be empty soon and blow away." She turned away. "When?" she asked.

"Tomorra night."

"We need to get Beck to see ya."

"I know."

"And me."

Why?

Comfort froze. What could she mean? Did she want Beck to see her like this too?

"He lock us in here together, 'cause he think we got the pox, he might just send us away from here." She was shy all of a sudden, as if she thought that Comfort might think her crazy.

"Or burn the cabin down," Comfort said.

"I thought of that," Fillis said, "but Mistress ain't gonna burn what she can still use. When Master beat my boy to death, they took the pants off'n the body and gave 'em to another slave," she said in a cracked whisper.

Comfort rose and went to her. The two women held each other a long time. Then Comfort went to a small bag she had made before her finger was broken, and took some of the hackwood leaves out and handed them to Fillis. "Maybe you oughtn't to chew as many as I did."

Fillis took the leaves and put them in the pocket of her apron.

Then the door swung violently open and Beck climbed to the top step. He looked blindly into the darkness. "Anybody there?" he spat. Comfort walked very slowly across the room and emerged into the light with her forehead shining and the boils, angry and pustulant on her naked arms, looking for all the world as if God himself had cursed her. Her hair hung vine like and her clothes were in tatters.Beck backed down the steps. "You in there, Miss Fillis."

"I am."

"You gonna come into the light too?"

"Naw."

"Why?"

"I don't think you could take it, boy."

"Why?"

"Do I have to tell ya?"

"No'm," he mumbled and walked away.

Comfort turned to her. Fillis stood in the dark, just now coming back into focus for Comfort. She was chewing a leaf, waiting, as if she expected any moment for sweat to burst forth, or boils to erupt plague-like on every surface of her body, and to pirouette, like Comfort had, into unconsciousness.

Comfort took her hand and patted it. "It's a long time comin'," she told her. "I chewed all afternoon."

"Did it scare ya?"

"Scared me 'cause I didn't know what to 'spect. But you've seen what happens. I standin' here just fine. I jus' look like somethin' the cat dragged in and the dog wouldn't eat."

"Well, maybe Clancy would," Fillis joked.

Comfort smiled at her. "I jus' hope Isaac ain't scared to death when he come in from the field."

"Maybe the dark will help," Fillis offered.

CHAPTER 76

Once Beck turned the corner where Comfort could no longer see him, he burst into a run, as if he could not get the information to Master fast enough. He was a keen observer of some things, the things that were important to Master. He had been chosen and trained from an early age to be the eyes of his owner, to see what he was instructed to see and report every detail clearly and simply. But Beck had early on learned the power of exaggeration. The greater the sin he reported, the greater the praise he received. And even that grew in his mind until he believed that someday it would all result in a great reward. It hung in his future like a brilliant star that he moved faster and faster toward him with every word of appreciation.

His report about Comfort the day before had been graphic and detailed. Perhaps the boils were a little bigger, the pus a little greener, the sweat more copious than it already was, but he had stuck to the facts, fearful that Master might go for a look himself. Now there were two, twice the report to give, triple the details he had actually observed. He puffed down the wheel ruts and dove into the copse of trees where he had deposited Master before his trip to Comfort's cabin. Master's ears perked up when he heard the crashing of feet, and the snapping of limbs and branches.

"That you?"

"Yessir. It's me all right—with a tale to tell."

"What now? Don't tell me that Virginnie died. I jus' paid a hundred twenty five dollars for her. She ain't made me nothin' like that yet. Damn her black hide."

"Ain't dead," Beck assured him.

"Still sick?"

"Yessir. Sicker, I'd say. Boils still leakin' and sweat runnin' like a river off'n her. She the color of ashes."

"Dammit," he bellowed rising from the base of a tree where he'd sat cursing the heat and listening for the familiar sounds from the field. Anyone dare to sing, and he would growl from his lair, "Put that energy into workin'. I won't have no songs on my plantation." And near silence would return punctuated by the click and scrape of hoe blade on poor, played out soil barely able to eke out plant and fruit every few feet.

Beck prepared to deliver the second blow. Master grabbed his arm and stomped about the small clearing, cursing and threatening anyone he could think of. He sounded as if he would be happier if she had died. Beck waited for an opening. It took a few minutes for the tantrum to level off. Beck grabbed the moment.

"They's somethin' else," he said, grinning. "Like what?" Master barked.

"Fillis." He delivered the report one word at a time, he knew what the result would be, and he had learned long ago, when it was all out in the air, to step aside or duck or wind up on the ground. Master was a puny man, but in his anger his attack was ferocious and powerful. But it didn't stop Beck from creating some suspense.

"What about her?"

"Sick," he said, and quickly backed away. "Boils and fever too?"

"Yessir. And worse I think than the other one."

Master let go of a sound born in his gut and shattered by the passage out of him. It was high pitched and strangled the very air around him. It was as if God himself had reached down and delivered an insult. His face turned the color of raw venison, and his eyes bulged. Beck, who ducked behind the tree, was secretly pleased with himself. As displays of anger and pure hatred went, this one strutted and flailed and everyone in the field stopped working and looked toward the long, inhuman wail that erupted from the woods.

No one dared laugh, but it had the effect of massaging the cramps and aches out of everyone's day. Rhythms seemed a little quicker as everyone willed the day to a close so they could gather and speculate what demon, housed in the miscreant body of the Master, had escaped, and what had provided the obviously painful key.

Comfort watched Fillis carefully. When sweat began to bead on her forehead and along her upper lip, she advised the older woman to sit down, to take a gourd of water and let the symptoms gather and grow. Let the body send its defenses.

Fillis smiled.

Isaac did not gather with others when Beck and Master limped from the field back to the decaying fortress. He went directly to Comfort's cabin. He knew the next day would be the dangerous one, and he wanted to see if she was prepared, to see if she had gained back any of her strength.

The whole episode in the afternoon had only reminded him of Master's fury when his property was not all dedicated to his service. He would not hesitate to whip Comfort and tell her he was driving out the demons of illness, though he wondered if Master would be foolish enough to get close to someone with a disease he could not name. Perhaps she brought it with her, he might conjecture and seek his money back upon her death. Or perhaps he might think it was among them all.

But even that little bit of meddling inside of Master's head had begun to make his own head hurt. So he stopped.

The evening had not squeezed all of the light from the air. Fillis met him at the door, and he fainted and fell backward into the dust, a few feet from the sleeping dog.

CHAPTER 77

When Isaac did not show up in the fields in the morning, Beck was quick to make it known to Master, who, just as quickly sent his seeing-eyes to Isaac's cabin. He wasn't there. Beck stood still and listened in the new light. There was noise from Virginnie's cabin, but he hesitated. What he had seen the day before was the stuff of nightmares for years to come.

But what to tell Master?

He had no answer. No wild tale to unravel. He walked slowly toward the door. Before he could make up his mind, it was made up for him. The door swung open. Filling the space was Isaac, his face disfigured with boils that oozed, hands rendered useless by the same sores. Fillis appeared at his side. Not a word was spoken, but Beck could see that Virginnie was not joining them and assumed there was some very bad news in the darkness of the cabin. He walked away, the question of what to tell Master twisting in his brain like a tiny worm.

Isaac closed the door and hugged his wife. Comfort came forward. She held a bundle she had made up from sacks Fillis had pillaged over the years. In it were all of the things she had come south with, all she had with her when Joe Johnson grabbed her in daylight without a word from Cuff. The thought of how she might kill her husband had sometimes sustained her nights when sleep was as elusive as freedom. Now it might be accomplished. She set the bundle on the floor. It was a long time until the new dark set in, when the wagon would be waiting on the road to take her home.

Through a chink in the wall, Isaac saw Beck and Master coming from the field. "Comfort, lie on your pallet and don't move. Fillis, cover her up, all but her face." It was done in a nonce. And when the door shot open, the three of them had assumed exhausted poses. Fillis sat on a stump with a rag dipped in cold water hanging from her hand. Isaac sat slumped against a wall, eyes barely open, mumbling. Comfort's eyes were shut, and she slowed her breathing until her chest rising and falling were hardly discernable.

Master was led into the room. Beck positioned him in front of Isaac, and he leaned close until the white hair came into focus, and then the face, only inches away, blistered and grotesque. Master darted back, his breath sucked in hard and fast. He fell backwards on his buttocks.

"Get me out of here," he demanded. "This is an unclean place. Death already fouls the air. Get me out!"

Beck led him to the door and down the stairs. He had not exaggerated, it was as gruesome as he had described. Everyone who had come in contact with Virginnie had contracted the sickness, and it spread, it seemed, in hours, not days.

Martin Osborne's hand trembled as it held the crook of Beck's arm. He took illness among his slaves as a personal affront, an attack upon his life and fortune. His face distorted as he spit forth a string of epithets, some of which Beck had never heard before, in fact may have been created for the occasion.

It was only mid-day, but Master had no more taste for Beck's droning narrative of the goings-on of the fields. He insisted he be delivered to his rooms where he might further destroy his eyes by reading the one book he had ever allowed himself to purchase. Inches from his eyes the King James translation of The Word swam into a foggy view, but the words calmed and comforted him as he read of the slaves of Egypt.

The farewells were brief. Comfort thanked Isaac and Fillis for their friendship. She felt a twisting in her stomach. It was the pain of separation, the fear of what was to come and the sweet anticipation of Rose returning to her arms.

Comfort took most of the remaining hackwood leaves from her pocket and gave them to Fillis. "Any good comes from these, pass them on. I got little more use for 'em, I hope."

Isaac smiled at her and nodded his big white head. "Did ya see Master this afternoon? He looked like he stared Death hisself right in the face. I mus' be a sight."

"You a sight all right," Fillis poked him.

"You think he was scare't or disgusted, Comfort?"

"Don't know," she said, "I was too busy playin' dead 'case Beck come snoopin' aroun'."

"Soon enough for that," Isaac said, "soon enough."

Comfort scooped her bundle up from the floor and looked at the old couple. "Got to go." She opened the door a crack and stared into the dark. No moon. She turned back one more time and offered up a half smile. Then she walked quietly down the stairs past the black dog in the dust, and picked her way slowly down the wheel rut toward the road.

CHAPTER 78

Comfort cut across the familiar field lit only dimly by starlight. She could not see five feet ahead. If Esther and Pompey and Rose were waiting for her, she could only hope.

She clutched her bundle to her chest and prayed nothing tangled her feet or slithered along the rows.

She stopped to catch her breath. Behind her the buildings hunched, rooflines dimly outlined against the sky, their bulk simply black against gray. She waited until her heart slowed. Her eyes were slowly adjusting to the light, but still she could not see the wagon, or even the clump of crepe myrtle. She merely aimed in the general direction and knew she would eventually find it.

Neither heat nor humidity had drained with the darkness. Her fever had gone, but the boils itched and she wanted to take handfuls of dirt and rub them on her arms and legs, or lean into a tree and let the bark scratch the discomfort away. But there were no trees, so for the time being she let the rough cloth of her dress do the job.

Pompey stood beside the wagon and stared in the direction of the farm. He saw a form moving through the field long before it saw him. He waited. She made out the stand of crepe myrtle, then the wagon, then the man, and finally the woman seated in the wagon.

Comfort wrapped a makeshift shawl around her shoulders and face and walked the last few paces toward the wagon slowly. Pompey greeted her with a brief hug and a nod. Esther took her hand. They were, all of them, awkward and afraid. Pompey gestured at the belly of the wagon. Comfort looked confused and shrugged her shoulders. Pompey dropped to his knees and crawled under the wagon. Comfort followed.

In a few seconds, Pompey emerged from under the wagon

alone. Comfort was secured in the web with one rag tied over her mouth, and another over her eyes. For the time being, she lay facing the underside of the wagon, arms crossing her belly like those of a corpse. The dust from the road billowed around her, and the horse's steps ticked like a clock.

Pompey held the reins a little tighter. They were heading north. For a few more hours they had the dark to protect them. But soon enough he would need to find woods to pass the day in. Food. Water.

Every few miles Esther bade him stop the wagon. She climbed down and peered under the wagon. "Comfort, you all right?"

"Umm hmm," she said through the rag across her mouth.

"You ain't chokin' on the dust?"

"Un uh," she mumbled.

Not far off, Esther could hear a horse galloping.

CHAPTER 79

Beck pushed open the weathered door to Comfort's cabin and stood framed in daylight, but would not go in. He wanted only to do what he had been ordered to do and get away from there. If he did not risk a vicious beating for refusing, he would have refused. So he had shuffled across the field, the fear a burden he could barely shoulder.

Isaac had seen him coming. He and Fillis moved into the darkest corner of the cabin. His heart pounded, the water bucket had gone dry earlier and his mouth was dry, but he would not go out in daylight. His boils wept onto the clean white shirt Fillis had laundered for him, and the blood turned black when it dried.

Beck appeared faceless, only a black spot against the glare of the sun. "Come where I can look atcha," he barked, more out of fear than any sense of authority, of which he had none.

Isaac moved slowly, as if his very joints were as diseased as his face and arms. He loomed out of the dark and stared down at the younger man with as little expression on his face as he could manage.

"Now your woman."

"She can't."

"Whadya mean she can't? She that sick?"

"Partly 'cause of that."

"Partly? You're talkin' riddles."

"Death ain't no riddle."

"Your wife, dead?" He stepped back and the sun blinded him. The sky was white, and cloudless, and the heat again, was merciless. He put his black hand above his eyes to shelf them and to better see Isaac.

"Naw, she ain't dead."

"Virginnie?"

Isaac inhaled deeply and paused. He looked at the floor. He was about to lie, and if master insisted on seeing the corpse, then she would not be the only one dead. "Yes," he answered.

"Master Osborne will be very angry." He said, as if Isaac

or Fillis or both, had killed her, or not saved her from dying.

That blind anger Isaac had witnessed many times before, would he become irrational and stomp into the cabin demanding to see her? He swallowed hard and waited.

Beck walked away slowly, muttering. "Prob'ly beat me for her dyin'." He was in no hurry to reach the cabin, now he was in no hurry to reach the woods. The shadows seemed blacker in this light, even the leaves and trunks were drained of their color and seemed only a charcoal silhouette against the sky.

Master heard Beck coming and looked toward the sound. "Don't bring me bad news," he said when Beck was still a ways off.

"I can't help it. But it ain't my fault, neither."

"The girl, Virginnie, was it her?"

"Yessir."

"Dead?"

"Yessir."

He did not strike out, did not loose another animal growl into the air, did not change his expression at all. He did, to Beck's amazement, nothing.

"Please don't send me to look at no dead woman."

"I can't do it myself. You're my eyes."

"But Isaac look worse than death, and he still alive. Dead people ain't nothin' to fool around with, Master."

"The dead are dead, hollow, empty, used up sacks of flesh."

"The dead ain't always dead. I seen it once't in Haiti. Man

walked right pass' me with them dead eyes, and slumped over like his legs could hardly hold him up, shoulders hunched. He staggered. He was dead. My grandmamma say he been walkin' 'round like that for a year or mo'. I don't wanna see that again."

Martin Osborne shook his head in pity.

Beck knocked politely on the cabin door. Isaac and Fillis looked at each other through the darkness, and both felt a chill blast them in the stomach. The lie hung in the air between them like a black hole, an ouroboros, the black snake swallowing its own tail. Isaac had never seen that look on her face before, or the ashen tint. Isaac exhaled and braced himself.

He opened the door. Beck stood quaking before him. "Master sent me to see the body."

Isaac's mind raced. Was there anything he could say that would run him off? Anything? "You don't believe Isaac?" he said, stalling.

"I believes ya, but Master send me to see for him. Then you got to bury her. Master say put a rock, a big rock on her chest to keep her down. Then he laughed. He didn't believe when I tole him I seen the dead walkin' oncet." Beck fumbled for words, anything to keep him talking and not looking at a dead woman.

"Then you don't wanna come in here, boy."

Beck backed away another foot. "You say she dead, it's like I seen her with my own eyes. You're an honest man."

He walked away, relieved, emboldened, and far from realizing the lie he had inherited, black snake forever devouring itself.

"Bury her," he said over his shoulder. Then turning, he said, "and Master said you ain't no damned good to him no more. He don't want you dyin' here. Get out. That cabin will be burned at sunrise. Less you wanna die sooner than later, stay put. Master say, God be with you." And he was gone.

Isaac closed the door, and lifted Fillis off the floor with a hug he didn't know he still had in him. She was smiling.

Isaac dug a hole the size of a grave and threw in some stones. He mounded the earth and covered the mound with rocks. He nailed two sticks into a cross and placed it at the head of the grave, facing east. When he was done, the field slaves walked by and bowed. Isaac watched through a chink in Comfort's wall. He wondered where she was.

CHAPTER 80

Wheels and horse's hooves churned through the dirt and threw up choking puffs of dust that seemed to Comfort worse when she laid facing up, and worse when she laid facing down. Mile upon mile her conscious mind knew she was heading north, but something nagged at her and every time the wagon slowed, or she could discern voices, she went rigid and her imagination became the enemy. Ten, twenty times a night she was carted off in chains, Esther, Rose and Pompey right behind her. She could have sworn she could hear the tinkling of chain links playing over every bump and rut in the road.

It didn't matter that it was dark, the rag tied across her eyes kept light out anyway, and the one across her mouth kept some of the dust at bay. So except for the sounds that were magnified because of her blindness, she had little of the world to apprehend, so the world of her mind molded and shaped every thought, turned each to view every angle, then moved on.

There was the world of freedom which gave her an inkling of hope, but which came infrequently to her fancy. It was a daylight world, bright and blue and giddy with sights and smells and textures smooth and lush.

And there was the world of bondage, the daily trudge toward nothing but tasteless food and dreamless sleep and the numbing sameness that refused to delineate one day from the next, one week from the next, one year from the next. This world spun into her orbit frequently, and she was helpless to avoid it. It was what it was, like the cold world they drove toward, she could only give in to it, let its images creep their awful creep across her mind, blast her with chilly reality, grind their roughness into her skin, and screech and stink around her until she was sweating again, the wide sweep of terror and hopelessness complete.

And there was this world of dust and darkness.

She could not sleep and blot the world away. The rare moments her mind calmed, the wagon bumped, stones leapt up from the wheels and pummeled her. The only good she could summon was the fact that her boils, despite the jarring and jolting, healed as they ground their way north.

The days, holed up in makeshift shelters and woods or abandoned farms, were filled with the fear of being found. They could not explain this odd assemblage of Negroes and a white woman, child and adults, man and women. No matter how hard any of them thought, no explanation made the least sense. Esther may have scared off one halfwit with her talk of magic and Pompey's seeming invisibility. But that was luck, and they all knew it.

CHAPTER 81

Comfort woke feeling the heat radiating from her daughter. It was still daylight and she thought for a moment that it might be the sun making her so warm. But the thought quickly passed. Rose was sweating and squirming in her sleep, restless, her face twisted and pained. She was, Comfort knew, caught in a nightmare loop, the same non- sense playing out over and over.

Rose coughed a small dry cough. It was enough to wake Esther who dozed nearby. Comfort and Esther's eyes met, then shifted. Esther could see the perspiration beading on the child's forehead. The coughing woke Rose up. Esther looked around the little clearing surveying the plants that grew there. They had stopped the wagon just before daylight in a clearing near an abandoned farm. What grew was a combination of plants native and those introduced by the farmer or his wife. Esther noted flax growing. That might work on the cough, she thought. And if her eyes weren't misleading her there was Balm of Gilead growing at the end of the fallow field.

"Esther help you," she said getting up and heading toward the plants.

A breeze picked up and made Rose shudder. There was a chill on the wind as the sun dipped toward the horizon. Esther returned with different plants. "We'll need to boil these when it's safe." Comfort could smell the balsam from several feet away. She nodded. Esther had also found some gnarled apples and picked as many as she could carry in her skirt. Comfort ate hungrily, but Rose refused even the bite her mother offered. Worry crossed Comfort's face like a shadow.

Pompey, who had appeared without anyone noticing, leaned against the wagon. He had a flour sack at his feet. When Comfort and Esther saw him, he grinned and offered them sweet potatoes from the sack. They were a meal.

❧

She knew it was very risky, but she had no choice. Esther sent Pompey into the woods to find a copse of dense trees that would prevent her from being seen. She asked him to build a compact, smokeless fire for her and find some flat stones. She would boil some water and make an infusion with the Balm of Gilead. With the flat rocks she hoped to grind the flax seeds into powder.

Both would be difficult to get into Rose, but they had to try, the child was getting sicker by the day, her cough more thunderous and the whistling intake of breath was alarming. After a coughing fit that might go on for many minutes, she would collapse into her mother's lap and sleep for hours. Pompey would pace when a fit came on her. He strutted and worried because he had had whooping cough as a boy; it had stolen his voice and kept him sickly for years. He watched the girl with sadness in his eyes. He would do anything for her, but there was little anyone could do to help. Not even Esther's Roots could help now, he thought.

He stood by waiting to be sent on another errand as Esther added deadwood to the fire. He watched and bit his lip. He paced until Esther sent him off to seek Purple Knockweed—he made her nervous.

Comfort climbed back into the web beneath the wagon soon after nightfall. Esther had made up her mind that she had to risk sitting in the wagon with Rose, the child needed to be held. If anyone happened upon them, it would be all the more suspicious, but she hadn't a choice. So far they had run three nights and saw only two Negroes who bowed slightly in passing, but said nothing and did not slow down. Not since the encounter in the woods—was it days or weeks ago?—had Esther dealt with a white person, but she knew that luck couldn't last forever.

Tonight they would make it into Sussex county, and it was ground they all feared more than anything. It was the home of Joe Johnson and Patty Cannon. Caught by them and they might as well plead for death. So they tried not to think about the danger and pulled the darkness around them like a blanket. They could feel the chill returning to the air.

As the horse took its first step, Rose began spasms of coughing that seemed endless. Esther held her loosely as the thunderous bursts collided with the calm of the night. Then the high whistling intake of breath came. When she was done, Rose collapsed in Esther's arms and did not move for hours.

CHAPTER 82

The rider approached, slowed, then blocked the road as if he could see through the oily dark lit by a moon that seemed no larger than the whiteness rising at the base of a thumbnail. He stared in the direction of the wagon until Pompey saw him and pulled the reins and stopped the horse. The stranger climbed down from the horse just as the first tendrils of sunlight slid through the trees. He walked around the wagon and surveyed what he'd found.

"Can we help you?" Esther finally asked, her heart galloping loud enough for all to hear.

"Morning," he grudgingly offered.

"Morning," she responded.

"This your nigger?" he asked, his head nodding toward Pompey.

"Yes, sir," she said as boldly as she dared.

"Who's sleepin' in the back?"

"His daughter," she said without hesitation.

"A bit odd, ain't it?"

Esther froze. "Odd?" she said, sounding perplexed by the question.

"Yeah. White woman. Negro man. Negro child. Driving a cart at night. I'd call that odd. Or suspicious. Got nothin' to hide, why not ride in the day time?"

"I, umm, I was in a hurry to get home."

"That so?"

"Yessir, that's so. I been to my brother's in Virginia for two weeks. I want to get home now."

Beneath the wagon Comfort followed every syllable that was spoken. As each one burst into the air, the story sounded lame. Don't think I'd believe it neither, she thought.

The stranger gave the horse a slap as he walked by it, still inspecting the wagon. He took his Harper's Ferry flintlock from the saddle.

"What you got that for?" Comfort heard Esther ask. It sounded ominous.

"Cause I think you're up to no good."

"We been up to good," she said defiantly, "we almost worked ourselves to death helping my brother when he was sick and had no one to run the farm."

"Hmm," he said and walked next to Esther. In a flash he had Esther's hand and inspected for cuts or other wear and tear. They were smooth. "Farm work, you say? What was you doin', milkin' cows?"

Pompey had, from the time they stopped, sat stock-still

and tried to blend into the dark. The stranger kept a close eye on him thinking he might run.

Rose sat up suddenly in the back and called out, "Mama."

Esther closed her eyes. It was over. Done. The whole foolhardy plot was cracked and crumbling as they sat in the sunrise.

The stranger stood still. He was right. He had no idea how right he was, but the whole mix of people and situation was just out of balance.

"That nigger child's not yours."

"No, I told you she's his."

Pompey nodded a slow, scared nod. "Why doncha speak, boy? You ashamed of that little girl?"

"He's dumb," Esther said, "Mute."

"Uh huh," the stranger said. "Here's what I think. I think he stole that child, his or not, from some innocent plantation owner, and you're an abolitionist helpin' him. Do I have that about right, cause I think I do?"

"No, that's not right. I told you the truth."

"Why'd that child call out for her Mama?"

"She died. Recently." Esther said. Her mind spun and fumbled. Her indignation dissolved in the full blare of sun pooling in the soft sand. Comfort waited. She was trapped. Every bit of control she had was being drained and an irrational voice in her head told her to climb down and run away. Her fists gripped the web, then relaxed and untied the rag from around her eyes. She was facing down, she could see the man's boots. He was facing Esther, she knew that, and except for him everyone else was still in the wagon.

"Mama," Rose cried out again. She seemed terrified of the man with the gun and she wanted Comfort for protection.

"I ain't stupid, Ma'am. I know somethin's goin' on here. I just ain't got it figured out yet."

"I have not lied to you," Esther insisted.

"You have," he said with confidence, "and I'll prove it. Next time that pickaninny hollers for her Mama, I'm gonna shoot her."

Comfort gasped.

A grin came to the stranger's face. "My, my," he said. He walked to the side of the wagon and dropped to his knees. He looked up past the wheel into the shadows. Comfort stared into his face and then at the rifle.

"How many more you got hid away?" he asked rising and smiling.

CHAPTER 83

Comfort climbed from the web in panic. The stranger staggered back when he saw her face. Some of the boils still wept and the dirt from the road clung to the pus. Even Rose screamed when she saw her mother—when they sheltered during the day, her face was washed clean and she was not the horror she was now. Esther sat still, constraining herself from reaching out to the child. It wouldn't look right, and we're already in trouble, she thought.

"What are you gonna do to her?" Esther asked the stranger.

"Where'd you steal her from?"

"We didn't steal her. I tole you."

"Then why you hidin' her under the wagon?"

Esther stared at him. She suddenly remembered that she was a white woman talking to a white man. "Why do you think?" she snapped at him.

The man only stared back.

"Because we were just trying to get her back to Wilmington without problems like this one." They could not run, she knew that. She wished Pompey might hit the man in the head, but when he came to he would be on them in no time.

Pompey thawed from his statue like posture and looked at the man. He pointed at the stranger then motioned as if he were cradling a baby.

"Me?" the man asked. "What?"

"He wants to know if you have children. "What's he care?"

"Guess he wanted to know how you'd like your child ripped from you like Rose here was from her." She pointed to Comfort.

"What are your sayin'?"

"Joe Johnson."

"What about him?" he seemed shaken just hearing the name.

"Her husband gave her to Johnson for a gambling debt. Johnson sold her. She's a free woman."

He looked at Comfort who had cleaned some of the dirt from her face and held Rose tightly to her chest and calmed her. Esther looked at the man's eyes. Comfort, too afraid, stole only brief glances. She wondered how many times a human heart could be broken, because hers was pounding again, and she feared it might burst.

"I got three children," the man said, his voice distant, and suddenly sad. "Two others died tryin' to be born."

"I'm sorry," Esther told him.

"It was a long time ago," he said. "My wife's dead now too."

Esther watched him carefully as he changed before them from one who would shoot a child, to one who mourned the deaths of two children from long ago. His eyes softened, they were a father's eyes now, not those of a hard stranger.

Esther slid Comfort's manumission papers from her pocket and unfolded them as the stranger stared off into a distance she could not see, and hoped she'd never know. She thought how odd it must be to be a man and show none of the softness they must have had once, but must callous over early to be a man. She knew when he returned this part of him, perhaps buried or scarred over since his children died, she would watch him transform yet again, tuck himself into the part he had created for himself in the world, and they would be no closer to escaping this encounter than they were when he first stopped them. She looked to Comfort and saw panic, and fear and sadness play across her face. She wanted to hold them both if this were going to be their last minutes together. But she stiffened her back, and waited.

Slowly his gaze returned from a long-ago sadness, to the trees beyond the road, to the faces around him. Esther held the manumission document toward him.

"You Comfort Mifflin?" He looked straight at Comfort and Rose.

"I am," she said looking down.

"Look at me," he said. She looked.

"This paper says you're a free woman."

"Yessir."

"Only a few months ago."

"I paid my freedom price. Then Mistress died."

He handed the paper back to Esther, and nodded. They waited and held their collective breath, a huge ache gathered around them, pulled tight like a snake slowly draining the breath from them. Killing them. Letting them feel the death coming to them all.

The stranger placed his rifle back in his saddle. "I'll ride on ahead," he said so quietly they almost didn't hear.

"We to follow you?" Esther asked in a controlled panic.

"Ma'am, Joe Johnson's known in these parts. I'll ride ahead at least into Delaware."

"You ain't takin' Comfort?"

"No Ma'am," he said and rode off.

CHAPTER 84

Isaac and Fillis nibbled on the hackwood leaves just enough each day to keep their skin erupting and a slight fever just in case they were stopped. Isaac doubted the hurried document Master Osborne had thrown at their feet was legal or complete to keep them out of bondage if someone chose to capture them. But the few folk they passed, black or white, simply gawked at the two of them and passed as quickly as they could. They were pleased.

They had bundled their few belongings minutes after Beck left them with Master's demands. They had taken only a few potatoes and some beets. Everything not in the bundles was on their backs. They knew only that they were following the north star toward freedom if they could hold out.

The second morning, a scarred man on horseback approached them and slowed. Clancy, without a moment's hesitation, melted into the landscape. The horseman wiped his eyes thinking he had seen something, but there was nothing, certainly no black dog. Their appearance didn't seem to affect him as it did the others. "You got papers?" he demanded.

"Yessir, we got papers done up by Master hisself before he threw us off the farm a' his for bein' with the plague, or the pox or whatever we got."

"Where do you think you're goin'?"

"North to die, I 'spect. We ain't got nobody here no more."

"I could get fifty-sixty dollars for the two of you just down the road."

"Yessir, I s'pose you could at that. But Master already buried one slave, he didn't want the responsibility of buryin' us shortly."

"One dead?"

"Yessir, a young, strong woman too."

"Any others?"

"Don't know. Could be the whole farm's infected. It come on us sudden when we cared for the girl."

"Where's this farm?"

"Down the road, a day's walk or so. But we move slow."

"Prob'ly a couple hours on horseback," he mused out loud. Isaac looked at the man and the ugly black scar that crossed his face and snaked into the dirty hair.

"Who's your master?"

"Was Osborne 'til he throwed us out."

"Martin Osborne and that dump he calls a plantation?"

"Yessir. That be the one."

"Well I'm gonna ride there and if you been lyin' to me, and maybe even if you ain't, I'm comin' back for the two of you. I'll find you. I got a nose for niggers—free or runaway."

Isaac and Fillis both blinked and began walking.

Clancy emerged from the woods, teeth bared as he would at a snake.

CHAPTER 85

While Comfort hung beneath the wagon, she could hear Rose hack and rumble into another fit. Rose was not even waking up because of the coughing anymore. She was unconscious with the fatigue it brought on. Esther took a chance sitting in the back with Rose, but the child heaved and shook violently as the long expirations seemed as though they would harrow every sip of breath she had left in her. Then the suspirations would bring on the vomiting of bile, and then an unsettling calm.

The stranger heard the girl coughing far up ahead. He turned his horse and drove back to the wagon. He was going to admonish them to keep the child quiet, but when he saw her, he said nothing.

"There's a doctor in Seaford," he offered, "we're about ten miles from there." "Thank you," said Esther. "I think we need to find him."

Comfort heard the conversation, but lay helpless to do anything. She couldn't even bang on the wagon boards to let Pompey know she wanted out. She stared at the road dirt and felt her own breath sucked from her lungs.

Rose was going to die. Comfort could feel it, like a sad

dream, over take her thoughts and spin wildly inside her blindness and hopelessness. She hung upside down in the ropes, caught like a fly in a spider's web. Between the agony of Rose's coughing and her own bondage inside the web and gag and blindfold, she thought she might know the madness of her father before he gave up upon her mother's death and wandered off to God knew where.

Pompey, perhaps sensing something, pulled the wagon into a small wooded field and stopped the horse.

Comfort fell from the web tearing at her eyes and mouth, then grabbing Rose from Esther's lap and hugging the limp child close to her. Comfort fell to her knees and wept for the helplessness that was her sanity.

"There's a doctor in Seaford," Esther whispered, "the man said." But Comfort didn't hear her.

CHAPTER 86

Pompey jumped down from the wagon and seemed to effortlessly melt into the wooded countryside. Esther admired that ability, and his quickness of mind. What wonderful conversations they might have had that would have calmed many of their fears.

She took the reins and slapped the horse to get him moving. They trudged into town fifty yards behind the stranger who had become a kind of guardian, albeit at a silent distance. Comfort sat in the back holding Rose. The look on her face said the child was already dead. But she wasn't, and she had not had a coughing fit in hours. Esther continued to give her the Balm when she would take it. She tried to make her swallow the ground flax seeds, but she spit them out, and that tiny act seemed to wear Rose out. Esther thought it wasn't worth the effort.

Comfort moved mechanically through everything Esther directed her to do. She held Rose, mopped her brow, tried to make the child comfortable even though she seemed to be unaware of anything else in the world, that world had dilated to her tiny, sickly offspring, alternately conscious and unconscious, sweating and shivering, coughing and vomiting from the strain.

The stranger stopped his horse and waited for the wagon to draw closer. He pointed down a narrow street in Seaford, turned forward again in his saddle and rode off. He said nothing. Esther turned the wagon down the street afraid of what they might hear if the doctor even deigned to see the child.

The doctor was backing out of his office door as they drew up in front. He was an older man with bristly, long white hair and a large mustache. He squinted as Esther approached him.

"The child," she said softly and trying to keep a respectable distance from her slave and the child, "is very sick."

"With?" the doctor asked as if perturbed.

"I can only tell she coughs so hard she passes out, or

vomits, or both. When she finally breathes in she whistles like a giant bird."

The doctor narrowed his eyes. "Pertussis," he said sharply. He seemed to grow less severe as they spoke. He walked to the wagon and looked at Comfort and Rose. "Mother doesn't look too well herself."

"No, Sir. She's scared to death she might lose her child."

"Just might," he said. "They yours?"

Esther hesitated. She had gone over this in her head, but now the words would not

"Are they yours?" he repeated.

"Yes, yes they are," she said and blushed. They were eye to eye for several moments.

"Have you or the mother tried to treat her?"

"Umm, I tried to get an infusion of ..."

"Of what?" he snapped.

"Of Balm of Gilead," she said, "It was all I could find for coughs. She spit out the ground flax seed."

"Hmm," he responded. "Can't hurt," he mumbled. Then looking at Esther again, he said, "Probably do as much for her as what I can give her. Drive the wagon around back and I'll let you in." He turned and unlocked the door.

CHAPTER 87

Cuff awoke. He was in some woods. But he always woke in the woods now. He was just unsure which woods these were. His left hand went instinctively toward the jug he always left nearby. He patted the ground without moving his eyes from the sun dribbling in through the top branches of the trees. He shivered as his hand patted an arc.

There was no jug, but his hand came down solidly on a large object. It hurt too much to move his head so he attempted to lift whatever it was and bring it to him. He was not curious so much as he was annoyed that the jug was not where it was supposed to be. What swung into view was a skull, a dog's skull judging by its size and shape. Cuff studied it a moment then let it fall.

He rose from the ground without brushing the dirt and grass from his pants. The world swam into view as he steadied himself against the tree. There was no jug. Dammit, he muttered under his breath. Then he smiled.

He stooped and picked the skull up. The rest of the skeleton lay off to the side. "Tooth," he said out loud, and the whole world glittered with new possibility. Even his headache glowed and glinted new sunlight.

CHAPTER 88

An evening haze was settling over road and field and wood. But through it, Joe Johnson could make out the wall of trees to his left and knew this signaled he was coming on the Osborne place. He heeled his horse to quicken the pace. If the old man's story was untrue, and they were old runaways, he wanted to get started back toward them, though he would not reach them until the morning.

Beyond the trees were the hulking shapes of tumbledown buildings, a miserable collection of rotten wood that bespoke failure, or perhaps defeat. From anyone's perspective it was a mean place where spirits died and only shadows carried on a dark dumb-show of work. Johnson thought of Martin Osborne's blasted eyesight and feeble grip on his slave's arm. "Pitiful," he said out loud.

The wheel ruts ran down to the road, and Johnson turned on to them and cursed this Osborne for risking his horse's legs. There was no sound. This time of day would have still found the field slaves winding down, but they would be there, the scrape-scrape of their hoes marking off the seconds and minutes until another day's labor would end, and they could drift back to their cabins, eat a few moldy bites of whatever might be available, and fall asleep, a deep, dreamless slumber that would carry each and every one of them out of the hamlet of fatigue and into the city of rest.

The haze obscured some of the landscape, but enough sunlight filtered in for him to survey the fields. He wished he didn't have to go to the house. It was an evil place.

In the distance he could see two hunched shapes, and for a moment he imagined that Osborne had finally snapped and killed his slaves since he half-killed them frequently with whippings and beatings that could be worse than death. He dismounted and tied his reins to a sapling. He walked slowly toward the shapes hunkered in the field near the woods.

As he drew closer he could see more clearly. Two bodies lay close to one another, one seemed as if death had come as a complete surprise, the other appeared to have tried to escape. The white man, Osborne, lay on a pillow of his own blood. His scalp had been partially torn back, his face and neck bore the slashes and gouges of multiple attacks. His mouth lay open and Johnson could see teeth on the man's tongue and some hanging by nerves in the center of what had been a face.

The other was a black man, the one, Johnson remembered, who was always nearby if not hip to hip with Osborne. His head, too, was bloody, his legs were twisted when the first blow brought him down and he spun to see his murderer. A hoe was implanted in his back.

Abolitionists, Johnson thought. But they generally weren't violent. Then he wondered if the slaves had revolted. He shook his head, and felt nothing.

He led his horse carefully along the ruts watching the

clutter of houses for signs of activity. He saw nothing move. At the cookhouse he peered inside and spotted an old Negro woman cowering on the floor, another had climbed under a table. Both were crying.

He left them and walked to the main house, a nightmare of rotting clapboard bleached gray by the sun. The roof pitched dangerously and the steps were broken and stove in. Johnson could only imagine what the nearly blind man must have seen in his mind. Is that where a mansion and plantation resided? He knocked on the door. No sound. He wondered if the wife and children hid somewhere in the dark interior. He called out, but heard only his own voice bouncing through the halls and rooms and returning to him.

He walked slowly and carefully with each step expecting his foot to crash through the floor. In the parlor, as his eyes adjusted to the dark and shadows, a girl, perhaps six, lay face up on a tattered rug. She seemed to have taken only one blow— to the forehead. A long gash cut down to shattered bone.

Upstairs, an immense woman lay in her bed as if sleeping. But this was an eternal sleep. Parts of her had been simply hacked away and blood had dyed the entire bedspread a deep, royal burgundy. Even Johnson turned quickly from the image and proceeded room to room. In one he found a teenager who appeared to have fought back. His hands were crisscrossed with deep cuts and his jaw was shattered. In another room there were two younger boys. And Johnson had had enough. He did not know how many children Osborne had, but it was clear no one was left alive, not a breath to be found except his own and two Negro women in the cookhouse. He shook his head and climbed down the stairs. He had seen this once before when slaves had revolted on farms that were like distant outposts with no friendly whites for miles. And he knew they could not be far, running, giddy perhaps with the freedom of escape, terrified of the consequences.

Johnson sat down on the steps of the little porch and struck a plan to capture them and sell them deeper into North Carolina or maybe even South Carolina. Not a word of what had happened, just a solid price and a quick sale. The corners of his mouth curled up slightly. But he did not enjoy the chase through unfamiliar geography. It was work and fraught with luck both good and bad. They had killed once, they would kill again. He forgot about the old white-haired Negro man and the woman with him.

He stood and walked to the cookhouse. Both women were in the exact place they had been a quarter of an hour before as if frozen in place and time.

"How many were there?" he asked impatiently. "How many?" when they didn't answer instantly. "You," he said pointing at the cowering woman. She only cried more. He moved as if he would attack her, but the other woman spoke up.

"She can't count."

"You can?"

"Yes, there were five," she said, still on her hands and knees under the table.

"From this farm?"

"Yessir."

"All men?"

"Three, they did the killin'. The women just ran."

"How come you and her didn't run when you had the chance?"

She stayed silent for a long time. When she spoke she spoke more to the ground than the man, a gesture long instilled by servitude. "I don't know," she said, "I don't know."

CHAPTER 89

Esther guided the horse down the narrow alley. She saw a door open part way, and she stopped. The doctor stood in the shadow.

Esther stepped down and walked back to Comfort and Rose. She laid her hand on Comfort's shoulder, and Comfort startled into wakefulness, a look of confusion on her face as she hugged Rose closer to her.

"A doctor is going to look after Rose," Esther whispered.

"A doctor?" Comfort asked.

"Yes. Remember, he thinks I'm white and you're my slave. Don't say much."

Comfort nodded.

Rose woke with an explosive cough and the doctor hurried to the wagon and lifted the girl into his arms. Esther followed, not waiting for Comfort to climb down and catch up. When the spasms stopped, the doctor looked into her throat and listened to her labored breathing. "I think you've done about all you could have," he said to Esther. "I've got elixirs that might sooth the cough ..." He motioned her to a corner of the room.

"About the best I can offer," he said in a hushed voice, "is to give her something that will let her rest, but I think you'll be taking her home to die."

Esther tried not to let her shock seem too obvious. If Rose died, she was sure Comfort would die, too. There was a quiet in the room like a presence, a stillness that dilated and expanded like breath, like hope and hopelessness filling the room. All they could hear was Rose's breathing, the jagged little halations that ripped at the silence, frayed its edges and bound the four of them together for the moment.

"Don't you have medicine?" Esther finally asked.

"I'm afraid it has to run its course, over a month or two. I could give you an elixir, but mostly it will just let her sleep. He winked at Esther and said under his breath, "It's just a pickaninny."

Esther bristled. "What is that supposed to mean?" she asked.

"What it sounded like," he snapped.

"Thank you for your time. We'll be going."

"Where?"

"North."

"To?"

"Why do you want to know, so you can send the undertaker?"

"A courtesy question," he said, unperturbed.

"Wilmington," she said, "then Pennsylvania, I suppose."

"She won't last the trip," he said, nodding toward Rose. "She needs a bed and some quiet," he said loud enough for Comfort to hear.

"She'll get that soon enough," Esther said.

The doctor busied himself among vials and bottles. Comfort rocked Rose in the chair and seemed to stare off into infinity, a blank look on her face that spoke of nothing but concern for the child, a complete disregard for herself.

"Esther," the doctor said, not looking at her.

"Yes," she said. Then she froze.

CHAPTER 90

Esther did not turn to face the doctor. She looked at Comfort and Rose and felt a wave of fear pass by her. How did he know? What in their conversation had given her away?

She turned toward him, her head down. When she looked up, she saw the handbill and read the news: "Esther: Absconded: Fair: One blue eye, one brown."

"Your eyes. You can't hide those," he said with no look on his face that she could read.

She looked back at Comfort and a look of realization flickered in Comfort's eyes for a moment. For that moment she was not looking into her child's grave, not looking into a future of numbness and regret. She was hardening, determining that nothing, not even death was going to take her child. And they were not going to take Esther.

Comfort sat Rose on the chair and approached the doctor. She held out her manumission papers. "I am a free woman," she said with force.

"I see that," the doctor said. "But I have said nothing of detaining you."

"And what do you have to gain by holding Esther? She only been helpin' me. She went into Virginia to save me, now you 'spect me to give her up?"

"I could have the authorities here in a few moments. And I don't know if they would honor your papers or not. Your friend is a runaway. A noble one and a brave one, no doubt, but runaways are runaways and they are dealt with. Esther," he turned to the other woman, "you have stolen from your master. He has a right to have his property returned to him."

"Yessir," she said, numb. Her thoughts spun and collided. She tendered the notion of merely walking out of the door and driving from town. But she knew it would not be long before she was caught, and they might not be as benign as the doctor. She let the idea go. Comfort continued to talk to the man, but he was not budging. He had caught her when she passed all the tests.

"She is the woman advertised here, is she not?" Comfort read the handbill.

"Doesn't she have one blue eye and one brown?"

"She does."

"Is she fair skinned?"

"Yes, but she's white. I'm sure lots of white women have differ'nt colored eyes, ain't that so?"

"I suppose."

"Then can you be certain you ain't makin' a white woman's life hell until this master says it ain't her, or worse says she is when she ain't?"

"Two things gave her away."

Esther looked up. The conversation had an abstract quality to it. They were talking about her, but she drifted away, watched them talk, but refused to be the subject, the embodiment and flesh of their words. Now she was curious.

"She hesitated when I asked if you were hers."

"Good reason she had. She was indentured. She knows what's like to be owned."

The doctor drew back, rested his right elbow in his left hand and brought his right hand to his face. "I see." He looked at Esther. "That true?" he asked.

She nodded immediately. Esther started immediately to think of everything she could from Mistress Mifflin's story.

"And the second thing?" Comfort asked him, his certainty shaken.

"Roots."

"Roots?" Comfort asked.

"Yes. Whites don't know about Roots. It's a Negro knowledge, a slave knowledge—from Africa."

Comfort's shoulders slumped. She couldn't argue that.

"It began with the eyes," he said, not unkindly.

"He will kill her," Comfort said, almost to herself.

"Unfortunately," the doctor said, "he has that right

under these strange laws."

"Nobody has the right to kill another person," Comfort said indignantly, "and you a healing man."

"I didn't say I agreed with them. But they are the law, and we fought a revolution for the right to have those laws."

Comfort shook her head. "I have a sick child and I want to take her home. I would like you to let Esther come with us. I'll hide her and get her out of Delaware."

Her words hung in the small office until Rose heaved into a coughing fit. The doctor lifted a bottle of elixir from a high shelf and handed it to Comfort.

CHAPTER 91

Comfort nearly forgot to return for Pompey. She drove out from the back of the doctor's office and could not remember which way to go. Tears stung her eyes. She was leaving Esther behind, and there was nothing she could do. She might be taking Rose home to die, and there was nothing she could do.

All of the nights she lay in her Virginia cabin, she had never cried like this—not over the finger wrenched back and broken, not over the relentless sun after a summer of chill, not over the endless hours of drudge work in the field when she could not imagine seeing her daughter again. She had needed to hunker down and find a place in herself that would not surrender, would not admit that her free life, only weeks old, was over.

She had not cried so hard in the wagon going south, gagged and bound and heartsick that her husband could do this to her, to her and their daughter. But now she let it come, let the enormity of her loss, and her future loss, flow.

As quickly and effortlessly as Pompey had dissolved into the woods, he reemerged, took the horse by the harness and slowed her to a stop. He looked up at Comfort with a grave look on his face. Comfort slid to the passenger's seat and held the reins out to him. He climbed up and took them. He looked in the back and saw Rose bundled and unconscious. He didn't know what to think, nor could he find a way to ask it.

They drove north.

"Caught," Comfort managed between the heaves of this storm, and the onrush of tears, and tears, and tears.

CHAPTER 92

Esther sat primly in a small chair intended for a child. Her hands were clasped in front of her and she appeared dazed. She stared beyond the neat little room where she was kept. Something, a figure or shape far off very slowly was coming closer. The sunlight coming through the high window was speckled and the motes danced.

What was coming toward her, she wondered, then realized it was of her own creation. She could not see out of the room, or down the hallway or out of doors. She was staring into her own future, and slumped into the chair with the realization.

In the parlor, Dr. Samuel Jefferson sat down hard on a chair and put his elbows on his knees, then his head into his hands. He rubbed his eyes hard with the tips of his fingers, and stars shot through the darkness, lights of different colors bloomed and faded.

His wife watched him. "How long are you going to make her wait?" she nodded toward the little room down the hall where the girl named Esther was kept.

"Not long," he said. "Don't want to be cruel. Just want to give her time to settle down."

"She won't eat, not enough anyhow."

"I know, I know," he said, rising and crossing the room.

"She's been in there a day and half. I go in, she's sitting and staring. I try to talk to her and it's like I'm not even there." Like her husband, her hair had turned white, but she wore it today like a younger woman, loose and falling below her shoulders. She wore a snood, but not a knotted one like Esther's."

The doctor nodded. "She's convinced her master will kill her."

"And you want to prolong that agony?"

"No, of course not."

She looked at him as she would a problem child who could not see the problem. He stood. "Bring her out here, would you please?"

She nodded and walked off down the hall.

❋

Esther stood in front of the doctor and his wife, she refused to sit. He cleared his throat several times.

"Esther," he began. "I'm very sorry we have kept you confined for the past day and a half, but we wanted to give you time to gather your thoughts. If those thoughts have been a jumble of fear and confusion, for that, too, I'm sorry."

Esther glanced up for a moment, then dropped her eyes again. It was fear, she thought, but it was more. It was shame. She stood here an owned woman. These people were either secretly gloating that they had caught her, or they were pitying her. Either way, she wanted to shrink to a tiny dot and dance with the other motes on the air of her temporary room. There they would not be able to tell her from the rest and she might go on dancing and being anonymous until she died. To remain herself meant a beating at the very least, and probably death.

His voice broke into her thoughts. "It is important that you listen to what I am going to tell you."

She returned slowly to the room and the hum and halt of his voice.

"You have obviously passed convincingly for white for many weeks now." She nodded an almost imperceptible nod.

"It is not easy to do. Too many light skinned Negroes delude themselves into believing that just because their skin is pale that they can fool a society hell bent on enslavement."

It was, to Esther's ears, an odd statement he was making.

After all, what did it have to do with him, or his wife, or to Master Clendaniel who would soon enough be on her with a whip, perhaps raping her first.

"Do you follow what I'm saying to you?"

"No," she mumbled.

The doctor looked at his wife in frustration. She nodded toward Esther. "Just tell her—without all the words."

He cleared his throat again. "There is a community, a small one hereabouts, of Negroes passing as whites. Some are freemen, some are runaway slaves. Some have been passing for years, some a good deal shorter. I have identified them all when they've come to my office. Their secret is safe with us," he said, pointing to his wife.

Esther's eyes rose to meet theirs. "There are more like me?"

"Like you," he said, "and like us."

Esther's breath caught and her eyes grew wide. "Us?" she repeated.

"I have been passing since the Revolution, my wife for twenty-two years." He stood in silence and let the information sink in.

"We can help you into that community," his wife said, "if you want to go."

"Why do they want to pass for the rest of their lives?" Esther finally managed.

"Some are quietly working for the cause of abolition. Some know they can hide out more successfully in full sight. We could move you in among them as a cousin or niece. The rest of the community never thinks anything of it."

Esther was dumbstruck. She was not going back to Clen-daniel, that much seemed clear to her, but she had no desire to play a part for the rest of her life and run the risk of one day saying or doing some little thing that might betray her.

"You don't have to answer right away. Take your time to think about it. It will be a complete change in your life."

She had already made up her mind. She needed to be with Comfort and Rose. Esther needed to help doctor the child because Comfort could not lose her. It had broken her heart when Comfort drove away, both stunned into tears and gestures of desperation.

"I need," Esther began slowly, trying to pick her words carefully. "I need to find Comfort and Rose. She is almost like my child too."

Esther slowly told the doctor and his wife the story of the past few months. When she was done, both stared at her. "We will take you where you need to go, you can travel as our niece," the doctor's wife said.

CHAPTER 93

Cuff held the dogtooth in his palm along with the half-penny and the nail. He could feel the power returning. His senses keened. He would soon be back on top. He could feel the world brightening around him. It would be good to have bags of money again, the still going and blue flame flowing. Maybe he would go south, he thought, and try to find Comfort. His head filled with ideas and plans, a long line of them marched inside his head. Then others came along and moved the earlier plans aside. It was exhilarating, like selling his first batch of blue flame, like picking the undersized cock to win, then winning. Picking the untried filly, and winning big.

Cuff fairly danced. He smiled his first smile in weeks—or was it months—he had lost track. He thought suddenly of Rose, and winced. He would buy her things—clothes, toys, whatever she wanted. He remembered her smile and how she would jump into his arms. And the smile faded.

He had long ago given over his fancy suit for his old raggedy clothes from his days in the Mifflin household. But nothing said he had to dress for the races. That was part of the foolhardiness of the past. He would go as he was and if somebody had a problem, it was their tough luck.

The track was quiet. The fall races did not attract the same summer crowd. And it was cold, colder than the cold summer by degrees. He stood at the edge of the woods and watched the scene. Men milled about as they always did at the races. Some looked over the horses, some talked in small groups. The man who took bets sat on his log stump and waited for the money. His son tended the meat-roasting pit.

It felt like it had. It felt good.

The bet-taker watched Cuff as he came near. "What you want, boy?"

Cuff smiled at him. "Don't you remember me?"

"Can't say as I do. Why would I?"

"Blue flame?"

"Where's your suit. Don't recognize you without the suit, and mute."

"Aw, both of 'em's long gone. And good riddance."

"Got yer flame with ya?"

"Naw. Still's been shut down awhile," he said sheepishly, looking at the ground.

"Damned shame."

"It'll be back, real soon. I'll bring you some." And he walked off toward the horse corral. His hand in his pocket felt the magic—the tooth that bit, the nail that scratched and the halfpenny that dimpled his fingers when he squeezed it tight. The power surged up his arm, and he thought his hair might stand on end.

Cuff watched the horses carefully as they grazed or whinnied when someone patted their neck or flank. There were no horses he recognized. He worked his way around the outside of the corral, paying no attention to the stares. He was the only Negro among them, and with no blue flame to calm their distrust, he moved slowly and carefully, drawing as little attention to himself as he could.

He held the magic trinity cupped in his hand. As he drew his hand down one neck after another he got or did not get signals, like the horses were speaking to him, or refusing to speak. He paid very close attention to the tingling in his forearm, the numbness when the horse refused the touch.

Without warning, the tooth bit his finger, and Cuff jumped back from the horse and stared at her. Yes, he thought, that one. That one has spirit.

Then there were hands on his shoulder, and someone was yelling in his ear. "What the hell are you doin', boy?" More hands took his arm roughly and forced his hand open.

"What the hell is that, boy?"

"T'ain't nothin, jus' some things I picked up off'n the road."

"You been runnin' that hand by all the horses. Why?"

"I didn't mean to do 'em no harm."

"So why you do it?"

"Ain't nothin,' I said."

Then another voice: "You doin' some kinda voodoo on them horses, make 'em break a leg or pull up lame?"

"I don't know no voodoo. I'm just here like you to bet on the races. I don't want no trouble. I'll just move off and watch. I don't want no trouble."

Word of voodoo moved like a wave through the gathering that shifted from their little clusters to see what the commotion was about. "That boy doin' voodoo?" they asked. Within minutes it was no longer a question.

The first fist struck Cuff firmly on the side of the head. The second knocked the wind out of him and his legs gave out. Then it was no longer fists, but boots that struck and struck and struck until Cuff lay unconscious. The tooth, the nail and coin were scattered in grass and dust, powerless to do good, or any more harm. Had the bet-taker not seen what was happening and come to Cuff's aid, they would have killed him. He did not come to for an hour, his teeth were loosened or left as jagged shards in his mouth, his eyes swelled shut and blood ran from his nose and ears.

CHAPTER 94

Comfort was back in the chill air and the day was wringing out the last of its stingy light. She watched her hands closely as she tried to teach them to knot again. But the broken finger was painful and did not want to obey her commands. She threw the tiny piece of work down, but picked it up again immediately. "You won't keep me from my work," she addressed her middle finger. "You will not beat me. I been beat, but I won't allow my own body to hold me back. I got to make money."

Rose must have heard her and roused from her sleep. The coughing came less frequently in the past few days, and Rose slept a little less, did not seem as fatigued as she had during the worst of it. Comfort didn't know if it was the elixir, or just time that healed. But for the first time in weeks she felt hopeful. Hopeful and sad when she thought of Esther and the sacrifice she had made. She passed the Clendaniel house some days when she took Rose out to get some sun. But she saw no sign of Esther.

Rose laid her head on Comfort's leg. She slipped her hand into the little girl's hair and felt the dampness at the roots. "How you feel?" Comfort asked her.

She shrugged her shoulders. "Mama, I still sick," she said.

"You gettin' better."

"Poppa?"

"No, Rose. Poppa is gone. Aunt Esther is gone, but we might see her sometime." She felt the lie go deep. Clendaniel would not let them be together if he let her live.

"Want something to eat?" she asked to avoid thinking further about Esther. Rose wagged her head no, and pointed at her throat.

"Still hurts?"

Her head bobbed yes. "I'm sorry."

"Water."

"All right. And I'll have some too." Rose gave a hint of a smile.

Comfort poured water and watched her daughter drink. "You see," she said picking up the beginnings of a knotted piece, "Mama is knotting again. Gotta teach these ole hands to work small. This one doesn't want to help me out," she said pointing to her broken middle finger.

"Why?" asked Rose.

"Oh, it got broke—down there," she said pointing south.

Comfort raised the finger up before her face and spoke to it again. "You have to help me out," she said in a tiny voice.

"No, I don't," the finger replied in Comfort's deepest voice. "Yes, you do."

"Why? I can just sit here and feel sorry for myself."

"'Cause I owns you."

"I ain't your slave," the finger said. Rose was now giggling each time the finger spoke.

"No, you ain't. Let's call it 'dentured servant. How about

that?"

The finger twisted and bent slightly as if trying to decide. "Come on, said the other fingers, work with us like we used to ..."

There was a knock at the door. Comfort picked Rose up and put her on the chair. As long as she was home, she feared Cuff might come for her, or worse, come for Rose. "Stay here," she said to the child.

Comfort's palms began to sweat. Everything in the house now was in deep shadow, only the little oil lamp glowed where Rose sat drinking her cup of water.

She opened the door slowly. Esther smiled.

Comfort stood motionless for a very long moment, disbelieving. She didn't even notice the tears coursing down her cheeks and wetting the front of her dress.

CHAPTER 95

Esther and Comfort gathered the household items: clothes, a pot, a pan, Rose's freedom clothes and Comfort's. Pompey had secured a few wooden crates and some rough cloth unsuitable for anything that might come into human touch.

Esther kept to the interior, and most often to the deepest shadows, for the Clendaniel house was not very distant, and handbills seemed to be everywhere as the doctor and his wife, with Esther between them, approached Wilmington in their wagon.

Pompey, with Comfort helping, carried the boxes and bundles to the street. They didn't have much, so there was room in the far back to set up a pallet for Rose, who would no doubt sleep much of the time.

It had gone unspoken, but accepted, that Pompey would go, too. Cuff had been about all that kept Pompey here, so he could just as well continue his gregarious but solitary ways anywhere they might settle. His was an uncomplicated life, with little anticipated or planned for. A day to day existence, he thought to himself when he allowed such thoughts to come and ripen. He would then mentally shrug and move on. The trip south had unnerved him, but he never let it show. He was, now, happy to be heading farther north.

The wagon filled with Comfort's and Rose's possessions, by midday the contents of the house had all been transferred. The four of them sat on the floor looking relieved, but somewhat bewildered. "Got jes' one more thing to do," Esther said.

"I know."

Pompey's ears perked up. He looked around and saw only bare walls and floors. There wasn't a stick, stone, knife, doll or handkerchief to be seen. He scratched at his chin, and then his head.

"How?" asked Esther.

"I don't know," Comfort said matter-of-factly. "I've forgotten more ways than I dreamed of."

"But you know his dyin' was the onliest thing kep' you livin' down there," she pointed south.

Pompey wished they would be less elusive in their conniving. It was clear something had to be done, but what? He was afraid to find out. It did not concern him, and he got up. Like a dream he vanished. Neither Comfort nor Esther saw him or heard him go. Only Rose followed his every move as he slipped into shadows and then out the door. It was several minutes more of vague conversation before either of them noticed he'd left.

"Somethin' heavy like a hammer, you s'pose?"

"Dreamed that one too," Comfort told her. "And rope, water, rocks and birds."

"So if you dreamed it, you can't do it that way."

"Naw, I could. But it's like it's been done a'ready. You know?"

"No," Esther said, squinting toward the voice coming out of the darkness of the house.

"Guess it mus' be some craziness I dreamed too."

"Ain't crazy, it just don't make much sense. To me, anyway," she added.

They sat silent for some unmeasured time. Rose had her head in Comfort's lap, and Esther smiled at the awkward lump they made in the shadows.

"Where's Pompey?" Esther asked as if he had vanished before their eyes.

Rose reared up and pointed down the hall. "Out," she said.

To Pompey Pennsylvania was unknown territory as much as Maryland and Virginia had been. He wouldn't be afraid there, he realized, but he also didn't know what they drank there, so he had gone off in search of Mingo and the finest rum made since Cuff went out of business.

He had drunk nothing the entire trip, hadn't even slept much, but now he was thirsty and he would deny himself no more. If Mingo would agree to sell him a whole keg, then he might just rummage up the devil himself and bargain for a down payment on it. But a jug or two would be all right.

Mingo was no Cuff when it came to business. He was hard to find and tougher to pin down on quantity and price. And complaining left a man thirsty.

Comfort and Esther scoured the house for forgotten things one last time. They found nothing. Comfort went back to her bedroom and pulled away a loose piece of window frame. Beneath it was stashed her Freedom price, every penny mistress had taken and saved for her. It was the last thing the house owed her and it paid up.

Pompey returned to Comfort's and stowed three jugs of no flame in the wagon and covered them with some Osnaburg salvaged from someone's old trousers.

"You're back," Esther said.

Pompey smiled the smile of those familiar with the obvious.

"I think I'll need to get in the sling under the wagon," she told him, "at least 'til we get farther north than Philadelphia."

Pompey nodded in agreement. He had seen the handbills posted on trees and fences. He could make out a few words, but the gist of the message was clear. He pulled the wagon to the back of the house where Cuff's shed tilted and the blue-flame still inside remained cold and dry.

When there was no one on the street, Esther slipped out of the house and disappeared under the wagon. Gone. Clean as one of Pompey's vanishings.

CHAPTER 96

Esther lay in the web beneath the wagon, her mouth and eyes covered just as Comfort's had been. Rose lay in the wagon and Pompey and Comfort sat side by side as they made their way out of Wilmington. He worried what he might have to do if they found Cuff. He could fight like a cornered dog if he had to, but he couldn't kill, he'd even always found it hard to hunt.

They were back to the drudge of travel. Houses gave way to scattered shacks and lean-tos. The woods grew thicker and people were scarce.

But Cuff Mifflin staggered out of those woods, and stood bewildered at the side of the road. His eyes were shot with bloody veins, his lips were swollen, his wounds had scabbed over and his hair was a nest of twigs and grass. Comfort almost didn't recognize him. But when she looked to Pompey, he nodded, and his stomach sank.

For Comfort, this was the moment she had dreamed of, here was the man she got up mornings for. Because of him she worked the fields and that let her know she was still alive and still had a purpose—to kill him. Cuff stared at the slowing wagon, barely comprehending what was taking place. Thoughts swam in his liquefied brain. He looked about to pass out from the effort to keep them all steadily in view. He tried to smile, but his lip burst open and he winced in pain.

Esther wondered why they'd stopped. There was silence, but she could make out a pair of shoes approaching, shoes like many slaves were made to wear.

"Comfort," he mumbled through tightly closed lips, "how'd you get back?"

She only glared at him and sat frozen in her seat, it was clear she could kill him with her bare hands. He nearly toppled over trying to stand still for a moment. Disgust flooded her brain and all of her senses breathed or tasted or felt an awful loathing.

Cuff walked to the back of the wagon. When he saw Rose, he reached for her, but Comfort was off of the seat and at him in a second. She punched him in the arm to block his reach. Her next volley hit him in the side of the head and in the chest and he staggered even harder.

"That's my child," he roared indignantly. "My blood."

"'Tain't your blood no more. You keep your hands offa her. She been real sick and she don't need no disease like her poppa to make her worse."

"You speak disrespectful to me," he said, raising his hand as if to deliver his own blow. Pompey threw his forearm across Cuff's throat and pulled him to the dirt backwards.

"Now you're where you belong," Comfort sneered at him. Suddenly Esther was glaring down at him from this semicircle of familiar faces. But he hadn't seen her in the wagon.

He wondered for a split second if he were dreaming, but the pain was real and the angry faces almost spit venom at him.

"Respect?" Comfort laughed.

"Respect," Cuff repeated with less force. "I am your husband."

"You were my husband, and that little girl is the only good thing to come outta that. Cuff Mifflin, you got to be a man to be a husband. You some dank swelled up thing in the dirt. I pity you."

Cuff rolled over and tried to stand. "I don't want your pity," he spat, "I'm comin' back, and I'll be rich again. Then you'll want to be my wife again. You'll see. I don't want your pity."

"But you got it. All of it."

Comfort returned to her seat holding Rose in her arms. Pompey looked up at her with a question furrowing his forehead. Esther seemed poised to help deliver a deathblow.

But Comfort had walked away. Death would only be a gift, now, she thought, already far from this moment and place.

READING GROUP EXTRAS

Questions and Answers
With the Authors

1. What attracted you to the "Reverse Underground Railroad"?

Maxson: I think the extremes of human behavior have interested me for a long time. Cuff demonstrates both kindness and depravity. Comfort endures unthinkable harshness as well as love and consideration from many people. Freedom and slavery are another diad. The "Underground Railroad" itself represents those two extremes as well.

2. How do the characters in Comfort support the plot structure?

Young: The characters of Esther and Comfort obviously needed to value freedom and independence, but they also needed to be resilient and strong. Their courage was necessary to confront their predicaments and find their way to freedom. Cuff's greed and ambition became the obstacle that set the plot structure in motion. The catalyst, however, is Pompey. His unwavering conscience sets him apart from Cuff and supplies the assistance and direction Esther needs to rescue Comfort.

3. Is there a historical character of Comfort?

Young: There is no "real" historical character of Comfort, but her situation was a very real issue. While hundreds of runaway slaves worked their way north along the Underground Railroad, there were numerous unsavory individuals who would kidnap free blacks and others of color, smuggle them south and sell them to plantation owners. The selling of these individuals was lucrative because the importation of slaves was banned after 1808. Any individuals with even slight coloring to their skin were at risk. This Reverse Underground Railroad is not well known, but was definitely real.

4. What does Rachel Mifflin represent to you?

Maxson: Rachel is one end of the spectrum of slave owners. In Frederick Douglas's and Solomon Northup's books we are introduced to slave owners who treat their slaves with respect—though not enough to set them free—and slave owners who treated them worse than animals and had no regard for their comfort, health or protection. Rachel has experienced, as an indentured servant, much of what a slave experienced. She has wisely learned from her experiences.

5. Why is the book set in 1816?

Maxson: 1816 was the "Year without a Summer." On April 10 (my birthday), 1815 (not my birth year) Mount Tambora in Indonisia erupted—the worst volcanic eruption in 1,300 years.

It caused a Volcanic Winter event across most of the Northern Hemisphere. It was also the last decades of the Little Ice Age. So it was a cold and hungry time. It has always seemed an apt metaphor for the coldness of the institution of slavery. It was also the summer that Percy and Mary Shelley visited Lord Byron at Lake Geneva. Because of the cold, a contest was suggested. The result was Mary Shelley's Frankenstein.

6. Maxson, you and your cousin Claudia have written seven historical novellas for young readers. Is Comfort also historical fiction?

Maxson: Comfort is historically accurate in several places: there was slavery in the U.S. in 1816; the information about tatting is accurate (our grandmother Peeden tatted, that's how we knew about that art); and the information about "Roots" is accurate, as is the eruption of Mount Tambora and the Year without a Summer. All of the characters are fiction. The town names are real Delaware towns, but we made no attempt to discover if the streets mentioned in the book existed then, or ever. As Edward P. Jones said in an interview once that he didn't do research on everything in his book (*The Known World*) because he didn't want facts to get in the way of truth. We wanted the book to be realistic but not get bogged down in details that don't matter much in the end.

7. Why is Comfort set on the Delmarva Peninsula?

Young: The Underground Railroad was very active on the Delmarva Peninsula. Harriet Tubman, its most famous conductor, was born on the eastern shore of the peninsula and helped many slaves wend their way northward through Wilmington, Delaware—a hotbed of abolitionism. However, the Reverse Underground Railroad was quite active in the more southern parts of the peninsula. Patty Cannon and Joe Johnson were notorious for their kidnapping and smuggling of free people, then selling them to plantations further south. While the Reverse Underground Railroad was undoubtedly active in other locations, our research strongly supported the location of the Delmarva Peninsula as our setting.

8. Comfort was allowed to work weekends tatting collars etc. for other women. Was it common for slaves to have even limited freedom to earn money?

Maxson: Rachel is fictional; Comfort is fictional; hence, their relationship is fictional. We made it up. It seemed like a kindness that Rachel would be capable of. I have just recently read Solomon Northup's very fine *Twelve Years a Slave* and discovered in fact that he often played violin at gatherings, while he was a slave, and was allowed to keep at least the tips, if not his actual pay for the event. It seems if the Master hired him out to someone else, the Master kept the pay. But the performing seemed to be handled differently. Some slave owners gave garden plots to their slaves to grow vegetables. If there was excess—a rare occurrence—they were allowed to sell the excess. So I guess Comfort's being allowed to earn her freedom price was not far off the reality mark.

9. The rider who confronts Esther, Pompey and Comfort as they make their escape is an unusual man for his time in the

South. He might be described as a Renaissance man because of his views on slavery and family. Comfort's rescue and Esther's escape could not have been successful without his help. What other present day forward thinkers have changed lives on a local rather than a global level?

Young: Leigh Anne Tuohy, portrayed by Sandra Bullock in the movie the *The Blind Side*, was a woman who saw a situation that needed to be rectified. She did not see the issues of race that many of her peers saw. Her intervention into the life of Michael Oher was life changing on a local and personal level. While globally people like Nelson Mandela work for racial equality, Tuohy acted locally. In my view, her forward and unselfish thinking places her in the category of a Renaissance person.

10. Esther passing as white is one key to the plot. Were there many blacks who passed for white at that time? Was there a real town?

Maxson: I don't know if there were a lot of slaves or free blacks who passed for white. Our reasoning was, some slave owners raped, had affairs with or even married their female slaves. So there must have been at least some offspring who could pass for white. How many? I don't have any idea. Was there such a town? No, only in our imaginations.

11. Pompey is an unusual character. Where did he come from?

Maxson: Pompey is a trickster in the ancient tradition of the trickster myths. He's not a shape-shifter, but he does seem to magically disappear at times. He is clever and resourceful and extraordinarily intelligent. Despite the fact that he spells like a young child, it's only because he was never taught. And that is not something one teaches himself generally. With a little urging and guidance he would probably become quite adept at anything he set his hand to.

12. Compare the legal practice of indenture to the situation in Ireland faced by poor farmers paying exorbitant rents for land, as recounted by Rachel.

Young: Indenture was a form of legal slavery. Indentured people had few if any opportunities to improve their lot in life. Irish farmers in the late 1700s often faced extreme economic hardship. They rented land from absentee English landowners who often charged exorbitant fees. When the fees could not be paid, the farmers were brutally forced to leave with few if any options to improve their circumstances. The lives of both the indentured persons and the impoverished Irish farmers were oppressed legally by wealthy aristocracy and the economics of their time.

13. What effect did Pompey's disability have on the outcome of Esther's plan to rescue Comfort?

Young: Pompey was mute. People ignored him because they assumed he was lacking in intelligence because of his disability. He was able to use that common assumption to protect Esther and Comfort. He was a loyal protector for the two women who could not have made the arduous trip without him. Unfortunately, even today people with disabilities are assumed to be lacking in intelligence or worth. People with disabilities are forced to prove themselves before they can be accepted with their true value.

14. Cuff has a lucky charm, or a group of objects he considers essential to his continuing luck. Why the charm and why those three objects?

Maxson: I believe the coin was there as kind of a stone in "Stone Soup," it started him on the path to more coins. The nail came from a church, the only building to survive a hurricane. Maybe that was luck, or just solid construction. And the dog tooth was just for fun. I have read that many slaves were religious or superstitious, or both. So, since Cuff grew up in Rachel's home, and she was Roman Catholic, it stood to reason that he would have some religion. Making him superstitious was a way to give another angle to his personality that the reader might not expect. Besides, he's a secretive guy.

15. Rachel reads to Comfort as she goes about her chores. Most slave owners didn't want their slaves educated in any way. Why does she broaden Comfort's horizons?

Maxson: For a couple of reasons: she knows that Comfort is industrious and ambitious. She knows she is coming to the end of her life and she wants to be sure that Comfort will survive in a difficult world. After emancipation in 1865, many slaves were so awed by the responsibilities that went with freedom that they were unable to live in the world and actually went back to their former masters and asked to be taken back as a laborer on the farms and plantations that for many was all they had ever known. Rachel knew freedom and she knew servitude. She is preparing Comfort carefully and quietly without Comfort ever knowing.

16. Were Patty Cannon and Joe Johnson historical persons?

Young: Patty Cannon and Joe Johnson were indeed historical persons. They lived in the southern sections of the Delmarva Peninsula, traveling back and forth across state lines for protection. Patty Cannon was the leader of a gang who kidnapped free blacks and others of color, selling them to plantation owners further south. Joe Johnson was her right hand man. This practice was lucrative for them because Congress had made the importation of slaves to the United States illegal in 1808. The value of slaves grew very high because of this importation ban.

Patty Cannon eventually was convicted of murder and died in prison in 1829. Her body was exhumed in the 20th century and reburied near a new prison. Her skull was separated from her body and placed on public view in numerous venues including the public library in Dover, Delaware. She was notorious for her cruelty.

17. Why is Cuff's moonshine dubbed "blue flame?

Maxson: If you are a collector of trivia as I am, you pick up all sorts of useless information that one day suddenly comes in handy. Somewhere along the years I read, saw or heard that to test their product moonshiners set a match to a small amount, the closer the flame is to blue, the purer the product.

18. Was Cuff held accountable for his actions?

Young: Cuff decided to sell whiskey for extra money, even though he knew the risks. He saw gambling on cock fights as a means to increase his profits. Though he was successful at first, he quickly fell victim to his own greed and ambition. When he could not control his losses, he became desperate. The only thing of value at his disposal was his wife. Essentially, he had to choose between his own life and that of his wife. When he chose to sell his wife, he chose not to be accountable for his own actions and it destroyed him. In the end his shattered life was his accountability.

19. What did Comfort discover about herself to help her survive?

Young: Self discovery is a life changing force. Comfort's life was turned upside down when she was betrayed by her husband. Cuff's betrayal fueled her anger and resilience. She discovered an inner strength to help her survive physical and psychological abuse and return to her daughter. She learned to use her own instincts of who to trust and who to ignore. She never gave up hope that she would be rescued.

20. How did fear affect Esther?

Young: Esther experienced fear of huge proportions. Her owner was a sadistic man who raped her repeatedly. Fear and desperation can immobilize you or it can motivate you into action. Buying her way to freedom could not happen because her owner manipulated her indenture agreement. Instead of accepting the abuse as her fate, Esther makes a plan to escape. Esther finds great courage to save herself and rescue Comfort. She uses the power of her fear to solidify her resolve to find a way out of her desperate situation. Esther uses every skill she possesses to find her way to freedom and a better life.

21. Discuss forms of slavery in the United States in 1816.

Young: Before 1815 the most common form of slavery in the United States was indenture. Two copies of the indenture agreement were written and signed on one piece of paper. The paper was then cut in an irregular pattern, ensuring that no changes could be made by either party. Both pieces of paper had to fit perfectly for the payment claim to be legal. The person indentured then worked to repay the debt and retake his or her freedom. The indentured person was completely at the mercy of his or her owner. While indenture was legal, little care was taken to determine the legal status of the person at sale.

After 1815, the most common form of slavery in the United States was lifetime slavery where the person enslaved could only become free through manumission. This was a huge change from indenture, where a person could work his or her way to freedom. Cotton farming in the South was becoming a major industry with a need for large numbers of laborers. Slavery was a means to meet those labor needs. The ban on the importation of slaves increased the value of slaves and complicated an already difficult situation.

Follow up question: Discuss forms of slavery in the world today.

✲

22. One last question. Someone once said, if you don't know what to ask about a book, ask about the dog—because there is

always a dog. What about the dog in Comfort?

Maxson: Clancy. Well, I had an old black lab named Clancy and he died during the time we were working on Comfort. I wanted to give him a chance to live at least in the book. Then we had to invent the story about all of the Irish men being called Clancy. So, at least for me, he's always there. I think a number of writers put things in their books and poems just for themselves. It's a kind of game that's played over the long months or years it takes to write and polish a novel or collection of poems. Another example is Rachel's maiden name, McArthur. It is my wife's maiden name.

REFLECTIONS ON THE NOVEL COMFORT

By co-author Claudia H. Young

History is a good story told well. As a teacher I saw my students recall the historical details of an engaging story, but immediately forget the material they read in a standard history text book.

I taught elementary school for sixteen years and loved every moment. After many years teaching first grade I changed over to a third grade classroom. Aside from the obvious differences in curriculum, I realized that my third graders were transitioning from an emphasis on learning the process of reading to learning the concepts of science and social studies by reading books and articles. They were like little sponges, eager to absorb information from their reading. My challenge was to meet the standards the state of Delaware and satisfy those thirsty brains at the same time. Social studies standards included specific goals for Delaware history—and here I was confronted with a dearth of materials with suitable vocabulary and reading level for my students. It was a huge frustration for me.

One evening at dinner with my cousin, Max, and his wife, I lamented this lack of appropriate social studies materials. It didn't take long for us to decide to start researching Delaware history with the goal of writing for children. Our venture blossomed into a small publishing company, Bay Oak Publishers. Over 13 years we wrote and published seven historical fiction books for children, each with a corresponding resource guide for teachers. We also published numerous books of poetry, one novel and two memoirs. One of the memoirs, *Dancing in the Garden*, was written by William Jay Smith, former United States Poet Laureate. It was an exciting and fulfilling time.

Our historical fiction titles for children were well received in the Delaware public school system. Our books are still in use in more than one third of the public elementary schools across the state. Max and I often gave talks to students about our Delaware history books. We described how we started each book with a field trip and research. We visited historical sites across Delaware and Maryland and met many wonderful people eager to help us find our information. Museum curators, archivists, ship captains, secretaries and history enthusiasts aided our research efforts. Students were enthralled to hear how we wrote a book together and how much time was spent editing. Max would bring his spearpoint collection to our presentations. He would describe how they were made and where they can be found today. Teachers would send us student written thank you notes that would inevitably refer to the spear points or arrowheads. These tangible artifacts made a significant impression on our young audiences. Our favorite note was from a student thanking us for sharing our "airheads." It is a reminder for us never to take ourselves too seriously.

In addition to historical site visits and interviews we read many books and articles on the history of the Delmarva Peninsula. Eventually we found a copy of *The Entailed Hat, Patty Cannon's Times* by George Alfred Townsend. Originally published in 1955, it was a cumbersome read. However, we were intrigued with the information about the notorious Patty Cannon and her companion, Joe Johnson, who terrorized Kent and Sussex Counties in Delaware in the early 19th century. They kidnapped, stole and murdered at will, often taking their victims to Richmond to sell at the slave market. Patty Cannon was noted for her physical strength as well as her horribly violent deeds. She remains the only person ever to be banned from the state of Delaware. One scene in the book stuck with us: a young black woman chained in a clearing, awaiting her fate at the hands of Patty Cannon and Joe Johnson.

At one of our many presentations to teachers we were asked about future topics for our children's books. We mentioned our interest in Patty Cannon and her exploits, but not as a children's story. A member of the audience—the keynote speaker, as we later discovered—asked if we had considered writing about the Reverse Underground Railroad—the selling of kidnapped men and women at slave markets. Much has been written about the Underground Railroad and Harriet Tubman, its most famous conductor. However, we found very little is written about the Reverse Underground Railroad. It's not pretty, nor is it romantic, but it is most definitely part of our history. Our story of Comfort came out of this conversation at our presentation.

Max and I discussed our plot structure for this new venture at length. Central to our thinking was character development. Comfort needed to be a resilient and strong survivor. Cuff, her husband, had his fatal flaws—his blind ambition and his gambling. Comfort's rescuer, Esther, needed strength of character. We decided she should have skills with herbs, both cooking and medicinal. Her courage made Comfort's rescue possible. Pompey, a mute with an uncompromising conscience, pulls the plot together.

History will always be a source for good stories. I have enjoyed this venture with Max to create Comfort's story. Perhaps adult readers can become more aware of this lesser known segment of our history. If not, I hope they simply enjoy the story.

H. A. MAXSON ON BECOMING A NOVELIST

What a long strange trip it's been

I began my writing career as a poet and as an occasional literary critic. My first three books were poetry collections. I continue writing poetry and publishing collections every few years. Early on I wrote a few short stories, but I delayed writing longer fiction (and non-fiction prose) for decades. Why? When I began writing in earnest, there were no personal computers. Everything was written long hand and then revised drafts were typed, and retyped, and retyped. I never learned to touch type despite the lessons in high school, so typing was a slow hunt-and-peck. I was not about to commit myself to seventy-five thousand words and probably years of typing a single manuscript. (Side note: I am now a demon on the keyboard, two fingers and a thumb a blur). However, I still write first drafts long hand.

So, I delayed writing my first novel, *The Younger*, until about 1988. By then I still had no computer, but I did have a Brother word processor with a two-line display. Better still I, had a full-time teaching job and enough money to pay a typist to produce a final draft. After researching dolphins, dolphin research, man-dolphin communications, and the bottle-nosed-dolphin die-off of 1987 for about four years, I plugged in my cassette tape of ocean sounds, sat down at my desk a few blocks from the Atlantic ocean, sharpened some number two pencils and opened my notebook.

I set myself the task of writing one thousand words per day, plus inventing dolphin history, culture, myth, laws etc. going back millions of years. Simple. No, but a workable text emerged and after a couple of years of rewriting, a publishable manuscript. was in the mail. The book was released in 1997.

In 2000 my cousin, Claudia Young, her husband, Dick, and my wife, Maureen, were having dinner at our house. Claudia was a public school teacher at the time, and she complained that there were no decent books available or appropriate for teaching Delaware state history to fourth graders. We had a pow wow in my den and quickly hatched the idea of researching and writing historical-fiction novellas on Delaware state history. So began a thirteen year collaboration that produced seven books and seven study guides for teachers under our own imprint, Bay Oak Publishers LTD. These books are now primary social study texts in about one third of the elementary schools in Delaware. We later published poetry and fiction by other Delmarva authors—including a memoir by a former US Poet Laureate, William Jay Smith.

Oddly, this leads me to Comfort. During the Bay Oak years we were often invited to speak to fourth grade classrooms and at writing conferences. At one of the adult gatherings we gave a presentation about our latest book (I can't recall which one). After our dog-and-pony routine, as we came to call it, there was a Q & A. We were asked what our next project would be. We said that were contemplating a two or three book series on the Underground Railroad—a significant portion of which ran through Delaware, including a stop in the governor's mansion.

In the audience was the featured speaker of the day, the author of either *Lies my Teachers Told Me*, or *Everything I Needed to Know I Learned in Kindergarten*—that was seven/eight years ago, I can't remember everything! Anyway, he said, why don't you write about the Reverse Underground Railroad. That stopped us cold. Since we had not yet begun researching the Underground Railroad, we were not familiar with the Reverse Underground Railroad. So we did what novelists do, we looked confused and then asked what the Reverse Underground Railroad was. He explained. We nodded. The audience nodded along with us. Then we went home and got started.

Our research was long and intense, especially since there are so many sub-texts to research as well—tatting; roots and spices; the eruption of Mt. Tambora in 1816, the year without a summer (the same year Mary Shelley wrote Frankenstein); geography, Joe Johnson (real life slaver and kidnapper of freed blacks, and by the way, one of the most reprehensible human beings in US, or any other, history). Since there are four stories being told, they had to be braided in such a way that made sense.

Our first draft of Comfort was chronological. When we landed an agent in California, he wanted more action in the beginning of the book, so we rearranged chapters (he has since retired due to health). A film script is being written based on the chronological version—same chapters, different order, under the title *Finding Comfort*.

Because of the braided narrative it seemed to make sense to write multiple short chapters rather than, say, twenty longer ones. That style suited me, as a poet at heart, just fine. There is a sense of accomplishment at getting a chapter draft done in one sitting.

Poet-novelist? Novelist-poet? Both bring with them a specific satisfaction. I cannot imagine abandoning either one. In fact in 2012 I published *Brother Wolf*, a novel in free verse. The manuscript had its beginnings as a book-length poem in the mid 1970's, was more or less abandoned, then lost for over 30 years. I found the notebooks in the 2000s, rediscovered why I had abandoned it—it wanted to be a novel—then rewrote it. So, full circle.

BIOGRAPHICAL NOTES

H. A. Maxson is the author of sixteen previous books—five collections of poetry (*Turning the Wood*, *Walker in the Storm*, *The Curley Poems*, *Hook and Lemon Light*); a book-length poem (*The Walking Tour: Alexander Wilson in America*) and a novel in free verse (*Brother Wolf*); a novel (*The Younger*); a study of Robert Frost's sonnets (*On the Sonnets of Robert Frost*), and seven works of historical fiction for young readers, co-authored with Claudia H. Young. Over eight hundred poems, stories, reviews and articles have appeared in periodicals, journals and anthologies. He has been nominated several times for Pushcart Prizes. He holds a Ph.D. from the Center for Writers at the University of Southern Mississippi. Married to Maureen Maxson, a nurse and photographer, they are organic gardeners in Milford, DE.

Claudia Young was born and raised in coastal New Jersey. After living in many locations across the country as a military family, she and her husband and children settled in Dover, Delaware, where they still live. Claudia retired from teaching elementary school but still enjoys classroom visits. She and her husband spend time traveling, golfing and enjoying their children and grandchildren. She is an avid reader who enjoys researching and co-authoring books with H.A. Maxson, her cousin.